Then Ash came back to me, his eyes burning into me.

"I meant what I said, Sophie. I have business in London, and I want you to come with me." I didn't understand. Why, in God's name, should he want me with him? "You and me—it's not possible. You know it's not possible."

He moved closer. He put his arms around me; he held me very close and he said, "You promised me devotion in your letters. Didn't you mean it?"

Oh, more than ever. "Yes," I breathed. "I meant it, every word."

"Then come with me. Stay with me."

All I Want Is You

By Elizabeth Anthony

All I Want Is You

All I Want Is You

ELIZABETH ANTHONY

www.redhookbooks.com

Redhook Books/Orbit
Hachette Book Group
237 Park Avenue, New York, NY 10017
hachettebookgroup.com

First U.S. Edition: October 2013
First published in Great Britain in 2013 by Hodder & Stoughton
An Hachette UK company

Redhook Books is an imprint of Orbit, a division of Hachette Book Group, Inc. The Redhook Books name and logo are trademarks of Hachette Book Group, Inc.

The publisher is not responsible for websites (or their content) that are not owned by the publisher.

The Hachette Speakers Bureau provides a wide range of authors for speaking events. To find out more, go to www.hachettespeakersbureau.com or call (866) 376-6591.

Library of Congress Control Number: 2013912424
ISBN: 978-0-316-25481-6

10 9 8 7 6 5 4 3 2 1

RRD-C

Printed in the United States of America

All I Want Is You

Prologue

'Oh, Belfield Hall,' people are fond of exclaiming at the fashionable London parties and restaurants with which I am now familiar. 'It really is the most amazing place. Home to the dukes of Belfield for centuries, you know – it's truly one of the grandest houses in England . . .'

After a while I find I'm no longer listening to their chatter, for my mind drifts away, and I am there. I see the lush beech trees unfurling their leaves on a spring morning in a peaceful Oxfordshire valley. I see the river winding through sheep-dotted pastures, I see the familiar drive that leads through the woods to the Hall itself, with its mellow stone gleaming and its windows sparkling in the sunshine.

When I was a child, it was a place of mystery to me. My family was not wealthy, far from it, and I imagined those who lived in the Hall to be different in every way: stronger, wiser, more beautiful than we ordinary folk. Such were my fancies, but disillusion set in when at thirteen I became a scullery maid there. With time I grew used to rising before dawn every morning, to scrubbing floors, lighting fires and scouring pans till after ten at night, while my meagre existence was hidden away from those who lived in grandeur above stairs. I learned so much, so quickly. But nothing – *nothing* – could have prepared me for what happened to me next.

I learned, you see, that when love arrives – physical love, physical desire – there is a complete surrendering of all the normal rules of existence. You do things, you allow things to be done; there is a time – it may be a year, a month, or one night only, perhaps – that becomes unforgettable. That is etched on your memory for ever.

When I met him, it was an awakening. A time after which nothing could be the same again. The man I loved and had thought unattainable was scarred, in both his body and his soul, and I longed for my love to heal him; indeed I believed my love *could* heal him, which was why I gave myself to him so completely. *You are mine*, he used to say as he lay beside me in the darkness, his body aroused and blissful against my delicate underwear, against my skin. Sometimes, when his mood was lighter, we danced together, because he loved music and so did I. *I've told you – you are mine*, he would breathe, holding me tenderly in his arms. *Don't leave me.* And I would say, *Never. Never, my love.* Even though his eyes were shadowed with secrets, and often so impenetrable that I had to turn away shivering, I would have done anything – *anything* – for him.

All I want is you, just as the song says. When he was far away from me I would cry out his name in my loneliness, in the night: I heard his voice; I saw his face. And oh, I'd waited for him for so long. For so very long.

Chapter One

My name is Sophia, though most people call me Sophie. My father Philip called me his little sparrow, because I was always chattering and singing, he said. He worked at the village smithy, and sometimes, when there was a house party at Belfield Hall, the grooms would bring the fine horses down to him for shoeing. Will and I would run to peep at them, marvelling at their beauty.

My mother worked four days a week as a laundry-maid at the Hall and I remember that I used to be upset by the soreness of her pretty hands. But she would smile and shake her head and say there were servants there who had to work seven days a week, from six in the morning until half past ten at night.

'Imagine that, Sophie,' she would say, brushing my long fair hair as I sat on her knee. 'Imagine that.'

I was born in 1903 and when I was five I started at the village school. Every day on my way there and back I would gaze at the gates leading to the Hall, though of course you couldn't see the building itself because of the woods. But sometimes in summer I would run to the top of Win Hill nearby, so I could see the windows and turrets all gleaming in the sun, and to my mind it was a fairy palace.

Will Baxter was my best friend. He was two years older than I was, but the Baxters were our nearest neighbours and because I was an only child he was like a brother to me. He and I would run races on the way to school and he would do things like hop on one leg so he didn't beat me. Will was kind and made me laugh. And in class I would help him with his letters, because I was quicker than he was at learning, and sometimes he minded it.

My father didn't see much need for learning, not in our kind of lives, he said. But my mother owned a few treasured books and often, when I was small, she used to read to me from *The Tales of King Arthur*. As I listened to her calm, clear voice, I would look at the pictures, and I used to imagine that people at the Hall must be like that, the ladies beautiful as the princesses, the gentlemen as brave as King Arthur's noble knights.

One hot June day when I was eight, the Duke of Belfield gave a party in the Hall's gardens, because the new king had been crowned in London. All the servants and their families were invited, and I still remember the trestle tables laden with food set out on the lawns in front of the Hall, while the men were given free beer. A band played music for dancing, then the Duke, a whiskery man, made a speech of which I don't remember a word because I was watching the butterflies dancing in the herb garden, and I danced too, thinking no one could see me there amongst the lavender bushes. But a gardener's boy chased me, and I ran into a thicket of trees and got lost.

I was a little afraid, I remember, and the scent of the

herbs my skirt had brushed against seemed suddenly too strong in the heat. Then I heard a man's voice, softly calling nearby. 'Where are you? Where *are* you, you mischievous thing?'

I shrank back behind a tree, thinking he was calling to me; then I saw that the man was the Duke's son, Lord Charlwood. People said he was very handsome, but I didn't like his black moustache and his shiny black hair. Then he laughed and said, 'Ah, there you are, Florence. You little tease, to run from me just when I was getting to know you.'

And I realised that he was speaking to my mother.

She was in her prettiest white blouse, and her long hair, as fair as mine, was falling a little from its pins. I thought she was the loveliest person in the world, but I was confused. She did seem to be running from Lord Charlwood, but it was obvious to me that she wanted him to catch her, and even as I watched she stumbled slightly and Lord Charlwood caught her in his arms.

He was kissing her on the mouth, and then he was putting his hand between the buttons of her pretty blouse. When she laughingly pushed him away, he stooped to lift her skirt and started running his hand up her leg.

I was frightened because, young though I was, I knew I was seeing something I ought not to see. He was pushing her back against a nearby tree, then kissing her again. I squeezed my eyes shut, but I could still hear my mother making strange sounds at the back of her throat, and though she'd put her arms around him, I was afraid he was hurting her. His lordship was breathing hard and calling her his sweet Florrie, his lovely Florrie.

I thought, *Her pretty blouse will be all spoiled by the bark of the tree.* I ran blindly to get away from that place and Will Baxter found me. 'He's hurting her, Will!' I sobbed. 'It's my mother – Lord Charlwood is hurting her.'

Will's face changed – I think he must already have known about Lord Charlwood's pursuit of my mother that summer. He put his hand awkwardly on my arm. 'It's all right, Sophie. It's just a sort of game – a secret game, that the grown-ups wouldn't want us to know about, do you understand?'

In those days I didn't understand at all, but Will's mother gave birth to a new baby almost every year, so he was bound to know more than I did about such things. Will's father was a farm labourer and he hated the rich – the toffs, he called them. Sometimes, when I knocked at Will's door on my way to school, I could see that their cottage, as well as being full of children, was dirty, which embarrassed me; I couldn't help but notice the grubby floor and the broken windowpanes that never got mended.

Will's father used to say everything would change soon, and I wondered how. I imagined a great storm, I think, like in the Bible, perhaps blowing all the rich people away, but I knew it couldn't really happen, because the rich owned the world, and the vicar preached to us in church every Sunday that if we honoured and obeyed our betters we'd get our reward in heaven.

There were a lot of funerals at the church, often of small children, and the vicar said that they were going to paradise. But I used to think they would be happier by far playing in the river meadows on a sunny day, like me and Will.

When it was time to bring in the hay harvest, my father would drive me out with him to the fields in the blacksmith's old cart, and I would carry the canvas bag with our lunch of bread and cheese. I was given a switch to keep the flies off the horses' heads as they stood so patiently, while the men and boys, shirtless in the heat, loaded the sheaves on the wagons.

Will would come to me to talk every so often – to stop me feeling lonely, I think – but I was never lonely in those days. Once, when I was stung by a wasp, Will ran home and came back with a small jug of vinegar, which he poured onto my clean handkerchief and pressed to my skin. 'Brave lass,' he said. 'Brave lass, not to cry.'

I think the war began with me hardly noticing it. I was eleven, and everyone said it would be over soon; besides, I had other matters on my mind, for my mother had started to look ill and I was terribly worried about her. She always used to wear a black dress to go and work at the Hall, and she put her lovely fair hair under a cap. But I could see that her dress was too big for her, and the black of it suddenly began to frighten me, because it reminded me of the funeral services at church.

'Don't wear that dress,' I used to beg her. 'It's ugly.'

'Sweetheart,' she would say, kissing me, 'I have to wear black for work. All the maids do.'

My father was quieter than ever, and often in the

7

evenings he would just sit outside our cottage, smoking his pipe.

One autumn day we heard that the Duke had given permission for the Hall grounds to be used for army training, so my father and I hurried with the other villagers to the top of Win Hill to see the cavalry galloping across the fine lawns, and the gun carriages being pulled by strong horses.

The men were so smart, in their red uniforms. The Duke had given thousands of pounds, it was whispered, so their outfits and horses would do the county proud. And that day we heard that Lord Charlwood, the Duke's heir, who was riding about amongst the cavalry men looking very pleased with himself, was going to the war in France with the soldiers. He had married recently; the wedding had been in London, and there'd been no great party at the Hall, because of the war. I wouldn't have gone to the party anyway; I hated him, because of that time I'd seen him with my mother in the garden.

My mother hadn't been well enough to climb the hill and watch the cavalry parade, but when my father and I got back she was sitting eagerly waiting for us outside our cottage door. It was a warm day in October, with some late roses still blooming in our small front garden, but I remember she was wrapped in a thick shawl. 'How was it?' she asked. 'Did you see the soldiers, Sophie darling?'

I told her all about them. But my father, though he listened, didn't say a word.

★ ★ ★

All I Want Is You

When I was twelve, my mother lost her job at the Hall, and because my father didn't earn very much, she took in washing at home. I helped, because I'd left school by then, but my mother grew paler and was always coughing, though not when she thought I could hear her. As the months passed I became more and more afraid of her illness.

The war didn't finish in months, as everyone had said it would, and one day the following spring, soon after my thirteenth birthday, my father told us he was leaving. 'I'm going to join up,' he announced. He said it as if he was proposing to do a little work in our small vegetable garden, or to take a stroll to the village alehouse. 'They're recruiting in Oxford. I'll pack a few things and leave tonight.'

I remember that he held me tight and gave me a quick kiss on my forehead before leaving us. I never saw him again. My mother said nothing, did nothing; I wanted her to plead with him to stay. But her face was white, and she was shivering badly.

His going shook my world. I remember I made my mother some tea, but she didn't want it. 'Read to me, sweetheart,' she whispered, so I did; I read her a story from *The Tales of King Arthur*, but grief was choking me because my father had gone – didn't he love us? Didn't he love *me*? I wondered if he knew about my mother kissing Lord Charlwood at the summer party years ago. How would we manage, without him?

'Tomorrow, Sophie,' whispered my mother, 'we'll go into Oxford, you and me. We'll buy you some pretty things: some ribbons, perhaps, and some new lace-edged handkerchiefs.'

9

'No, Mama,' I pleaded. 'You're not well enough.'

A tight cough racked her body. She squeezed my hand. 'Please, Sophie.'

The last time we'd gone into Oxford we'd seen a gypsy girl dancing for money while a man played wild, whirling music on his fiddle. I'd longed to dance as that girl did, with her full red skirts flying, and I hoped she'd be there again. But instead in the market square there was a man playing on a flute, and while my mother queued at a stall to buy some ribbons, I went to listen. Finding a sunny spot a little away from the flute player, I began to dance, and soon people were watching, I realised. Some of them were smiling, and a few even dropped coins by my feet. What the man playing the flute thought I don't know, but I danced on to his tunes, humming under my breath and letting my feet lightly follow the rhythms.

Then I saw my mother, watching.

She was smiling proudly, but I was suddenly very frightened because she looked so ill. Her cheeks had red spots on them, her eyes I thought were feverish. I hurried to find her a bench to sit on, but though she was clearly struggling for breath, she sat only for a matter of minutes. 'We must carry on with our shopping, Sophie,' she said, putting her hand on my arm. 'I want to buy you some more pretty things.'

She got to her feet, but almost immediately she collapsed to the ground. We were in the market place surrounded by crowds, and she lay quite still on the cobbles with her eyes closed. I called out to the people around me, 'Please. Please help my mother.' But no one did. I crouched at her side, and I could see she'd coughed up some dark stuff, like blood; it had got onto her white cotton gloves, which she kept for best to cover her poor chapped hands.

The flute player had gone by then, but suddenly I could hear more music, the sound of a band, for some soldiers were marching through the town in their splendid uniforms, and everyone had gathered to watch. People were saying that the Duke himself was in Oxford as well, to welcome the troop's officers to a grand reception. As the soldiers went by, the crowds cheered, and some well-dressed women walked around the square carrying baskets full of white feathers which they were handing out to all the young men who weren't in uniform. I thought these women might take pity on me, and I ran in desperation towards them. 'Please, will you help my mother? She is sick, and I don't know what to do. *Please.*'

I was so frightened. I pointed to my mother, still lying on the cobbles; but a woman with a stern face who carried a Bible as well as a basket of feathers said to me, 'Child, you're hampering us in our work. God punishes those who break His divine laws.'

I couldn't believe her cruelty. I ran back to my mother, who had opened her eyes and was trying to get up; I struggled to get her seated again on the nearby bench, but I was really shaking by then. A couple of men walking by looked at my mother and me as if we were part of a sideshow.

'Blow me if it ain't Florrie Davis,' one of them said to the other. 'She used to be a bit generous with her favours when she was a lass, didn't she?'

'Aye. She caught poor Phil Davis right and proper.'

I didn't understand what they meant. All I knew was that they peered at us once more without pity, then they moved on. I had my arm round my mother's waist but her eyes were fluttering shut again and I really didn't know what to do. Then I saw that the crowds had parted to let a man in a smart grey coat walk past.

To this day I don't know what made me do it. What made me think that he of all people might help me. But there was something about him, something I later tried and failed to put into words; certainly a kind of desperation overwhelmed me as I called out to him, 'Sir! Please will you help us, sir?'

He turned and looked at my mother leaning against me on the bench, her face deathly white. 'Surely she needs a doctor,' he said.

Something in me broke then, I was so frightened. I cried out, 'Do you think I don't know it? All these people, I've asked them to help. I've *begged* them to help. Would you let this happen to your wife or your sister, sir? Would you?'

He'd drawn closer now, frowning. 'Are you her daughter?'

I was trying hard not to weep. 'Yes, sir. My name is Sophie.'

'Has she been sick for a while, Sophie?'

She had but, oh God, she knew she couldn't afford what a doctor would cost, and that was the truth of it. Instead she'd been saving up so she could buy things for me. So she could buy me ribbons.

The rich man looked grave. 'Come,' he said at last. 'We'll take her to the hospital.'

He was younger than Lord Charlwood. He had thick dark brown hair and blue eyes, and I thought his eyes were sad. I remember that one of the women thrust a white feather at him saying, 'Call yourself a man, and not in uniform?'

Everything happened so quickly after that. He had a big shiny motorcar parked on the far side of the market, with a driver waiting in it; he must have been walking towards it when I stopped him. He ordered two bystanders to carefully lift my mother and put her into the back seat, then he sat in the front while I sat next to my mother and held her hand, which felt cold, so cold. 'It's all right, Mama,' I whispered. 'It's all right.'

That was my first time in a motorcar. At the hospital my mother was taken away, and we waited in a green-tiled corridor that smelled of antiseptic. I've never afterwards been able to breathe in that smell without feeling utter dread.

Then the doctors came back and said to me, 'We're sorry, but your mother's died. She was very ill, didn't you know that? She should have seen a doctor long ago.'

In that moment my whole world came tumbling down. The rich man with the blue eyes grasped me by the arm because I was trying to run to where they'd taken her. I was saying to him, to all of them, 'She couldn't afford a doctor. She couldn't afford to stop work, even though she was so ill.' My eyes were burning with tears; I tried to punch his chest. 'Didn't you see her hands? Her poor hands, they were red and rough from working for people like you, and she had no money to see a doctor.'

The rich man held my shoulders as tears poured down my cheeks. I remember his hands were beautiful; I remember the faint lemon scent of soap on his skin, when most men I knew smelled of sweat. 'You must go home,' he said. 'To your family.'

My family? My mother was dead; my father had gone to the war. 'I've no one,' I told him. I felt bitter grief. 'No one else.'

'How old are you, child?'

'I'm thirteen,' I whispered.

The man with the blue eyes told me to wait for him, then went away to speak to the doctors again. I found out later that he paid for everything so that my dear mother wouldn't have a pauper's burial but had a small carved headstone in our village churchyard, but I didn't thank him for what he did that day. I didn't know how to; besides, I thought I'd never see him again. He led me outside to his motorcar and he said, 'You can't live by yourself. I'll get a letter sent to the housekeeper at Belfield Hall. Her name is Mrs Burdett and the letter will explain that you need a job.'

I shook my head. 'My mother worked in the Belfield laundry. They sent her away because – because—'

He interrupted, 'Mrs Burdett will take care of that. You'll be safe there, at least until you're old enough to decide what you want to do with your life. Is that all right, Sophie?'

I thought of my hands, getting as red and raw as my mother's. I thought of Lord Charlwood pursuing my mother in the gardens. But I nodded because I could think of nothing else to do, nowhere else to go.

The tears rolled down my cheeks. 'I loved her so much.'

He bent down so that his head was level with mine, his blue eyes searching mine. 'I can see that,' he said gravely. 'Save your love, Sophie. Remember that people judge you by the value you place on yourself. Work hard at the Hall and in a few years you can start making your own plans, living your own dreams. Do you understand?'

I scrubbed away my tears and gazed up at him. 'Yes, sir. I understand.'

'Good girl. Now – ' he straightened up – 'have you a friend or neighbour? Someone who'll look after you for a few days before you go to the Hall?'

'There's Mrs Baxter,' I whispered. 'And Will. Will is my friend.'

'Then go to them,' he said. 'I have to leave you now, Sophie, but remember what I said, won't you?'

I suddenly didn't want him to leave me. 'Do you live at the Hall, sir? Shall I see you there?'

'You won't see me there, no.' Bitterness suddenly filled his eyes. 'But listen.' He got out a sheet of paper and wrote down a London address. 'Write to me, will you? Even if it's only every few months or so, send me a letter to let me know you're all right.'

'You haven't put your name,' I pointed out.

'My name is Mr Maldon.' He scribbled that too, beneath the address. 'Now, do you promise to write?'

I knuckled the tears from my cheeks. 'I promise.'

★ ★ ★

His driver took me to our village in the smart motorcar, which caused a great commotion. I told Will's mother what had happened and she hugged me tightly while all her ragged children clustered round, wide-eyed.

Will walked with me to our cottage, where I packed up my few possessions and my mother's half-dozen books, and I gave Mrs Baxter the white blouse my mother had worn for that party at the Hall. I didn't cry again.

But I never forgot a single thing that happened that day and, years later, when I knew what I know now, I remembered that they gave him a white feather. I couldn't get that from my mind. *They gave him a white feather.*

Chapter Two

'If you please, I've come to speak to Mrs Burdett.' My voice faltered as the stern housemaid looked me up and down.

My mother's funeral had taken place three days before, with myself and the Baxters and a few of our neighbours gathered at the local church. It had been cold and raining and the birds had stopped their spring song. I had thought that no one could see my tears, but Will had touched my hand in silent sympathy.

Now I stood at the back door of the Hall, lonely as could be beneath the gaze of the housemaid who glared at me so. I was a scrawny little thing in a patched-up brown dress, and the housekeeper Mrs Burdett, when I was taken to her sitting room, looked disapproving also. 'Are you Sophie Davis?'

'Yes, ma'am, that's to say—'

'I've received a letter,' she interrupted.

'From Mr Maldon?'

'Mr Maldon?' She appeared puzzled. 'No,' she went on, 'from the bank manager in Oxford, Mr Isherwood. He says you're of good character and I'm to find you a place if I can.'

My fear gave way to confusion – why hadn't Mr

Maldon written to her himself? But I thought it better to keep quiet, especially as Mrs Burdett's face didn't look particularly kind to me.

'Your mother Florence Davis used to work here in the laundry, didn't she? Thinking of using her name, were you? Well, don't,' she said. 'You'll be paid ten pounds a year, you'll start as a scullery maid, and we'll call you Sophie Smith.'

I think the colour flamed in my cheeks, because I was remembering my mother and Lord Charlwood that day in the gardens long ago, and guessing this woman knew of it too. Mrs Burdett was eyeing me sharply. 'Do you want the place, girl? Or don't you?'

'Yes, ma'am. Thank you, ma'am.'

'Then I'll take you to the kitchen and introduce you to Cook – she'll be glad of an extra pair of hands.'

This meant I had somewhere to stay at least, and the chance to earn my living, however pitiful the pay. I followed Mrs Burdett to the door, eager to please, but I couldn't help stopping by a black-framed photograph on the wall, which was a portrait of a man in army uniform.

Mrs Burdett saw me looking. 'My brother Wilfred,' she said. Her voice was suddenly different. 'He was killed in the fighting in France last year.'

So I was set on as a scullery maid, lowest of the low, and told I would sleep in the attic dormitory with six other maids, all older than me. I was told I had to get up at five to clean the kitchen and scrub the range every single day and, apart from giving me orders, most of the maids never troubled to talk to me at all, except to tease me.

Though if Mrs Burdett overheard she would speak to them sharply. As Mr Maldon had implied, she did, despite her brusqueness, take care of me in her way. I found out years later that she and her brother had been raised in an orphanage, and that perhaps gave her some sympathy for me. But apart from Mrs Burdett, all the upper servants – Mr Peters the butler, the Duke's long-serving valet Mr Harris and the Duchess's personal maid Miss Stanforth – took no notice of me at all.

After my first week there I wrote to Mr Maldon. In the servants' hall after our supper we sometimes had a little free time before the evening chores started, so one night I sat at the table with my pen in my hand, but I didn't know what to say. In the end I wrote, *Dear Mr Maldon, I am working at Belfield Hall now in the kitchen. I am very grateful to you because I know I owe my position here to you, though I am a little confused because Mrs Burdett says it was a Mr Isherwood who recommended me. I trust this finds you well. Yours sincerely, Sophie Davis.* I paused, with a lump in my throat. I scrubbed out *Davis* and put *Smith* – I was Sophie Smith now.

Carefully I copied his address – *Wilton Crescent* – from the sheet of paper he'd written it on, and I tried to imagine him in London, a city that sounded like a far-off magical place to me. Would he even remember our meeting? I posted it on my next afternoon off and to my surprise the following week I got a reply. The post was always handed out by Mr Peters the butler at breakfast, and I think I blushed bright red.

'Our little Sophie's got an admirer,' sneered Betsey, one of the maids whom I didn't like.

I opened it with fumbling fingers. His writing was beautiful and even, in black ink.

Dear Sophie, Mr Isherwood is a bank manager in Oxford, and a friend of mine; I asked him to write to Mrs Burdett. Are they feeding you well? Is Peters still a tyrant, and do the Duchess's cats still drive everyone to distraction? Tell me more next time. Yours, etc, Mr Maldon.

I folded the letter in some consternation. He knew the Hall, though Mrs Burdett had not even recognised his name! He knew Mr Peters the butler, and he knew that the Duchess's dozen or so cats – which were truly a law unto themselves – annoyed the staff exceedingly with the hairs they left everywhere.

I wrote back to him that very evening, telling him how Cook had chased two of the Duchess's cats out of her kitchen with a broom only yesterday – they'd licked the cream off a trifle and she was furious. I wrote, *Please tell me about London.*

In his next letter he described some of the fine shops, and also told me about the cavalry that rode up and down Horse Guards Parade. I wrote eagerly back, and for many months his replies to my letters came regularly. I kept them all. I still have them.

Of course the war was darkening everyone's world by then. So many men were being lost in the fighting, and in the autumn of 1916 Will joined up too, my good and dear friend Will, who had been working on the home farm since leaving school. He came to tell me he was off to France and talked eagerly of being in the army, but I think he was also hoping I'd beg him to stay. Lord Charlwood was still in France; he was a captain, aide-de-camp to a general, they said, and covering himself with glory. The Duchess loved to talk of her war-hero son, but it was muttered often in the servants' hall that his was a safe job, well away from German guns and gas.

Sometimes I heard the servants talking of London: of the fashions, and the wonderful parties the rich people still gave in spite of the war. I listened to every word. There was a footman called Robert, who hadn't joined the army because he had a weak chest – asthma, he said. Sometimes Robert would sweet-talk Mrs Burdett into letting him carry an old gramophone she owned into the servants' hall, and he would wind it up so we could listen to her records of Caruso and Nellie Melba while we ate our supper. The music filled me with pleasure, but Robert would croon the songs in a mocking sort of way once Mrs Burdett and the rest of the upper servants had retired, as they usually did, to her private sitting room.

Of course, apart from the servants' mealtimes, the male and female staff were meant to be kept strictly apart, but the footmen were a topic of constant gossip amongst the maids and I quickly realised that Robert was a particular object of admiration. One night in our dormitory the other maids started to tease me when they noticed I was listening. 'Little Miss Holier-Than-Thou,' they taunted. 'Don't you sometimes look at Robert and think what a nice-looking fellow he is, eh? Oh, wait till you're old enough.'

They often talked like that, though not in Cook or Mrs Burdett's hearing, and they loved to bait the new kitchen boy, Dan, who was even younger and shyer than I was. He bumped into Betsey once by mistake and she accused him, as a joke, of trying to feel her up. 'Now, our Dan!' she cried. 'I'm after a man's prick, not a boy's that's no bigger than my finger.' He blushed furiously while they all laughed and, because I didn't join in, Betsey whispered something about me to the others that made them laugh even more. Robert, the arrogant footman, persecuted me in different ways. He would wait till I'd just cleaned the kitchen floor and then he would spill something – coal-dust, or scraps saved for the pigs. He would give his mocking smile and say to me, 'Oh dear, Sophie. You've not made a very good job of that floor, have you?'

My face flaming, I would get on my knees and start again.

On one bleak mid-January day I realised that Mrs Burdett's efforts to keep my identity secret had been in vain. There was often whispering in the servants' hall about Lord Charlwood's reputation; he was a *philanderer*, they said. I always tried desperately not to think of him and my mother in the garden, but on that particular day, as I was clearing away the pots after our lunch, all the servants started talking about Lord Charlwood again, just loudly enough for me to hear.

'It's true,' Betsey was saying in a raised whisper while pointing at me. 'Little Miss Holier-Than-Thou over there – yes, her mother was one of his lordship's favourites for a month or two. Used to work in the laundry. Florrie Davis was her name, and in Coronation year

Florrie came running whenever he so much as smiled. His lordship's Coronation Special, Florrie was.' They all laughed loudly.

I dropped a plate, Mrs Burdett roundly told me off, and after that the maids got on with their work, though Robert came to help me pick up the broken pieces. At first I thought he was being kind, but as he bent close he whispered, 'Never could say no to a man, your ma. Thanks to some old boyfriend of hers, you were on the way before she even met your so-called dad, Phil Davis. But then, by golly, she married poor Phil quick as she could, then told everyone once you were born – him too, poor fool – that you were an early arrival.'

To be told in such a way that I wasn't the child of the man who'd raised me was cruel indeed. I remembered what those men in Oxford had said – *She caught poor Phil Davis right and proper* – then I thought with pain of my father leaving us so suddenly. Yet I faced up to Robert. I knew by then it was the only way.

'Well, aren't you a know-all?' I replied calmly. 'You think I didn't know?' I got on with my work, but I was crying inside, for my mother and for the man I'd thought was my father.

I dreamed of getting away, and of course I wrote to Mr Maldon. I didn't tell him about the other servants' cruelty over my mother, but instead I told him of the jobs I'd learned to do, and how Mrs Burdett was very pleased with me. I told him too about Robert sometimes borrowing Mrs Burdett's gramophone, and also how one of the Duchess's cats had brought a live mouse into the kitchen, which had Cook shrieking and climbing onto a chair while Mr Peters tried to shoo it out.

But he only wrote back once more, to tell me that he'd be away for a while. *I want you to still write to me though, Sophie,* he said. *I want you to still think of me, and to think well of me.*

These words of his mystified and upset me. How could I not think well of him, when he'd been so very kind to me? I kept his letters tucked inside one of my mother's precious books, and I still wrote every week to his address in London. I missed getting his letters badly, but I took comfort in the thought of him getting mine.

I wondered often why he'd been in Oxford that day last spring when my mother had died, and why he seemed to know the Hall so well. But I had a feeling that if I tried to find out too much, all my memories of him would vanish, just as the figures in a dream will fade away to nothing if you try too hard to remember them.

Life at the Hall went on, and my only friend was a new maid called Nell, who had been raised in the workhouse and was just a few months older than me. None of the menservants noticed either of us except to torment us, since Nell was slightly lame from birth and I still looked scarcely more than a child in my black servant's gown. As for the Duke and Duchess – well, we might as well not have existed. One of the first things I'd been told was that if – by some dire accident – I should spot any member of the family or their guests approaching down a corridor, I was to turn to the wall and stand very still until they'd gone past, so they didn't have to see my face even, let alone speak to me.

Sometimes there were grand house parties, and we might catch glimpses of the Duke and Duchess and their finely dressed guests as they went to and fro. The Duchess was gaunt and sharp-nosed, and for these house parties she loved to create vast flower arrangements, which were the bane of the servants' lives since they were always dropping leaves and getting in our way. The Duke was a little jollier, though to me he did not resemble his son Lord Charlwood in the least, but was short and stout, with red, puffy cheeks. In his younger days he'd apparently enjoyed riding to hounds, but now he confined himself to hosting shooting parties and playing billiards with his friends in the library.

Over the Christmas of 1917, the Duke arranged for a jazz band to be hired for one night for his guests, and we servants crept as close as we could to the half-open doors of the great hall to watch the young ones performing some modern steps, which were called the ragtime and the tango, Robert told us. I loved it all, and later when I was alone I practised by myself; but I couldn't remember much of it, so I danced in my own way, as I'd danced in the gardens as a child that summer afternoon so long ago.

I thought of my Mr Maldon, always.

In the spring came the shocking news that Lord Charlwood had been killed. He was supposed to be safe behind the lines with his general, but he wasn't; a stray German shell had landed on him.

'Must have blown the bugger to bits,' breathed Robert almost reverentially. 'Just think, all over the shop he'd be, him and all his medals . . .'

'Robert,' cried Mrs Burdett, 'you keep your mouth shut for once! Oh, my goodness, it'll be mourning everywhere, black draperies to be put up, and there'll be dozens of house guests for poor Lord Charlwood's funeral . . .'

'Some funeral,' muttered Robert slyly to us all after she'd gone. 'How are they going to find enough of his lordship's body to fill a coffin?'

I said nothing, but I wrote to Mr Maldon to tell him about Lord Charlwood's death, and how the Hall was plunged into mourning. Every week I walked to the village on my half-day off to put wild flowers on my mother's grave, then to post my letter to him.

And I still hoped that some day he would reply.

The old Duke was stricken by the loss of his only son. The Duchess, never known for the sweetness of her temper, went around with a face that would turn milk sour. Who was the new heir? That was something that everyone except Nell and me seemed to know, and we were indeed swiftly told by the other servants that the Duke had a much younger brother, who'd died eight years ago, leaving a widow and just one child – a nine-year-old boy known as Lord Edwin.

Lord Edwin came to the funeral with his mother, who seemed a quiet mouse of a woman; Lord Edwin was plump and frightened-looking, I remember, and all dressed up in a stiff knickerbocker suit of black velvet.

The Duchess, the servants muttered, was absolutely desperate to keep her husband alive for as long as possible so she wouldn't have to make way for this child.

'Otherwise,' Robert told us at the servants' supper, 'I reckon she'd poison the old Duke herself to be rid of him.' Cook heard him, and warned she'd report him to Mr Peters next time he spoke like that. I was realising by then that this wasn't the only rumour about the Duchess – they said, for example, that there was a locked room leading from her private parlour, which no one but her elderly maid Miss Stanforth was supposed to enter; no one but Miss Stanforth was supposed to clean. But Betsey told us that she'd once peeped inside the forbidden room, and there were lilies all around in vases; white lilies, for death, Betsey whispered.

Lord Charlwood's coffin was brought home from France with great pomp to rest for five days in the Hall's marble chapel. All the reception rooms of the Hall were swathed in black draperies, and the bell of the village church tolled from dawn till dusk. We servants had to file past the coffin and I thought of my mother as I made my curtsey. I thought of her grassy grave in the village churchyard, with the birds singing in the leafy trees overhead, and I knew I would far rather have her place in the earth when I died, than be put in the family mausoleum like Lord Charlwood.

That summer, because so many young men had gone off to the war, the garden and grounds were allowed to run wild where they weren't visible from the house, and we maids had to do much of the work that the men had once done, carrying the coals all around the house in heavy buckets and trimming and filling the oil lamps. We were especially busy with the approach of the funeral, because so many house guests would be staying. The day before the funeral itself, there was a great fuss because Lord Charlwood's young widow was arriving. 'About time too,' said Cook sourly.

Nell and I were cleaning the dining room on our own. It was as gloomy in there as in the rest of the house because the mirrors were covered and the blinds were drawn and I longed to be out in the sunshine. We were meant to be brushing the carpets, but Nell had peeped out of the window because she'd heard a motorcar arriving.

'Oh, look.' She turned to me, her eyes shining. 'She's so beautiful.'

'Who?'

'Her. It *must* be her. Lady Beatrice. Lord Charlwood's widow.'

I hurried over to the window too, and saw that the chauffeur had opened the door to let Her Ladyship out. Lady Beatrice was dressed in mourning, of course, but her coat was shorter than we were used to, and her lips were painted red, and for some reason my heart began to beat a little faster, especially when she stood and gazed up at the Hall with a knowing little smile.

That night Her Ladyship's maid – Margaret – dined with us in the servants' hall and told us that Lady Beatrice got all her gowns from Paris. Margaret was a cut above all of us as a lady's maid. She had a small white scar on her left cheekbone, and I wondered how she had got it. She had, of course, her own bedroom adjacent to Her Ladyship's suite, and after supper in the servants' hall she retired, as was to be expected, to the housekeeper's sitting room with the other upper servants to take tea and join in their superior talk.

On the day of the funeral, Lord Charlwood's hearse was drawn by six black horses with black plumes fastened to their harness while six mutes, clad all in black with their faces veiled, accompanied the cortege on foot. 'Fair give me the creeps, those mutes do,' Nell muttered at my side.

Then we walked, all of the servants, to the church for the solemn service. Hundreds of mourners lined the route, and inside the church we saw the little heir in the front row, looking pale and afraid.

Lady Beatrice, Lord Edwin and his mother left a few days after the funeral but more visitors came daily – lawyers from London, Cook told us. Cook was less discreet than Mrs Burdett, and she told us also that what with the war and declining rents, certain 'economies' – she pronounced the word with doom-laden weight – were having to be made.

But my friend Nell was starry-eyed. Recently the Duke – though he still kept his elderly valet, Mr Harris – had hired a new young manservant, Eddie, to help him get around now his mobility was so poor. And Nell told me that on her afternoons off she'd started walking out with this Eddie, who also drove the Duke's motorcar. Because he was good-looking and had a mouth as smart as Robert's, Eddie was what was known as a catch.

A few weeks later in our dormitory, as we lay in our narrow little iron beds next to each other, Nell reached out to touch my shoulder and whispered, 'I've done it, Sophie. With Eddie.'

'Done what?' I was exhausted; I'd had to wash all the copper pots twice that night with a mixture of flour, salt and vinegar, because Cook had said they weren't clean enough.

'Gone all the way. *You* know.'

I was wide awake suddenly. My pulse had stopped, then started again jerkily. 'Nell . . .'

'Oh, I know what you're going to say. But it was wonderful, Sophie. I thought it might hurt a little, but it didn't really.' She was silent a moment. 'When he kissed me – when he felt me, down there, and was so gentle with me – it was wonderful. I love him, so much.'

Again I felt a tremor run through me. 'Nell. Aren't you scared?'

'About having a baby? No, he told me I was all right, so long as we choose the right time of the month. Anyway, my Eddie says he'll marry me, Sophie!'

I said nothing else, but I thought of my mother, and how the man I'd called my father had left her. I thought that anyone who gave themselves as lightly as Nell had done was a fool, though I didn't have to worry about men anyway, because no one was interested in me.

With Nell in love, I was lonelier than ever. I still wrote to Mr Maldon, even though he'd told me he wouldn't be writing to me any longer. I'd already told him about the funeral, and how poor Lord Edwin was so very young. *Mrs Burdett was extremely angry*, I wrote to him on a lighter note, *because she caught Robert the footman showing Betsey how to do the foxtrot in the dining hall the other day . . .*

Then I put my pen down. I wanted to write, *I wish I could tell you how much your kindness meant to me, on the day my mother died. I wish we could meet again.* But I didn't. I finished my letter, and then it was time for me to do the washing-up in the scullery.

I looked at my hands and suddenly realised they were as red and work-worn as my poor mother's had been.

Chapter Three

In September that year there was a big house party for
Lord Edwin's tenth birthday. The Duke, confined to his
bath chair by now, made an effort at jollity, but the
Duchess was as poisonous as ever to the young heir.
When he arrived with his mother, and the footmen were
all lined up in full livery outside the main doors, Robert
heard her greeting him with, 'Dear little Lord Edwin!
You've not grown any taller, but goodness, how stout
you are – what do they feed you on?'

Quite a few children had been invited to the house
party – to keep the young heir entertained, the Duke
and Duchess explained graciously – and on the morning of his birthday the Duchess personally insisted the
children all go out riding in the grounds. Most of them,
the girls as well as the boys, were already confident on
horseback, but Lord Edwin was terrified of horses. Billy,
one of the grooms, told us about it afterwards.

'Her Grace the Duchess came along and insisted we
put him up on the most evil-tempered cob in the stables.
By gosh, when his little lordship was thrown in the first
five minutes and started crying for his nurse, I'll swear
the old witch smirked.'

That was what they called the Duchess, *the old witch*,

though never in the butler's or the housekeeper's hearing.

At the birthday tea, we maids and some of the foot-men served sandwiches and jellies in the downstairs parlour, then afterwards Robert organised games for the children, like blind-man's-buff and pinning the tail on the donkey. Lord Edwin was poor at *everything*, and the Duchess's cats, which were all over the place, made him sneeze. Some of the bigger boys got bored with the donkey game and wanted to play at killing the Hun instead, so Mr Peters announced they could go outside, and they charged about the lawns with their arms outspread pretending to be British airmen, while the girls gathered in a huddle to talk about their frocks and their ponies.

Lord Edwin was left sitting by himself. I felt sorry for him.

After a while the adult guests went out into the garden also for their afternoon tea, and I, together with the other maids and footmen, waited on them. The men who'd gathered around the Duke talked solemnly at first, not only about the war, but about a strike through-out the country by the miners and railwaymen. But they stopped their conversation and turned to stare when a blue two-seater motorcar came steadily up the drive and crunched to a stop on the freshly raked gravel – Lady Beatrice, Lord Charlwood's widow, had arrived once more from London.

And my heart skipped a beat.

She fascinated me, with her short dark hair and her daring clothes. Last time we'd seen her she'd been in black for her husband's funeral, but now she was wearing a cream hat and a lovely swirling silk coat in shades of blue and gold. The servants all gossiped about her during supper and Betsey the kitchen maid reckoned Lady Beatrice must find it stiflingly dull here in the country after London.

'Perhaps Her Ladyship feels closer to her dead husband here,' said Mrs Burdett. 'And that's enough disrespectful talk about your betters, Betsey, my girl.'

Poor Lord Edwin, he was sick the day after his birthday tea. Robert muttered that the Duchess had probably poisoned him, but Cook pointed out that was unlikely, since the man who would be next in line if the young heir to the dukedom died was, she said, an even worse prospect than Lord Edwin.

'Why?' asked Nell.

'He's a distant cousin, and a bad lot, you mark my words,' Cook said darkly. 'They say he's got business interests in America.' In Cook's eyes this clearly amounted to a criminal offence.

'He must be well-born, though,' put in Betsey.

Cook shrugged. 'I've heard his father was an English lord. But this lord brought shame on his family by marrying a common Frenchwoman, and then the two of them got divorced in France – a fine old set-up.' Cook had a particular aversion to the French, ever since the Duchess had started ordering her to put some more of the newly fashionable French dishes in her daily menus. So that was the distant cousin dealt with, and duly condemned.

Anyway, the ailing Lord Edwin had to be driven off

home with his ever-anxious mother, but the other guests stayed on enjoying themselves, and during the beautiful summer days that followed I watched for Lady Beatrice. She played tennis on the lawns, wearing a long white skirt and lace-trimmed white blouse, or drove her friends out into the country lanes in her gleaming blue motorcar. And I didn't think she looked like a grieving widow at all.

I watched her whenever I could, because I thought she was beautiful.

In November that year the war ended at last, and there was a thanksgiving service at the village church, which all the staff were given permission to attend. I'd heard from Mrs Baxter that Will was safe, though not home yet; but I was so sad for all the men who never would return home, and I was sad too because I was beginning to realise that I would probably never see my Mr Maldon again.

I tried each night once the lamps were out to remember his face and his voice, but my memories of him were fading. And what if I did some day meet him? What could I expect of him? Nothing, except the chance to thank him for the kindness he'd shown my poor mother and me in Oxford that day, and to thank him for securing me this job at the Hall, for he'd been right; I was safe here, even if I was lonely. And I did feel that Mrs Burdett, as he'd said, watched out for me.

I was sixteen the following spring. By then Robert had fixed up a crystal set in the servants' hall, and he would fiddle around with it each night until, after a lot of noisy hissing, he would get some modern music. Mrs Burdett was disapproving at first; she still loved to listen to her Caruso records, but one evening a tune on Robert's crystal set caught her fancy – 'Rockabye Your Baby with a Dixie Melody' – and she went quite pink with pleasure when Robert caught her by the hand and did a few smart steps with her.

'Come on, Mrs B,' he coaxed. 'You love it, really. And you dance like one of the chorus girls at The Gaiety.'

I loved the music, and I listened to Robert with almost painful concentration. 'What's The Gaiety?' I asked him afterwards.

He winked at me. 'It's a theatre, little Sophie. A fancy theatre in London, where they put on shows with girls who dance and sing, and rich folks pay a fortune to see them.'

I searched for the name in the advertisement pages of the London newspapers, which were cleared away from His Grace's library each night, and true enough it was there. 'The Gaiety, London,' I whispered to myself.

And that was the day I started to dream of becoming a dancer.

Sometimes when I was dusting the big mirrors in the drawing room I would study myself, and I saw that I had over-large green eyes while my face was small and pale. My hair, which was fair like my mother's, was always pinned up out of sight beneath my big cap.

We maids weren't encouraged to show any vanity – far from it. We did have our own bathroom, down the corridor from our dormitory, where we had a flushing toilet and even had piped hot water to fill our copper bath, though the water was more like a lukewarm trickle by the time it reached our attic.

I would bathe myself carefully whenever it was my turn. I would also wash my hair and rinse it with a little vinegar I'd taken from the kitchen. There was no mirror, but sometimes as I stood and dried myself I would look down at my body. I was too thin, I knew, and my breasts were too small. And I wouldn't be in there long before someone would bang on the door and shout, 'Sophie! Are you going to be in that blessed bath all night?'

I wrote to Mr Maldon about the crystal set. *Robert danced with Mrs Burdett to 'Rockabye Your Baby with a Dixie Melody'. Do you know it? I imagine you hear all the latest music, wherever you are.* But I wanted to write, *I miss you. I think of you.*

Now that the war was over there were more parties at Belfield Hall than ever, even though the Duke was an invalid; and in the June of 1919 I remember there were forty guests staying for two weeks. It was a long, hot summer and, often, as the younger ones played tennis in the cool of the early evening, I would catch a glimpse of them through a window – we all did, as we scurried round the house like invisible creatures, rushing to complete our many lowly tasks and be out of sight before the guests came back in.

The footmen, hot in their full livery, served iced lemonade and gin and tonic out on the lawns, with some savoury French delicacies that were called *canapés*, though Cook grimly pronounced them *canopies*. Lady Beatrice arrived one evening from London in her blue two-seater; a second motorcar followed behind containing her trunks full of clothes and a gramophone more modern than Mrs Burdett's, which someone placed in a ground-floor room so that with the French windows open, the music could be heard out on the lawns.

The younger guests got into the habit of dancing in the open air once they'd finished their tennis, and they played their favourite records again and again. During the warm nights, as the lamps inside the big house glowed, the music filled the gardens. I still remember those tunes note for note, especially 'I'm Forever Blowing Bubbles', 'Alexander's Ragtime Band', and 'All I Want Is You'.

On the sixth night after Lady Beatrice arrived, something happened. Whether it was because the guests were still outside so most of us were free of our duties for a brief while, or whether it was the sight of all the young people in their beautiful clothes dancing out in the dusk, I don't know. But for some reason quite a few of the servants – led by Robert, of course – began to dance too in the servants' hall, where the music was loud and clear as anything.

What had happened to the upper servants, who were usually so strict with us? The housekeeper Mrs Burdett had been taken poorly with the heat, that I knew, and was resting in her private room, which was some distance away. Where Mr Peters and Cook were, I can't recall. All I remember is that a lot of servants were jigging around to the music, and though I'd stood aside, suddenly Robert was grabbing my hand.

The tune was 'Jazz Baby, Be Mine', and I was so surprised. All Robert had ever done was mock me, and it was he who'd told me that the man I'd thought was my father was no such thing. But now he whispered, 'You're really getting quite pretty, Sophie, you little tease. How old are you?'

'I'm sixteen,' I told him.

'Hm. Sweet sixteen,' he grinned, and he pulled me into his arms. I think he'd half expected me to refuse, but I so longed to dance that I almost forgot it was Robert who held me.

I picked up the steps quickly because I'd seen the young people do them. Robert was startled and pleased. 'Sophie,' he said. 'How on earth did you learn to move like that?'

'I watched,' I said simply. How I relished the look of surprise in his eyes. 'I watched them all, every time there was a party here.'

He grinned and gave me an extra twirl. 'Attagirl,' he said. He liked using modern phrases like that.

And all of a sudden my dream didn't seem so impossible after all.

I was enjoying myself so much. I floated to the music. I danced up and down the hall with Robert, while the house guests were still outside. It must have been towards the end of June, and so warm that – even though the stars were coming out – none of the young people wanted to leave the gardens. Some footmen had taken out baskets of cold meats and salads so the guests could have what they called a picnic. How they all laughed, and were excited, to take their supper out there with lamps placed around the lawn and their champagne in buckets of ice!

Our dancing had stopped, and although the gramophone was still spilling music out into the night air, I knew I had all my evening jobs to do. Reluctantly I started on the washing-up in the scullery, putting on my pinafore and stacking the dirty plates. But when I went back into the servants' hall to collect more dishes, I froze.

Most of the staff, like me, had moved on to their usual tasks of damping down the fires around the house, trimming lamps and making sure there was hot water in all the bedrooms. But a dozen or so of the younger ones hadn't moved from the servants' hall. Someone had put out most of the lamps, and I realised, with a slow chill of alarm, that they were in pairs, kissing.

Nell was on her Eddie's knee in a corner, and I saw that he had his hand down her gown to feel at her breasts, while her hand was between his legs. I could feel a flush of heat rising from my pounding heart to my cheeks. Then someone – it was Richard, one of the new footmen – got to his feet and rang the servants' handbell. 'Time's up!' he called. 'Roll the dice again. Your turn to throw, Robert.'

Slowly – stupidly slowly – I realised what they were doing.

Robert shook a six, then each girl rolled the dice, and the first to get six – it was Harriet – promptly sat herself on Robert's knee, flung her arms round his neck and started kissing him. Richard, meanwhile, snatched up the dice and threw a four, then sat waiting, with a grin on his face, for one of the girls to shake a four and join him.

I shrank back into the shadows. I could see that Nell didn't want to let Eddie take his turn, but he shook her off with a laugh. 'It's a game, Nell. Don't be stupid.'

Robert, who still had Harriet tight in his arms, suddenly caught sight of me. 'Don't look so shocked, little Sophie – come and join us. You never know, you might enjoy yourself.'

My cheeks burning, I fled back to my washing-up in the scullery. I scrubbed those dishes, plunging my hands in the hot water and carbolic that would make my skin even more sore, and I felt real despair. My life was passing me by. My longing to get to London and be on stage seemed ridiculous and futile. I thought with a pang of Mr Maldon, and how each time I posted my letters to him, my heart grew heavier, because he was becoming only a distant memory, like a dream.

That night, as I say, was a strange night, and so hot as to become almost oppressive. I was in my bed by eleven, but the other girls from my dormitory were still downstairs.

I remembered them all giggling and dancing and kissing. I wriggled between my sheets and opened a book of my mother's, but I couldn't get comfortable and my calico nightgown felt harsh against my sensitive skin. *A waste.* That was what I was. A waste of a life and youth, with my foolish memory of the man with blue eyes, my stupid dreams.

Someone was very quietly opening the door to our

attic room and I sat up quickly. It wasn't Nell or Betsey but Lady Beatrice's personal maid, Margaret. Her dark eyes glittered and again I noticed the pale scar on her cheek.

'You're reading,' she said. 'Like books, do you?'

'It belonged to my mother.' My heart for some reason was thudding.

She picked it up and her thin lips curled. 'Poetry. La-di-dah. I'm in need of an extra girl to tidy Her Ladyship's sitting room. You'll do.'

On Lady Beatrice's last visit, for Lord Edwin's birthday party, Margaret had asked me if I'd press some of Her Ladyship's clothes. I'd agreed, because I'd thought at the time I could maybe learn about London ways if I helped Margaret, though I was well aware she was just using me to get rid of her own jobs.

No doubt that was her aim now. I got up to dress again – we maids were, after all, at the beck and call of our guests and their servants. But as I tugged off my old nightgown I was aware of her watching me. She seemed to be taking note of the slenderness of my figure, and I felt my breasts tingle suddenly under her gaze. Clumsily I pulled on my maid's gown, and once I was dressed she took my arm to lead me along the corridor and down the back stairs. 'Lady Beatrice doesn't believe in letting her life go to waste,' Margaret said to me. 'Be prepared.'

What? I stumbled on the next step.

She stopped and looked at me. Her teeth were white and pointy; the tip of her tongue slid a little over her thin lips. 'You've seen her, haven't you? My mistress? She knows life is for living.'

'But her husband died,' I whispered.

'And she's done her mourning. I'm just telling you this so you're not shocked.'

I froze. Shocked by what? She cupped my chin with her fingers; my pulse thudded again. 'You're pretty. Very pretty. Her ladyship's noticed you. Not done it with anyone yet, little Sophie? Who are you saving yourself for? Boyfriend lost at the war?'

I thought of the servants below with their kissing games. I thought of Will, but most of all I thought of Mr Maldon. 'There . . . there isn't anyone.' My words came out in a foolish rush and I moistened my lips, agitated.

'No one?' She grinned, and I thought I heard her murmur, *All the better*, but I couldn't be sure. It was so late, and I was very tired and low in spirits.

In Lady Beatrice's sitting room, several lamps were burning, and it looked as though a private party had been held in there, because the side-tables were littered with empty glasses and ashtrays, and the chairs were all out of place. But I remember noting through another door that the bedroom was pristine, the bedcovers unturned.

'We've plenty of time to clean up before Her Ladyship returns.' Margaret was looking around.

I nodded. 'Where . . .'

I was going to ask where Her Ladyship was, but I broke off in confusion, because I'd heard the other servants say how after the lights went out at these house parties the corridors were full of visitors tiptoeing around to each other's beds in the dark, then creeping back before dawn. My blood heated with embarrassment again.

By the time we'd got the room tidied, it was past midnight. I said, 'I'll go now. I'll just take these glasses and ashtrays down to the scullery.' I was bone-tired.

Margaret stopped me. 'Sit a while. Have a drink.'

Something held me there – despair, I think. In my tiredness, my usual obsession to make a better life for myself seemed quite hopeless.

She poured me gin, with something else in it – tonic, I guessed. It was not unpleasant though it made my head swim a little. Then Margaret was guiding me to a small settee covered in striped silk and with her own glass of gin in her hand she sat down, sighed and leaned against me. Her voice was husky in my ear and prickles of alarm ran up and down my spine. She whispered, 'Sweet little Sophie. Don't you ever get lonely? Don't you ever feel you're missing something? Don't you ever – *long* for something?'

All I Want Is You. Though the gramophone was silent now, its music still echoed in my mind. She put her hand on my breast and I jumped as if she'd shot me.

'Hush,' she said. 'Hush, now. It's all right. It's nice, isn't it? It feels nice, when I do that?'

Tremors of alarm and of something else, some indescribable sensation, were shooting up and down my spine. I hadn't had time, of course, to put on my corset and chemise, and she knew it. She undid some buttons of my black maid's gown and before I realised her intention her hand was sliding over my bosom. When her fingertip touched my nipple, I jumped again, as a bolt of startling awareness charged through me, then suddenly she was leaning closer, her hand still on my breast, but her lips were on my mouth. I trembled as her tongue slipped between my lips and teeth.

I could smell her musky perfume. She kissed my cheek and drew away. 'Stay there,' she said. 'Let me show you something.' She'd risen, one finger to her lips, and glided into Her Ladyship's bedroom to come back with a leather-bound book. Curling up beside me, she spread open the pages, one after another.

My heart hammered. The book was full of engravings: lewd portraits of couples engaged in intimacy, the likes of which I'd never imagined.

'This is one of Her Ladyship's favourites.' Margaret was pointing to a picture of a country churchyard – an idyllic scene, dotted with trees and ancient crosses. But if I looked closer, I saw that a lively looking youth was leaning back against the church wall with his breeches round his knees. He clasped a half-clad girl to him, whose skirt was up around her waist and whose legs were wrapped round his hips. I could see his aroused male member disappearing between her thighs and I felt a huge surge of shock.

'You like that one, little Sophie?' Margaret was whispering. 'Then see here, and here. You'll like these too.'

She was turning the pages with great care, and I saw some writing, but couldn't understand it; the book was French, I guessed. 'Now, *this*,' said Margaret, 'is what my lady finds the gents all simply adore.'

I was shaking as she pointed to a naked, voluptuous woman sitting astride a man's lap with one of her breasts lowered to his mouth. I was a country-bred girl, I heard the chatter of the servants day after day, I ought to know these things happened, but . . .

'You're such a sweet little thing,' Margaret was whispering as she turned the pages. She reached to kiss my cheek. 'Such a pretty little thing. Not had a man yet? Not let any of those louts of footmen get inside of you?'

I shook my head numbly.

'Oh, you're a prize then,' she went on, 'my lady won't half be interested in *you*.'

Lady Beatrice, interested in me? I could scarcely breathe, and something was churning and clenching low in my abdomen.

Margaret took the book away. 'That's your first lesson. But now, let me teach you a little more.'

The gin raced through my blood. She was humming one of the tunes they'd been dancing to in the garden earlier – 'Everybody's Crazy on the Foxtrot'. Her hand was sliding up my leg to where I was warm and wet and I shuddered at her intimate touch, but at the same time I drew in a deep, deep breath of longing.

Margaret stroked me there more swiftly, her finger-tips sliding against my furls of flesh until I felt torrents of sensation flooding through me. She'd also pulled my bodice down further and her teeth were gently rasping at my nipple; her finger coaxed at my sex, finding the hot little bud there. My body stiffened; my delight cascaded as I cried out.

She held me while I shook. 'There,' she whispered archly at last. She was still caressing my breast. 'You see how that sort of treat will do you just fine for a while?

No men, no mess, no babies . . .' She got to her feet and sighed a little, smoothing back her dark hair into its pins. 'Her ladyship is leaving for London tomorrow. But she'll be back, and you'll find that I know exactly what Lady Beatrice wants before *she* does.' Her eyes suddenly glittered. 'I haven't always been a serving maid, you see. I used to be a dancer. In London.'

'You were a dancer? On the stage?' Again my pulse raced.

'Oh, indeed,' she said. 'I was up there nightly, kicking out my legs and flaunting my finery with the rest of them. I had so many fine gents after me – until *this* happened.'

She pointed to the scar on her cheek. 'I was too ambitious, you see. I thought to play one gent off against the other, but one of them turned nasty and put paid to my looks with a beer glass. Since then – ' she regarded me thoughtfully – 'I've found my entertainment in other ways. Oh, and I'm in charge of keeping Lady Beatrice happy too.'

Suddenly she gazed intently down at me. 'Are you sure you're a virgin, Sophie? Ready to swear it on the Bible?'

I could barely breathe. 'I swear it,' I whispered.

She kissed me on the lips, then went to a drawer and pulled out a purse, which she pressed into my hand. I could feel the coins in it through the soft leather.

'Take it,' said Margaret. 'Milady pays me well. And you're my investment.'

I stumbled back up to my room with my ill-gotten gains. The other housemaids were by then in bed and

47

fast asleep; it was I who lay there awake, with the purse a dark secret under my pillow.

I was her investment, she'd said. What did she mean? Oh, what had I done?

He was dead, my Mr Maldon, he had to be dead, or I would have heard, I would have known. The next day I wrote to him nonetheless. *Something has happened. I wish I had someone to talk to. I know that I'm foolish, but I think of you all the time.*

Chapter Four

Lady Beatrice and Margaret left for London the next day, but I had little time to either be sorry or glad about their departure because after lunch Mrs Burdett called me into her room to tell me that Will Baxter was home at long last from the war.

'I know you and he are old friends,' she said with an unexpected twinkle in her eye. 'And look, Will's sent a note for you.'

I opened it quickly. *Dearest Sophie, I am back and I should be very glad to meet with you again. Yours ever, Will.*

His writing was clumsy, though I despised myself for noticing it. Meanwhile Mrs Burdett had gone to sit behind her desk again, putting on her spectacles before studying the day's work rota. 'Now,' she said after a moment or two, 'I think we can spare you.'

'Spare me?'

'For the afternoon, I mean.' She positively beamed. 'Go and visit your young man, Sophie.'

Will was outside the Baxters' tumbledown cottage with his back to me, mending a fence by the vegetable patch with his younger brothers and sisters all clustered at his side.

He was still in his army uniform. He had grown, of

course, and he looked so sturdy. But he swung round when I spoke his name, and I noticed how his face lit up in the old way. Quickly he sent the young ones packing, then we walked down the hill to a place where we used to sit, near the river.

He told me he and thousands of other soldiers had been kept on in Germany after the war, in somewhere called the Rhineland. 'We'd been ordered there in case the Boche decided to play any new tricks,' he declared, with a swagger he'd not had before. 'But then we were told we could go home, and about time too.'

He recounted the journey by ship from France to England, and how half the soldiers had been seasick. He told me that to celebrate their return to Blighty their captain had bought them each a pint of bitter and some jellied eels in Dover, which, he laughed, made many of them even sicker.

But once Will had told me all that, he began to look serious and so sad. 'Sophie,' he said, 'Sophie, I saw things in the fighting that I don't want to see ever again.'

'Oh, Will.' My heart turned over, for him and for all of them. 'Was it so very bad?'

He nodded. 'But tell me how *you* are, Sophie. Tell me what life is like at the Hall.'

So I talked to him lightly, but I didn't tell him anything really about how most of them – except Mrs Burdett – despised me. I didn't tell him about what went on downstairs sometimes late at night, and the kissing game they'd played. I didn't tell him about my dream of getting away from there and being a dancer, and what I'd let Lady Beatrice's maid do to me.

He listened to my stupid chatter about the menial jobs I did and the food I ate, then he said, 'I've brought you something, Sophie.'

He reached into his pocket. And I realised he'd bought a ring for me, a little silver ring. I whispered, 'Oh, Will. *No . . .*'

'I've been offered a job at the mill,' he broke in eagerly, holding my hand. 'Once we're married, you can leave service. Oh, I won't earn a fortune, but it'll be enough to rent a small cottage and keep you and our children . . .'

His voice trailed away. He said in a different sort of voice, 'You don't want that, do you? Even though it's all I've ever dreamed of. You don't want . . . *me.*'

I couldn't answer. My throat was thick with sorrow. I was lying to myself when I'd thought he'd changed. He'd not changed at all – but I had.

'Sophie,' he said, in a voice I'd not heard him use before, 'Sophie, it was a living hell out there, with the guns and the bodies and all that. I only kept from going out of my mind by thinking about you.'

I swallowed down the lump in my throat. I touched his hand, then got to my feet, whispering, 'Will, it's just that we're both so young.'

He stood up too. 'I've killed men,' he said in that different voice of his. 'And I've seen men younger than me die. I'm old enough to know there will never be anyone but you.'

'I'm sorry,' I said blindly. 'So sorry.'

And I hurried away, leaving him standing there.

I heard a few days later that there'd been a fight in Oxford between the demobbed soldiers and some miners from the Gloucestershire pits who were marching to London. The miners were striking all across the country for more pay and a seven-hour day, and the soldiers were angry because of course most of the miners hadn't been in the war.

The soldiers had won the battle, as you would expect, but several of them spent the night in the town gaol, including Will. The soldiers had all been heavily drunk, I heard, and I was dismayed to think of Will going to the alehouse and downing pint after pint to drown his grief at my callousness.

I'm sorry, Will.

I was still desperate to better myself in any way I could. I secretly borrowed books from His Grace's library to read in my bed at night, and I practised dancing when I was alone, trying so hard to remember how the guests had moved to the music they'd played on Lady Beatrice's gramophone. I hummed those tunes to myself with longing and I dreamed, oh, how I dreamed. If a man with blue eyes came into those dreams of mine, who could blame me?

Dear Mr Maldon, I wrote that night. *I'm still writing as you told me to, although I don't think now that my letters reach you. Will Baxter my friend is back from the war at last. He asked me to marry him and I said no. Will is kind and good, but I don't love him, you see.*

I crossed out what I'd written about Will and started again. I told him how Harriet and Betsey had been to see *Her Heritage* at a picture house in Oxford and hadn't been able to speak of anything else for days. I told him how we'd heard there was some union for servants being started in London, but the Duke had said that any servant of his who joined it would be dismissed without pay.

The Duke was already filled with rage over the miners' strike. The Belfield estate, Mr Peters informed us in his important way, had owned vast coalmines in the Midlands for over a hundred years. During the war, the government had taken all the mines into national ownership so they were no longer the Duke's responsibility, but His Grace still took the miners' dissatisfaction as a personal insult.

Everyone thought the end of the war would make things better, I wrote to Mr Maldon. *Everything is changing here at the Hall, and so much is different. But I promise you my devotion, as always. Your Sophie.*

'Save your love, Sophie,' he'd told me on that day long ago in Oxford. And I did. For him, God help me. For him.

We heard in the New Year that the Duke's heir, Lord Edwin, had become very ill, and as usual Robert was our source. 'It's said His Little Lordship won't last out the month,' he declared gleefully in the scullery. 'So it's just as I predicted – the old witch has cast her curse.'

'Hush your wicked gossip, young Robert!' Mrs Burdett had come into the kitchen just then and she knew he was referring to the Duchess. 'The poor little lad maybe has a touch of fever. He'll pull through, that's for sure.'

But Lord Edwin died in the spring of 1920, when I was seventeen.

The funeral took place at Lord Edwin's home in Chichester, but of course the Hall was cast once more into mourning. I wondered if Lady Beatrice had attended the funeral, but didn't ask, chiefly because talking about her reminded me of Margaret, and I'd been trying to forget Margaret and the things she'd done to me that night in Lady Beatrice's sitting room. Were it not for the coins she'd given me, I'd have thought it all a dream.

Will had got his job at the mill on the Belfield estate and somehow all the servants knew what had happened between him and me. 'They say he's not smiled since you turned him down,' they muttered. 'Poor Will.'

Only Nell remained my friend, and she was still head-over-heels in love with Eddie. 'Oh Sophie,' she'd say with glowing eyes. 'I quite understand, about Will. You want to feel *real* love like I do for my Eddie, don't you?'

I said nothing, because the other night out in the back courtyard, as I emptied the kitchen scraps into the swill bin, I'd seen 'her Eddie' kissing Harriet in the shadows.

Because of the mourning for Lord Edwin, there were no house parties. But there was always a service every day in the family chapel of the Hall, at which the Duke, confined to his bath chair, read out a Bible lesson, and the vicar led us in prayers that seemed to go on for ever. What the Duke and Duchess were really praying for, Robert slyly informed us one evening in the servants' hall, was for the new heir to meet with some disaster. 'Their Graces are absolutely furious at the idea of him inheriting,' Robert declared. 'But the London debs are wild with excitement.'

'Why?' asked Nell.

He looked at her pityingly. 'Use your sense, Nelly. This man's already filthy rich, he's unmarried, and some day he's going to be a duke.'

'How old is he?' asked Betsey. 'What is he like?'

'Who cares? He could be fat as a tub of lard and as old as Methuselah, he's still easily the biggest catch for years . . .' Robert broke off and looked at the wall clock. 'My goodness, is that the time? Now listen, everybody. Listen to this . . .'

Robert was beckoning us over to his crystal set, where with great drama he fiddled about until, after the usual crackling and hissing, we heard a lady's voice faintly singing 'Home Sweet Home'.

'That's Dame Nellie Melba.' Robert grinned. 'How about that? The lady herself, singing in Chelmsford, right this minute.'

'You ain't half a clever-clogs,' muttered Betsey.

Mrs Burdett had come in and was listening in amazement. 'Chelmsford? How . . .'

Robert began to explain about radio transmissions, using words none of us could understand. I just listened to the music, entranced, but soon enough the bells began to summon us upstairs, and we all went rushing off to do our jobs again.

One day when we were in the sluice room, Nell pulled me aside. 'Oh, Sophie,' she said. 'Oh, Sophie.'

Tears were running down her cheeks. I went quickly

55

to close the door, after checking nobody else was around outside. 'Nell. What is it?'

She told me she was pregnant. My spirits sank, but I tried to say what I thought best. 'Eddie loves you, doesn't he, Nell? He'll marry you, he has a good job as the Duke's chauffeur . . .'

'He's saying it's not his.' She began sobbing noisily.

'Not his? But . . .'

'He told me that I'd – that I'd been with lots of other men for all he knew. But it's not true!' She looked distraught. 'There's nothing else for it – I'm going to have to get rid of it.'

'Nell. *Nell* . . .' But someone was coming; I could hear footsteps in the passage outside, and quickly we got on with our task of emptying the contents of the chamber pots down the drains then swilling them out. I worked in silent anger, because Eddie would get away scot-free just by saying she was a slut, and also because I'd heard terrible tales about women taking poisons like penny-royal in desperate attempts to end a pregnancy.

Later, when I got Nell alone again, I told her I thought there were church charities that would help girls like her; I said we could take the bus into Oxford on our next afternoon off, to find out.

But it was all too late.

Two days after Nell told me her news, I was up first as usual, for though I'd been here four years it was still my job to clean out the kitchen and scrub the huge oven before breakfast began. I'd just started to sweep the floor when the other servants came running in to tell me that Nell was ill in her bed. They were horrified, and asked me to come back upstairs to her. 'You're her friend, Sophie.'

Betsey actually offered to take over my tasks, and I hurried up the many flights of stairs to find Nell lying on her narrow iron bed in a pool of blood, her face as white as chalk.

'Oh, God,' I breathed. 'Oh, Nell . . .'

We did our best. We cleaned her, we made her sit up and drink a little hot tea, and someone found laudanum to ease the stomach cramps that seized her so badly.

'She was expecting a baby,' I told the others. 'She must have a doctor.' I think my voice was raw with despair; I didn't know if she'd taken something deliberately, or if it had just happened. And either way it didn't really matter, a doctor *had* to come to her.

But Mr Peters had arrived by then – I could hear his stern voice outside our dormitory. 'Doctor Blakey cannot be sent for,' he declared. 'That would mean Their Graces would have to know what has happened, and they would be shocked beyond belief. Besides, we are expecting important guests.'

It sickened me that Nell should be lying there in her own blood, possibly dying, and she was being ignored simply so that the Duke and Duchess shouldn't be troubled. Suddenly I realised how much I hated this place. I hated the Duke and the Duchess and all their grand visitors; all the people for whom I and Nell and the others had to turn our faces to the wall as they passed by because we weren't fit to look at them.

Nell continued to have terrible cramps all day and

was still bleeding. I wanted to tell Mrs Burdett what had happened, but house guests were indeed expected that afternoon and Mrs Burdett was closeted with the Duchess taking orders, which could take hours.

The other maids said they'd do my jobs, so I stayed with Nell up in the attic, and I grew more and more afraid for my friend. I changed her sheets, I held her hand, and as I toiled up and down the flights of stairs with hot water for her, I realised dimly that the guests had started to arrive. I hadn't even had time to wonder who they might be.

But on my way up the stairs yet again with a tray of tea for poor Nell, I suddenly heard Margaret's voice behind me.

'Why, Sophie. I've just been looking for you in the servants' hall . . .' She broke off. 'Whatever is the matter?'

Beyond caution, I blurted out Nell's tragedy. Margaret pursed her lips and hurried away; I thought – I *hoped* – that was the last I'd see of her. But we maids were just having our usual snatched meal before starting to prepare the guests' dinner when Lady Beatrice burst into the servants' hall, looking magnificent and furious.

Poor Mrs Burdett, who'd just come in, was unfortunate enough to catch Her Ladyship's full wrath.

'You've a very sick maid upstairs,' announced Lady Beatrice, her hands on her hips. 'You'd leave the poor girl to die? You want to pretend nothing's happened?' Mrs Burdett didn't know yet about Nell because I hadn't had a chance to tell her. 'My God,' said Lady Beatrice, 'would you all smuggle out her corpse and bury her somewhere at the dead of night?'

I rather thought that Mr Peters would. He stepped forward, adjusting his metal-rimmed spectacles, and started to explain, but in the end Lady Beatrice interrupted him and declared that she'd drive to town herself to fetch the Duke's physician. Then her eyes fell on me. 'You. Sophie, isn't that your name? Come with me – Margaret tells me you're the only one around here who has any sense.'

So I went with her, and though I was concerned for Nell, my mind was whirling. I knew that Margaret must have told Lady Beatrice about Nell, and I wondered suddenly if Margaret had told her mistress about the kisses and caresses the two of us had shared. My heart thudded, my cheeks burned.

I kept glancing all the time at Lady Beatrice as she drove. I noticed everything about her – I couldn't help it. Her short dress and matching coat – oh, in cream and coral silk, so lovely, her fine stockings and her shoes with their little heels. The way she drove her motorcar with such confidence.

I wanted to be like her. Not like Margaret, not a servant, but like her. She was humming as we careered down a narrow country lane – 'Rockabye Your Baby with a Dixie Melody' – but she was frowning, and I could tell she was furious about Nell. My pulse was racing.

I think somehow I knew that my life was going to change very soon.

Chapter Five

Doctor Blakey came back to the Hall in his car and he called an ambulance to take poor Nell to the Oxford hospital. After Nell had gone I went to find Eddie, who was out in the courtyard polishing the Duke's Rolls-Royce and whistling.

'You are scum,' I told him. I was so angry. 'Scum, to abandon poor Nell, and to speak to her so cruelly.'

Eddie cocked his head insolently. 'Could be me, could be one of quite a few others. She put it about a bit, did our Nellie.' He started whistling again and turned back to the shiny motorcar.

'She loved you,' I insisted. 'You know she loved you.'

He came close, smelling of sweat and car polish. 'Well, Miss High-and-Mighty. You're really turnin' out to be quite sweet-lookin', ain't you? But they say you're too stuck up to be interested in any courting. You kept poor Will Baxter dangling, then went cold on him. Know what you need? What you need is a bit of *this* inside you . . .'

Before I realised what he was talking about, he'd grabbed my hand and put it on his crotch. With shock flooding through me I realised he was aroused; he wanted me, or thought he did. I kicked hard at his shin.

He cried out in rage. 'By God,' he growled. 'By God, you bitch. You really *do* need a lesson, like the others say.'

He grabbed me and hauled me against him while his mouth clung greedily to my lips, but I kneed him, I caught him where it really hurt, as I'd heard the other maids describing. Then I ran inside, shaking with helpless fury.

Two nights later, Mrs Burdett called me in to her private sitting room. She needed, she said, to warn me that the other servants were complaining about me. Why, she wouldn't say; but I guessed that on top of the whispers that I'd been cruel to Will, Eddie was spreading his lies. What grieved me above all was that Mrs Burdett, who had always been kind to me, had now turned against me.

Mr Peters happened to be passing as I left the housekeeper's room, and he eyed me askance through his metal-rimmed spectacles. 'Sophie, there you are. Lady Beatrice has asked if you'll take a tea-tray up to her private sitting room.'

Why me? Why not Margaret? My mind in a whirl, I took the tray up and went in; *oh my*, I remembered that room well, the settee where Margaret and I . . .

Lady Beatrice told me to sit down on that very settee, while she strode around in her long blue evening gown, impatient and agitated. 'I'm going to be staying for a while,' she told me. 'There's a great deal going on here at the moment, Sophie, and I *need* to be here.'

Though she was their son's widow, she had never shown much sign of affection to the Duke and Duchess, so I wondered what had caused her change of heart, but of course it wasn't my place to ask.

'The thing is this,' she went on. 'I need a second maid while I'm here, in addition to Margaret, and I'd very much like a girl who's utterly familiar with the household, yet on whom I can rely. I want you to work for me, Sophie, for the next few weeks at least. Would you be interested?'

I think I probably stammered my reply, I was so overwhelmed. 'I-I don't know, my lady. I would have to ask Mrs Burdett—'

'I'll do that,' she interrupted. 'And I'll make sure she agrees.' She gazed at me thoughtfully from top to toe, then lit a cigarette; she smoked it using a long ivory holder. 'Margaret will still be my chief maid, of course,' she went on, 'but I need someone who is good at sewing and at caring for different fabrics. You like clothes, don't you, Sophie? You like *my* clothes?'

I wondered if she had noticed me watching her and taking in everything she wore, every detail. All I could do was nod, but she smiled, looking as satisfied as one of the Duchess's cats with a bowl of cream. 'I thought you did,' she said softly. 'So you'll agree to the job?'

I felt both fear and excitement, mingled with relief that Margaret must have said nothing about the time I'd spent with her here, in Lady Beatrice's rooms. 'I would be honoured, my lady.'

'Then start looking at my clothes, why don't you?' She glanced at the ormolu clock on the mantelpiece. 'We have an hour before dinner. Pick your favourites. Try something on.'

What? 'I-I beg your pardon, my lady?'

'Choose a gown. And try it on,' she repeated impatiently.

I still remember that gown I picked out from her wardrobe. She'd worn it to dinner the previous night – it was of pink crepe de Chine and she told me it was made by Jeanne Paquin, a famous Paris designer. It must have cost hundreds of pounds and I thought it was heavenly.

She poured us both drinks from a silver tray; she must have had quite a lot already, but she appeared icy calm. She made me taste mine – it was gin and tonic, like the drink Margaret had given me, and as I felt the unaccustomed alcohol racing through my blood, I was suddenly enthralled by what was happening to me. By the possibilities that were opening out in front of me.

I had to take my maid's gown off while she watched, and I hesitated, looking down at my old chemise and corset – they were far too bulky for the exquisite gown. I felt her eyes skimming my figure, and her fingers with their scarlet-painted nails were suddenly resting lightly on my arm.

'Take those ugly undergarments off,' she said. 'You're about my size, thinner if anything.' She was already searching in a drawer. 'Wear these instead.'

She handed me an unboned, feather-light brassiere with matching lace-edged knickers in cream silk. Oh, how often I'd gazed at pictures of similar exquisite, delicate garments in the magazines that sometimes found their way to the servants' hall! I put them on, my heart fluttering with excitement, and she helped me. The brassiere and knickers were gossamer-soft against my skin, and I thought – or did I imagine it? – that I felt her fingers caressing my ribcage. I was about to carefully pick up the Jeanne Paquin gown when she stopped me.

'*No.* Put these on, Sophie!' She was thrusting a pair of cream kid gloves at me, and I blushed as I eased them over my rough, chapped hands, but she patted my shoulder. 'It's not your fault that they give you such demeaning work. Now. Let me see.' She was looking around again. 'Here, you'll need these too.'

She handed me a pair of beautiful silk stockings, quite new, and some lacy garters; then it was time for the gown. I felt transformed. She lit herself another cigarette then stepped back and surveyed me thoughtfully. 'Turn round,' she commanded. 'Yes. You need your hair to be shorter, and you need some make-up too. Then you'll be quite lovely. Some day you must come to London with me . . .'

London? *London?*

'But for now,' she went on, 'I'm staying here. You see, I want to find out what plans are being concocted for Lord Ashley.'

Some warning kicked inside me. 'Who is Lord Ashley?' I asked.

'He's the heir, Sophie.' She drew closer. 'The new heir to the title and all the Belfield estates, now that the sickly little nephew is dead. And they hate him. The Duke and Duchess simply hate him.'

The son of the English lord and the Frenchwoman. I nodded. 'I've heard, but I didn't know his name.'

'And I know what you'll have heard – that he's not

worthy of the title.' She smiled almost dreamily. 'He sets them a problem and I've come here, Sophie, to find out just what they intend to do about it. About – *him*.'

She drew on her cigarette in its long ivory holder. She put on a record, and started slowly to dance by herself. The song was called 'Jazz Baby, Be Mine' – I remembered it from the night they danced on the lawn. She was moving in time to it with her eyes shut, and was singing under her breath – she was more than a little drunk, I realised.

And so was I. I was sitting on the settee, watching her; I was wearing the beautiful French gown she'd helped me into, and the silk undergarments and stockings, and my insides shivered with forbidden excitement.

She's got everything I want for myself, I realised. She had knowledge and sophistication; she had money and independence – everything I could have desired in my wildest dreams. And she was talking about this Lord Ashley, the hated heir, as if he were part of her plans.

'Lord Ashley,' I repeated. 'Why should Lord Ashley matter to you, my lady?' As far as I could gather, her own income was secure; she came from an immensely wealthy family, which was why Lord Charlwood had married her. We all knew that was the way of things.

She sat beside me, and I remember her perfume was heavy and alluring. 'Sweet little Sophie. Why should Lord Ashley matter to me, you ask? Because, quite simply, I'm going to marry him.'

Shock jolted through me. 'But surely. Don't you—'

She interrupted. 'I know what you're thinking.

Shouldn't I still be grieving for my decent, ever-so-British husband? Really, he wasn't over-bright, you know. And, to be honest, he wasn't awfully good in the bedroom department.'

I blushed, and she laughed. 'Oh, child, some men are worth bedding and some aren't. Shall we say they can . . . *vary* in their attributes? Charlwood would have made a perfect old-style duke, I'd have provided him with the obligatory heir or two, but then, my God, I'd have escaped back to London, leaving him to his hunting, fishing and shooting.'

She put her arm round my shoulders, pulling me closer on the small settee. 'But – Ash,' she went on dreamily. 'I want him all right.'

My mouth was dry. *Ash.* 'You've met him, my lady?'

'Oh, I met him briefly a few years ago, in London.' Her lip curled as if at some private joke, and her smooth palm was suddenly cool and silky on my poor work-chapped hands. I clenched my fingers; she unfurled them and frowned. 'Such pretty hands,' she muttered. 'Such pretty hands.'

I was silent, but I remember that my heart was pounding, and the pink dress suddenly felt too tight and too hot.

Then she said, as if breaking a spell, 'Well. You'd better put on your hideous maid's outfit again, little Sophie. And remember, I trust you not to breathe a single word about what I say to you, what I tell you. Do you understand?'

And so I became Lady Beatrice's maid.

★ ★ ★

Margaret took me under her wing, her dark eyes gleaming whenever she looked at me, the scar on her cheek always giving her narrow face a slightly sinister appearance. 'You and I, Sophie,' she said softly, 'we're to share a bedroom.'

I felt a quick spasm of fear that must have shown, because she laughed a little then showed me the room. It led off my lady's private quarters, and in it were two narrow iron beds, a dressing table and a shared wardrobe. That first night I hardly slept, but to my relief Margaret didn't try to touch me again. It was as if she'd forgotten that we were intimate, but I could never forget – I jumped if her hand so much as brushed mine. Yet my blood surged with excitement, because I saw in all this my chance to leave the Hall at last. *London,* Lady Beatrice had said. *Some day you must come to London with me, Sophie.*

Sometimes I saw Lady Beatrice watching me, when I was sewing in her sitting room or helping Margaret to adjust one of her beautiful gowns. I kept my eyes down, I spoke only when spoken to, but was aware of her, always. And I absorbed every detail of those exquisite garments; the styles and the adornments she chose.

Skirts were getting shorter every season for the fashionable; Lady Beatrice wore hers with the most exquisite silk stockings and, instead of heavy corsets, she dressed herself in the kind of undergarments she'd let me try on: soft chemises and brassieres made of silk or satin in shades of cream and light caramel. I adored her clothes. I believed that even I could be beautiful in such garments.

She said nothing more of Lord Ashley to me. Meanwhile other guests arrived and left, as was the way in these grand houses; and in the early autumn the Duke hosted an important meeting, to which politicians from London and even New York came.

Mr Peters, in his haughty way, told the staff it was something to do with the huge war debt that Britain owed to the American government.

'Why not meet in London?' asked Betsey.

'Because,' said Mr Peters importantly, 'these people realise that they will get far more privacy here at the Hall than they ever would in London.'

Indeed the guests had their privacy, and they were also entertained on a sumptuous scale. Every day there were outings, every night there were vast banquets of twenty courses or more, and I gathered from Margaret that Lady Beatrice was in great demand because of her beauty and her sharp wit. She was friendly with a pale-haired, pale-eyed man called Lord Sydhurst, whom the footmen detested because he was so extremely arrogant. 'Lord Sydhurst,' pronounced Robert, 'likes to talk of his important work in the war. Which means, of course, that he sat on his backside in some government office in London and gave lots of orders.'

'So he shot about as many Germans as you, then,' said Betsey. Which put paid to Robert's smart talk for a while.

Lady Beatrice was also often seen in the company of an American called Guy Fawcett. Mr Fawcett was a dark, thickset man in his thirties – *a dish*, Betsey called him, but I'd hardly noticed him at all, until one night Margaret woke me. It was around two or three in the morning, I guessed.

'Shh.' Margaret put her finger to her lips and motioned to me to follow her. Very quietly she opened our bedroom door then led me – I was still in a fog of disturbed dreams – across the carpeted floor of Lady Beatrice's sitting room. We walked barefoot on tiptoe between the pieces of furniture, I remember, and when we reached Lady Beatrice's bedroom I saw that a soft glow came from beneath the closed door, showing that a lamp was lit within. Then I heard a sighing noise which puzzled me, and the rhythmic creaking of a bed.

I didn't understand what Margaret was intending, but my senses prickled in warning. Margaret bent to look through the keyhole, then moved aside. 'Your turn,' she mouthed to me.

My heart was beating so painfully I could scarcely breathe, but neither could I hurry away as I should have done. I bent to look, and in the shadowy lamplight I saw – oh, my, I saw Lady Beatrice, quite naked, kneeling on the bed beside Guy Fawcett. He lay on his back, naked also; his eyes were tightly closed, he had reached behind him to grip the headrail, and . . .

She had him in her mouth. She had his erect member in her mouth, and was sliding her lips up and down it.

Guy Fawcett was by no means attractive to me. He was heavily muscular; his chest and limbs were furred with dark hair. Yet I'd never seen an aroused, unclothed man before, and something deep inside me tightened and shook. I watched in horrified awe as Lady Beatrice caressed him with her tongue. And Margaret was watching *me*.

A sound came from the corridor outside. It was most

likely just a draught, but Margaret pulled me away and we stole back to our beds, though I think we both lay awake for a long time after that. I was badly disturbed, I longed to touch myself in the way Margaret had shown me, but I knew that was probably what she wanted, so I resisted, though I burned.

The next day the diplomats left and, in the afternoon, Lady Beatrice went to London, taking Margaret but not me. I tended to Her Ladyship's clothes, washing the more delicate items myself in grated soap and warm water and airing them in the drying room. I heard them talking avidly about Lady Beatrice below stairs, whispering that she'd had affairs in London with all sorts of men, married or otherwise, and even the discreet Mrs Burdett was heard to mutter that the way she treated the memory of her dead husband, Lord Charlwood, was nothing short of scandalous.

But I considered anew what she'd been doing with Guy Fawcett in the dead of night, and though what I'd seen still disturbed me, I thought, in Beatrice's defence: why should she waste her youth mourning for a man who was gone for ever, and whom she had never loved anyway?

We heard that Nell was being cared for in a charity home run by Anglican nuns just outside Oxford. I still wrote regularly to Mr Maldon, although I no longer believed he read my letters or even received them. I wrote: *Lady Beatrice, Lord Charlwood's widow, has come to visit. She is very modern. She wears clothes that you are*

probably used to in London, and she has asked me to help
her with her wardrobe, because I am quite good at sewing,
my mother taught me . . .

I stopped. I wanted to write, *I saw her. I saw her in*
bed with a naked man, giving him pleasure with her mouth
in a way I would not have thought possible. And I cannot
forget it.

One night, disturbingly, Mr Maldon became Guy
Fawcett in my dreams. Lady Beatrice was astride him,
coaxing him into intimacy, and I was terribly upset. I
wanted to push her away and scratch her smooth skin
till it bled and take her place. I wanted to protest to the
skies that my Mr Maldon was waiting not for her but for
me, me, me.

When I awoke there were tears in my eyes and my
throat burned.

Chapter Six

When Lady Beatrice returned from London, we all saw straight away that she had arrived without Margaret and I waited nervously for her summons. During her absence the Duke had suddenly become quite ill. Normally at this time of year the Duke and Duchess would host shooting parties and entertain a houseful of guests; but instead the Hall was subdued, and the early autumn mists that gathered in the valley at daybreak increased my feeling of being isolated from the outside world.

'One thing,' declared Betsey over tea in the servants' hall one day. 'If the old Duke croaks his last and we get this new Duke, we might see a bit more life around here.'

'Don't count on it,' put in Robert. 'If the new chap does become Duke, then from the sound of him he'll be living the high life in London, Paris and all over the place. Oxfordshire will be far too bloomin' quiet for *him*.'

I was silent, remembering what Lady Beatrice had said: that she intended to marry him. Then I had to leave, because Lady Beatrice had called for me at last. And she told me why Margaret wasn't with her.

She'd found out, you see, that Margaret and I had been watching her that night when Guy Fawcett was in her bedroom, and Lady Beatrice was so angry. I thought with desperate anxiety, *I will lose my job here. Everything is ruined.*

Lady Beatrice was pacing her sitting room while I stood by the door with my head bowed. 'That fool Margaret had no right,' she stormed. She'd had her black hair cropped very short while she was away; she was smoking her cigarette in its long ivory holder. 'No right at all to spy on me.'

I stammered, 'When she woke me and led me to your bedroom door, my lady, I didn't realise what was happening. And then – and then . . .'

My face flamed. I felt tawdry, making these pitiful excuses, but Lady Beatrice was suddenly standing very still. 'Did you enjoy watching, little Sophie?'

I could say nothing; she drew closer. The curtains had already been closed against the gathering twilight and I could smell her musky, expensive perfume.

'*Did you enjoy it?*' she persisted.

Lady Beatrice was my only chance, and I had to tell her the truth. I met her eyes steadily. 'You are always beautiful, my lady,' I said. 'But that night, I thought you looked like the most beautiful person in the world. I wish – how I wish – I could be like you.'

She let out a little sigh. 'Do you really?'

I nodded, my heart thudding against my ribs. She could dismiss me for my arrogance now, in daring to compare myself to her, a great lady. Then she touched my cheek almost tenderly, and sheer relief flowed through my veins. 'Why not?' she breathed. 'Why shouldn't you be as beautiful as me? Did Margaret tell you that Guy Fawcett wanted *you*, Sophie?'

My breathing stopped. Her fingertips were still stroking my face.

'He wanted me to bring you to him,' she whispered. One red-tipped finger stopped on my full lower lip. 'He wanted to take your virginity, in front of me . . . You *are* a virgin, aren't you?'

I nodded numbly.

'Lord Sydhurst was interested in you too,' she went on softly. 'But don't worry. I have other plans for you.'

Plans. Hadn't Margaret said something like this? *My lady won't half be interested in you.* Suddenly my ribs ached with the need for air. She'd already risen, and was walking across the room to pour herself another drink, but then she turned back to me. 'There are a lot of things you need to learn, little Sophie. And don't waste a minute worrying about Margaret, will you? My God, the woman was becoming insolent – I was looking for an excuse to get rid of her.'

Lady Beatrice had been asked to assist the Duchess with one of her enormous flower arrangements. She'd gone downstairs and left me in her sitting room with a day-gown that needed hemming, but my fingers were shaking so much I could not even thread the needle.

She'd said that the American had wanted to bed me, and no doubt there would have been a reward for me, like the coins Margaret had bestowed. That would make me a whore. All my plans, all my dreams – and the only opportunity that had presented itself so far was to become a whore.

Bitterness welled up inside me.

People judge you by the value you place on yourself, Sophie.

I suddenly let the sewing fall; I pressed my hands to my burning cheeks. If I was going to end up a whore, I preferred to choose my own clients and name my own price. But when Lady Beatrice came back an hour later, she looked excited, almost feverish.

'The Duke is more ill than I thought, Sophie!' Eagerly Beatrice sat on the settee and patted it for me to sit beside her. 'Ah, the old witch will be furious – her husband's not supposed to die till they've dealt with Lord Ashley. And I've found out the Duke and Duchess's plan. They're going to try and make out that he's not who he says he is!'

My mouth must have dropped open. '*What?*'

She lit a cigarette and waved her hand impatiently. 'They're going to claim that he's a changeling – was substituted at birth, in other words.'

I laughed aloud. 'That's ridiculous. Like a fairy tale . . .' My laughter suddenly faded at the look on her face.

'I agree with you – but that's what the Duke and Duchess are saying.' She'd drawn closer. 'Come along, now. I know how servants talk. What do you know about the new heir, Sophie?'

I tried to remember what Cook had said. 'His father was an English lord who lived abroad, and his mother was a French lady.'

'That's right. Ash's father was an impoverished English baron who fancied himself an artist. His French wife – a nobody – gave birth to Ash in utter obscurity, somewhere in the French countryside.'

She leaned closer. 'When an important heir's born, Sophie, there are always doctors and independent witnesses present to verify that the child is really the mother's. But in Ash's case, there was no birth certificate, there are no reliable witnesses to be called upon, and both Ash's parents are dead. After all, who would have thought that Ash might one day be heir to a dukedom? Lord Charlwood was born within the first year of the Duke and Duchess's marriage, and they could have been expected to have many more children. But they didn't.'

Her eyes gleamed. 'The Duke and his Duchess are fighting tooth and nail to get Ash's claim annulled. But Ash *will* inherit, he will!' Suddenly her mood shifted again. She was like that, was Beatrice: you would even see her eyes change from dark to light; you would see her pointed chin lift in defiance. 'Let's have some music,' she declared. She'd already jumped to her feet and was putting on her favourite, 'Alexander's Ragtime Band'.

With the music my earlier despair began to dissipate. Things *were* happening, my world *was* changing. She couldn't make me do anything I didn't want to do. But I would learn from her, oh, I would learn.

She'd started opening up a trunk of new gowns, each of them folded and wrapped in tissue paper, and was pulling them out to show me. 'Sophie, I've brought these from London – look at them, do.' Then she started dancing dreamily to the music by herself. The gowns were exquisite, but I preferred to look at her. She grabbed my arms to sweep me up. We danced together, and I laughed with pleasure. I don't know what dance it was, I didn't care; my feet just worked, and it was like flying.

'Oh, Sophie,' she breathed. 'Little Sophie. You're adorable.' She drew me to a halt. 'Take your horrid maid's things off.'

She'd asked me to do this before, and I'd obeyed. But this time my heart was pounding in warning. *Something had changed.* It was the way she'd danced with me. The way she'd talked about the American wanting me. I slowly took off my black housemaid's dress.

Under it I wore just a plain white cotton chemise. I couldn't bear to put on my old underwear, my boned corset and bodice, not since she'd said how ugly it all was. She gave me her cigarette to try but I coughed a little, I didn't like it much, so I simply took the holder between two fingers the way she did, until she smiled in approval, and I suddenly realised she was stroking my shoulder and sliding the strap of my chemise lower and lower until one pink nipple was peeping over the top.

I caught my breath and my pulse raced. I felt excited and a little afraid, but God help me, I wanted her to go on. I wanted to learn.

With her fingers she toyed with both my nipples, one after the other, and I felt a tremor go through me. Margaret had done the same, but this was different, because I thought Lady Beatrice was beautiful. I think I was slightly dazed with the strangeness of these new feelings, and I found I was squeezing my thighs together to ease the sudden ache down there.

She whispered, 'Are you thinking of Guy Fawcett, Sophie?' She drew me down onto the settee, so we were sitting side by side. I shook my head – *no*. She began to chuckle. 'You're thinking of someone, though, aren't you? A man. You want a man.'

I moistened my lips and managed to say, 'I don't want just anybody.' And I didn't. Not like arrogant Robert, or Eddie, who got Nell pregnant then tried to deny it.

As if guessing my thoughts she said abruptly, 'How's that foolish girl who lost her baby?'

'Nell? She's gone to some kind of home,' I said. But I knew they wouldn't keep her there for ever; she'd have to come back here, probably. Poor Nell.

Beatrice said curtly, 'Let's hope the girl's learnt her lesson. You'll have learnt from it too, won't you, Sophie? You're aiming higher, aren't you, my dear?' She stroked my cheek tenderly.

Yes. My God, yes, I am. Mr Maldon. If he was still alive, if he . . . I turned to her, my blood pounding, scarcely heeding my chemise falling from my shoulders. 'Tell me, please, my lady. What do the kind of men you meet want above anything?'

She leaned nearer, her hand still toying with my small breasts. 'They want adventure, my dear – they hate the predictable. They want oblivion from time to time, through sex, alcohol, sometimes other kinds of drugs. Some want a beautiful slut. Others want a girl who is a fantasy of purity, of innocence, theirs and only theirs to be taken . . .'

Suddenly Beatrice's arm had tightened round my shoulder. She was gazing at me as if she'd not seen me before; her kohl-lined eyes were glittering with excitement. 'Sophie. My God, all this shy innocence, and you want to learn, so badly. Do you know, I've just had the most wonderful idea.'

I couldn't tell what was going on in her mind, I couldn't tell at all, but I knew that the air was charged between us, as if a thunderstorm were about to break. She had pulled herself away then rose from the settee to look down at me. 'Sophie,' she said, 'you're pretty. Extremely pretty.'

No, I wasn't. I'd never be beautiful like her, with her sophistication, her clothes from Paris. 'I'm too thin,' I shrugged. 'Everybody says so.'

'No. No. Modern girls are meant to be slim, it's all the rage in London – look.'

I suddenly saw that she'd unpacked some new magazines, which she grabbed and pushed towards me. While I turned the pages, she was pulling out more gowns from her trunk: picking one in grey chiffon, she beckoned me to her and got to work. Off came my old white chemise; I shivered, but now she was moving too quickly for me to feel afraid of being naked in front of her. First came a lace-edged brassiere and French knickers, both in palest green. Then she helped me put on silk stockings and finally the gown, just like last time when she'd made me wear that dress of pink crepe de Chine. When she'd finished, she pushed me to stand in front of the long cheval glass.

The dress I now wore was by Worth, she told me; it was sleeveless and drop-waisted, and my legs, in the nude silk stockings, looked shockingly sleek to me.

'I was wrong, Sophie,' Beatrice breathed. 'You're not pretty, you're beautiful.' Still bursting with energy, she found some shoes that fitted my small feet perfectly – they were of grey kid, with one-inch heels and buttoned straps – and we giggled together as I took some unsteady steps across the carpet, then collapsed into her arms. It was the cigarette I'd smoked, I told myself; it was the shoes; it was the sheer, incredible excitement of seeing what I could be. *What this could mean.*

Whatever it takes, I said again under my breath. *Whatever it takes.*

I was still leaning against Lady Beatrice. We were still both laughing, but our laughter died as we looked into each other's eyes. Slowly she put me away from her, her expression intent. 'We need to see to your make-up next. Sit there, at my dressing table.'

Carefully she pulled out a selection of the pots and tiny silver bottles that had always fascinated me, and she began to apply a little of each to my face: powder, a touch of rouge, a line of kohl painted around my eyes, then coral lipstick. I gazed into the mirror while she went to put on another record. I hardly recognised myself.

'Your hair is wrong,' she frowned. 'It should be short, like mine. But for now . . .' She quickly unpinned and brushed out my long fair hair, then picked up a pair of scissors. I must have flinched, because she laughed and said, 'Wait. Just wait, and see.'

I thought she might cut it all, but she trimmed only a small section so it fell across my forehead in a straight line above my eyebrows. Then she pulled back the rest of my still-long hair to the nape of my neck and pinned it into a smooth coil. She made me stand up and walk arm-in-arm with her to the cheval glass again; she held me tight as we looked at ourselves. *Oh my.* I was starting to look like her. Sophisticated. Modern. Elegant. My heart drummed with such excitement I could hardly breathe.

Her eyes too were glittering. 'Look at us. One fair, one dark ... Oh, Sophie, you're so lovely.' She was a little drunk, I thought. The lamp flickered and the record had stuck. *Love is the sweetest thing ... Love is the sweetest thing ...* Her arm tightened through mine. 'Let's dance, again Sophie. I want to dance.'

She glided to the gramophone to start the record again. She was intoxicating, I realised, as she drew me into her arms. Suddenly hot, I cast my eyelashes down, watching our feet as they moved and breathing in her scent, a spicy, exotic mix of patchouli and musk. I loved being near Beatrice. I loved what she had done for me.

Yet I wanted so much more.

Her scarlet-painted lips were against my ear as we danced. 'Little Sophie, I know you want a new life and I'm going to help you. You're so wise, not to have given yourself to some oaf of a man who doesn't deserve you. And your innocence will be your greatest asset as we lay our plans ...'

We again. *My innocence.* Oh, God, what was she thinking of? What was she planning?

But I was reckless by then, you see, and we danced on together, laughing now. Yet this time, when the record stopped, she suddenly placed my hand against her breast – and my breath caught in my throat at the intimate warm feel of her there, at the slight peaking of her nipple under the silk of her gown.

She put her hands on either side of my face. 'Do you sometimes feel, Sophie – ' her voice was a mere murmur now – 'that you can't bear waiting any more? That you can't bear being without a man, I mean?'

I shook my head, bashful again. 'I've never been with a man. So I've no idea—'

'But my dear,' she broke in, 'I know what you did with Margaret.'

My stomach lurched. *Margaret.* Oh, no. The things she'd said to me. The things she'd done to me.

Beatrice was still gazing at me. 'Indeed,' she said softly, 'she was aware of my fondness for . . . playing games, you see. Especially with one as innocent and lovely as you. She used to tell me everything . . .' Suddenly her eyes narrowed. 'Though she made a bad mistake, not telling me straight away about Guy Fawcett. I don't like being spied on. But what you did, with Margaret – it's only a shadow of what it's like, Sophie, to be with a man. And there are ways, as you know, to relieve the tension you must feel . . .'

Her hand had slipped round my waist. She was leading me, I realised, into her bedroom, where only one lamp flickered and the curtains were drawn. Slowly she undressed herself except for her stockings, then put on a silk kimono; I tried not to look, but I glimpsed enough to be reminded that her body was beautiful, her breasts full and high. For I'd seen her naked before, with the American, and at the memory my blood heated anew. *Playing games.* She passed another silk robe to me with a knowing smile.

'Here. Put this on,' she said.

So I undressed, like her. I was afraid she was watching me, but then I realised she had gone across to a closet and brought out a lacquered case with a tiny gold key to unlock it. She put the case on her bed, then came back to me.

'Sophie, I need you in my arms. Lie here like this with me, darling. That's right.' She put her arm around me, drew me with her onto her bed, snuggled herself close to me then sighed with happiness like a child. Her bright silk dressing robe had fallen apart and I saw with a jolt of shock that she had rouged her nipples. Excitement and a warning of danger made my pulse race at the sight of those creamy breasts with their scarlet tips. A dark, sweet tension unfurled in my womb.

'Kiss me,' she whispered. 'Please, kiss me, Sophie.'

She lifted herself up on one elbow so she was hovering above me. Her lips touched mine, lightly, then with firmer pressure; her tongue darted into my mouth and my pulse began to pound. She toyed with my mouth for a while, licking my teeth and tongue, gently biting the inside of my lip; she pushed back my robe and her hands were on my naked shoulders as I tried to control the aching throb that had started inside me.

83

She lay back suddenly with a little sigh. I was afraid I had done something wrong. But then she turned her dark head to me and I saw her cheeks were flushed, her lips swollen, her eyes very bright.

'Kiss me, there.' She was pointing to her breast. I moved and tentatively put my lips to her nipple, but it felt so strange, the flesh was so stiff – I backed away, and she grabbed me. 'Let me show you what to do, Sophie.'

Almost instantly she was there at my breast; like Margaret, only so much better. *Oh, my.* Her tongue was doing what her fingers had done earlier; she was sucking my breast into her mouth, and I cried out as delicious sensations shot through me. I felt my legs writhing; my secret place was hot and shamefully wet. She had slipped her thigh between mine, as her teeth gently bit my nipple. If she went on like this, I thought, I didn't know what would happen; I was coiled tight, I was burning, I could not stand this, I wanted more . . .

She drew away. I moaned softly in disappointment and she smiled at me in the half-light. 'The first lesson, Sophie,' she breathed, 'is to take your time. And learn to give as well as to receive.'

She'd reached for her lacquered box and drawn something out, but in the shadows I could not see it – until she put it in my hand. It was a thick, cool wand of ivory, several inches long. *Like – a phallus?* My insides throbbed with exquisite tension. Oh, sweet God, she could not – she would not . . .

She took it from me again, and pressed its length

against my tingling breast. I arched and moaned. 'Let me show you,' she breathed.

She parted her own legs and stroked the ivory shaft's blunt tip up above her stockings, which she still wore beneath her silk robe. Her dark hair was trimmed there into a neat triangle; I could see the pink lips of her sex, the furls of moist flesh as she drew the tip of the phallus between them. My heart stopped. *I want it to be me. I want . . .*

Still stroking the phallus up and down her sex she rasped, 'Kiss me, Sophie. Kiss my breasts, as I kissed yours.'

I put my lips to her nipple. I sucked, I licked the hardened crest with my tongue until she groaned aloud. 'Don't stop. Sweet Sophie, don't stop.'

She had raised her knees, and as she let them fall shockingly apart I saw her ease the blunt tip of the phallus into her sex. She was moaning and breathing harshly, and I felt myself becoming even more desperately hot and wet as she moved that ivory shaft in and out of herself; slowly at first, then harder, harder. Her parted thighs trembled frantically, she was lifting her hips in need, then as she drove it deep I bit on her nipple; almost instantly she exploded, thrashing in my arms, her hips pumping around the ivory wand.

I was on fire. I was burning with need myself. Slowly she pulled out the thick piece of ivory then leaned to press it against my mouth so I could taste her juices. I licked its smooth length desperately.

'Sweet little Sophie,' she murmured. 'You want this so

much, don't you? But we are going to save you. For Lord Ashley.'

And suddenly I was scrambling from the bed away from her.

Chapter Seven

For Lord Ashley – *no.* I was almost at the door but she was coming after me and pulling me back. 'No,' I said. 'No.'

She was stronger than me and was pushing me firmly to the bed by keeping her hands on my shoulders. 'Listen to me, Sophie,' she said, as if explaining something simple to an obstinate child. 'I want Lord Ashley. I want him badly. But men like him have their pick of the most beautiful, most sophisticated women in the world, so I need to show him that I can offer him what no one else can.'

Again I tried to break away but she grabbed my wrists. '*Listen.* In the kind of world the aristocrats live in, it's considered an amusing trick to provide your male lover – or indeed your husband – with a small gift now and then. A pretty serving maid, for example, preferably an innocent, for him to enjoy while the donor of the gift looks on.' Her hands tightened round me. 'I'm going to offer him you and me, Sophie. Together.'

My heart stopped then started again, so jerkily that I felt sick. And as her words finally sunk in, I realised that the path she'd taken me on so far was nothing, absolutely nothing compared to what lay ahead.

'I'm being remarkably generous to you,' Lady Beatrice went on. An edge of hardness had crept into her voice. 'More than generous. My dear, had you hoped to choose someone yourself to take your precious virginity? Someone you imagined – ' she laughed – 'would *love* you?' She'd got to her feet; she was prowling restlessly again. I think she'd realised I was shaking.

'I admit it,' she continued, 'there's a dark side to Ash. He's successful and ruthless and he doesn't give a fig what people say about him – which is as well, since he's made powerful enemies. I can cope with all that. I can make him realise that he needs me, as his wife. And I'm going to show him that marriage to me will be a beginning, not an end.'

I'd risen to my feet again. I'd pulled the edges of my gown together and my blood ran cold. But I remember I said – calmly, I think – 'What if I cannot – *will* not – do it?'

Her face was even harder then. 'Use your senses. Do you think you would stand any chance at all of escaping from here without my help? If you do, you're stupider than I thought. Most likely you'd end up like Nell in a few years – worn out by unwanted pregnancies and hard work. What do you want? What do you really want, Sophie, more than anything?'

I thought in despair of Mr Maldon, but I knew by then that I would never see him again. I lifted my head and met her eyes. 'I want to dance on stage,' I said. 'In London.'

I expected her to laugh out loud, but instead she

began to smile. 'That's good. That's very good, Sophie. Listen, then.' She came closer and seized my hands. 'Once you've helped me to persuade Ash that marriage to me will be an adventure and not a trap, then I'll take you to London myself – I'll even introduce you to the theatre managers I know. So what do you say?'

Shivering, I sat on the edge of the bed. The impossible was happening: Lady Beatrice was showing me a way out of my world of drudgery, possibly my only way out, but the price was high indeed. She was going to give me to Lord Ashley; offer him my virginity. And he sounded hateful to me. I imagined him as some muscular creature like Guy Fawcett, taking me almost frantically – *would it hurt? It must hurt, when the man is so powerful* – while Lady Beatrice perhaps tongued my breasts and watched my face darkly.

As she was watching me now. Then she sat beside me and picked up the ivory shaft again. To my shame my blood still seethed with deep physical need, and the coolness of that ivory – she was wicked, she was drawing it now up and down my thighs, then across my breasts – roused me unbearably.

Her dark eyes gleamed as I wordlessly reached for it. She looked almost sorrowful. 'Not this for you yet, Sophie. We must keep you a virgin, for my Ash.'

In that moment I loathed her Ash. But suddenly she had knelt with her face between my thighs, her pointed tongue was running lightly up and down my sex, and I simply could not believe the exquisite sensation. I cried out her name, I clutched at her hair; she lifted her face

89

to smile at me then started licking again, faster, stopping every so often to thrust inside me; such delicious torment, and her tongue was softly rasping, like a sleek cat lapping at milk.

I sighed and moaned, I cupped my breasts with my own hands, pulling at my own nipples, my world spinning around me. She pushed her tongue deep; I soared and exploded. She clasped my thighs and laid her cheek against them, steadying me until I finally fell to earth again.

She pulled me onto the bed with her and held me tightly in her arms. I think I was only half conscious, but I knew she was gazing at me, admiring her work. 'My gift, to Lord Ashley,' I heard her saying with quiet satisfaction. And fear gripped me again.

But I agreed, God help me. I agreed to it.

All through that autumn Lady Beatrice stayed on. It was because the Duke was ill, she told everyone – *her dear father-in-law*, she called him – and she sat often in his sickroom beside his bed, praising his dead son to the skies. The Duchess was extremely fond of Beatrice, letting her help with those flower arrangements and stroke the cats, though I knew Beatrice privately loathed the creatures. I wondered what the Duchess would say if she knew of Beatrice's plans.

I only went below stairs when I had to take down Lady Beatrice's trays, or needed to use the sewing room to attend to her clothes. The other servants thought I was giving myself stupid airs now that Her Ladyship had taken me as her personal maid. I wondered what they would say if they knew what Lady Beatrice really planned for me.

Ill though the Duke was, Lady Beatrice's presence lifted the gloom from the Hall and visitors began to arrive at Belfield again, among them the pale-haired aristocrat Lord Sydhurst. Beatrice called him 'Dear Eustace', and the servants muttered that she would no doubt be planning on marrying him. But I knew better.

Another of Beatrice's friends who visited was a gentleman called Rupert Calladine, who owned a theatre, Beatrice told me, in London. Mr Calladine was a suave little man with eyes as bright as his brilliantined hair, who charmed the Duchess completely and persuaded her to hold an autumn ball. About a hundred guests arrived on the night, the gentlemen in evening suits and the ladies in dazzling gowns. Such was Beatrice's influence on the ailing Duke that she'd coaxed him into taking a keen interest in the ball, and she was often to be seen at his side during the long evening, explaining the new music and new dances to him.

All of the servants were frantically busy, of course, and Mrs Burdett had asked Lady Beatrice if she could spare me for an hour or two that evening to help prepare the bedrooms for the guests who were staying. But I stole glimpses of the ball from the upstairs gallery whenever I had a moment to spare. I watched the guests dancing; I noted all the steps, and the way the young women dressed and talked.

Among the guests were some soldiers from a convalescent home near Oxford; the Duke had grudgingly agreed to invite them, we heard, because his political friends had advised him it would be good for appearances. Several of them had lost limbs and were in bath chairs like the Duke; they wore their medals pinned to their uniforms and I saw them watching the dancing with strange, blank expressions on their faces. I pitied them with all my heart.

Two days later Lady Beatrice told me she was taking me to Oxford to see *The Maid of the Mountains*. She dressed me in one of her tea gowns, lending me also a sage-green coat and some heeled grey shoes. She herself wore a silk cream cardigan coat embroidered with tiny pink flowers and pearls, and when she drove me into Oxford that evening I felt I was walking on air. We had a private box, and from the moment the curtain went up I was filled with wonder at the music and the costumes; I remember how we drove back singing 'A Paradise for Two' at the tops of our voices.

Otherwise the rest of that autumn was a strange time, a time of waiting. Quite often Lady Beatrice would take me out in her motorcar on the excuse of buying gifts in Oxford for the ailing Duke, but she much preferred to drive round the country lanes with the roof down and the breeze fresh in our faces. She would sing, and I'd sing too. She'd stop whenever the fancy took her, and we'd run up a hill, or dabble our stockinged feet in a nearby stream.

I was supposed to spend hours throughout the day dressing her and doing her hair, and rushing about saying, *Yes, my lady, No, my lady*, but Beatrice's clothes were so modern and light, her hair so easy to manage, that she could almost, she laughed, do it all herself.

So she spent time on me. I shared her bath. She painted my toenails, and licked my feet: *Such beautiful feet, little Sophie!* With her rouge she reddened my nipples, like hers, and gave me silk underclothes to wear beneath my drab servant's gown. She taught me dances like the Turkey Trot and the Boston Waltz – they were from America, she told me – and we practised the steps together arm-in-arm in her room.

She made love to me often, and though I was still desperately unhappy about her plan to give me to Lord Ashley, I think I told myself quite simply that given the choice I would do this all over again; because if I was to be a dancer I needed to be beautiful. And she was making me beautiful, I knew it, for I saw the way all the men of the house were starting to look at me. Even my poor work-worn hands were better now that I was no longer a scullery maid; Beatrice had shown me how to use a poultice of honey and oatmeal, and she smoothed some of her expensive Paris hand-cream on them at night.

Lady Beatrice intended to use me. Well, though I feared Lord Ashley's arrival and he was a figure of dread in my mind, I was using *her*. And at night when the house was in darkness, I tiptoed to her bed, where she caressed me into bewildering ecstasy. 'But you're still a virgin, Sophie,' she would emphasize. 'Still a virgin, for Lord Ashley.'

I wrote for the very last time to Mr Maldon.

I don't know where you are now. I stopped with my pen in the air, struggling for words. *But wherever you are, you might have heard that the Duke is very ill, and I am maid-servant to Lady Beatrice. I might not be here at Belfield Hall for much longer.*

I gazed into the shadows, sadness coursing through me, then I dipped my pen in the ink once more and wrote on in near despair: *I wish you had written back to me. I wish you had come for me. I will not write again.*

That night I dreamed – as I did almost every night now – that he was lying beside me and holding me in his arms. I dreamed of his flesh against my flesh; I teased my painted nipples in the dark, alone in my narrow servant's bed.

I cried out a name I didn't know, but I heard his voice, I saw his face.

Soon the October frosts were crisping the lawns and the gardeners' bonfires sent spirals of drifting smoke into the chilly air. Nell had now returned, but to me she didn't look strong enough to work from dawn till nearly midnight, and I thought it hateful that she still had to see Eddie almost daily when he'd all but wrecked her life.

For the first few days of her return I didn't get a chance to talk to her alone, but I did learn from Cook that Nell had been regularly visited in the charity home by Will and his family, the Baxters. I wondered if Will was courting her and, one afternoon, when we at last had a chance to be alone in the laundry room, I asked her.

'No,' Nell said sadly. 'I think he visited me at first so he could ask about you, then he simply felt sorry for me. But it's you he wanted, Sophie. It's you he's *always* wanted . . .'

She broke off; she must have seen my expression of remorse and regret because suddenly she rushed to me and hugged me tightly. 'Oh, I'm sorry. I'm sorry.' Her voice caught and broke. 'I loved Eddie so much – it's all right, I'm over him now, but I loved him, Sophie!'

I held her silently while her tears fell.

Doctor Blakey came daily to see the Duke, who was no better. The family's lawyer drove regularly from Oxford too for meetings with the Duchess, who was still desperate, Beatrice told me, to prevent the title and the entire estate going to Lord Ashley on the Duke's death.

I saw less and less of the staff, but one evening as I went downstairs for some coffee for Lady Beatrice, I found my way to the kitchen barred by four of the menservants, Robert and Eddie amongst them. Something in their expressions made my heart hammer.

'Excuse me,' I said, 'you're in my way.'

'And you don't like folks getting in your way,' sneered Eddie. 'Specially not common folks like us. But . . . you and Her Ladyship, now. The things we hear . . .'

I froze. Then, trying to breathe normally, I pushed past them and hurried on towards the kitchen. I realised Eddie was following me. 'What you need,' he said, 'the two of you, Her Ladyship and you, is a good bit of cock up you. And some day, bitch, you'll get it . . .'

Suddenly I saw Mrs Burdett bustling along the corridor in our direction. Eddie sauntered off, whistling under his breath. I was shaking.

Mrs Burdett saw Eddie and frowned. She said to me, sharply, 'Take care of yourself, young lady. I know you think you're destined for better things, but remember pride comes before a fall.'

I dipped a curtsey. After Eddie's verbal assault I was still trembling badly. 'Thank you, Mrs Burdett. Good night, Mrs Burdett,' I whispered. I fetched the coffee and hurried back upstairs. But late that night the house was suddenly in a state of uproar. Lady Beatrice called to me through my bedroom door but I was already wide awake. The old Duke was very ill, and Eddie had driven off in the Duke's motorcar to fetch Dr Blakey, but it was too late.

The Duke died before sunrise. I sat alone in my room, knowing this meant change everywhere, for everyone.

The shutters of the great house were closed and funereal draperies were hung at the windows, as they had been for the deaths of Lord Charlwood and little Lord Edwin. The bell of the village church tolled across the mist-shrouded valley as I dressed Lady Beatrice in her mourning clothes. She was very calm, but I could tell she was brittle with excitement.

'They've failed,' she breathed to me. 'The lawyers and all the old Duchess's paid lackeys have failed to prove Ash is not the true heir.'

It was naturally assumed that Lord Ashley – the new Duke of Belfield – would arrive for the funeral, but where exactly was he? No one seemed to know. The old Duchess was in such a storm of rage and self-pity that everyone except Beatrice was frightened of her. She walked around the Hall with her stick banging on the floor, frightening her own cats away and demanding again and again if anything had been heard from Lord Ashley. She refused to give him his new title.

'How can the son of a wandering artist and a Frenchwoman – a man who owns *factories* – be allowed to become the duke?' she was heard to wail. The rumours about his unsuitability grew and grew. The servants still called him Lord Ashley, too, and muttered angrily, 'It's not right that we should have to call him our master.'

There would be hundreds of mourners for the funeral from all around the country, with dozens of house guests. I felt oppressed again, dreading Lord Ashley's arrival, but Lady Beatrice was exhilarated. One afternoon, when I was tidying her room, she got me to take off her black bombazine gown and help her into a new frock of palest yellow silk with pleats that swirled light as swansdown from her hips. 'Do you like this one?' she asked me eagerly. 'Do you?'

'I think it's exquisite,' I said.

She must have seen the sadness in my eyes, because she hugged me suddenly. 'Soon I'll be a duchess, Sophie, and everything will be so different, you'll see. Ash *must* be on his way.'

I think I shivered; she drew away from me, clicking

her scarlet-tipped fingers impatiently, then went to pull a pastel blue frock from her wardrobe. 'Put this on,' she coaxed, twirling it before me. 'Then you'll feel better.'

I did as she said, of course. Always now I wore the beautiful silk lingerie she'd given me, and she let her smooth white hands skim down over my hips with a sigh of satisfaction before helping me ease the blue frock over my head. She fetched two glasses from a cabinet and poured us both some gin.

The dress was divine. But... 'It's so short,' I whispered.

'And why not? Your legs are beautiful, Sophie. So slender and shapely. When you dance on stage in London, the men won't be able to keep their eyes off you.'

Then quickly she went to put a record on and swept me into a foxtrot. She did that often, reminding me of my dream when she guessed I was becoming down-hearted. I knew she was cynically using me, but her good humour was infectious, and as I thought again of my future in London my spirits soared. We giggled, we sighed, we kissed. Her mouth was sweet and warm; her tongue slipped between my lips, tasting faintly of gin and tobacco. By then we'd stopped dancing but her body was swaying slightly close to mine and she was rubbing herself against me. 'Sophie,' she murmured, 'all day I've been thinking of you. Have you missed me?'

Once again her silken arms drew me close and her tongue twined with mine. She drew me to her bed and we lay there, our lovely gowns rustling. Her fingers with their red-painted nails were subtle yet teasing as they glided up my thighs and found my secret flesh there, toying with me until I was gasping, clenching myself around her. She'd pushed down the narrow shoulder straps of my gown and my brassiere; her mouth fastened on my breast and I climaxed almost instantly, grinding myself against her hand, letting out little gasps of pleasure.

Likewise I pleasured her with my mouth, brushing my lips to and fro over her sex then driving my tongue deep inside her, thrusting steadily. She liked that best of all. She moaned, moving her head from side to side and calling out my name in her extremity, then we lay in each other's arms while the autumn sun lit the room and we heard the motorcars coming and going on the driveway outside as more guests arrived for the old Duke's funeral.

'Have you heard yet?' I asked her drowsily. 'When Lord Ashley is arriving?'

She shook her head. 'Whether Ash is here or not for the funeral, you will still be my gift to him.' She kissed my cheek. 'You and I together – how can he resist?'

Beatrice told me again and again what we would do when he did arrive. How when the time was right she would invite him up here to her rooms, where I would be waiting. We'd even chosen the garments we would wear. 'We must remember,' she reminded me, 'that he'll be enduring the funeral rites of a family that loathes him and wishes he didn't exist.'

I nodded, but my spirits were low. I was afraid, you see, that I would find him so repellent that I wouldn't be able to do what I was supposed to do; wouldn't be able to conceal my revulsion.

What a fool I was, now that I look back on it all. What a fool, not even to start to guess.

Chapter Eight

The news finally came that Lord Ashley would *not* be arriving in time for the funeral. The body had already lain in state in the Duke's cold bedroom for several days so that everyone could pay their respects; the funeral was imminent. But a message had arrived on the butler's telegraph machine to say that Lord Ashley had been in New York when he heard of the Duke's death, and though he had boarded the next transatlantic crossing he would, of course, be late.

Nothing, it seemed, could be a worse insult. The Duchess, Beatrice told me, was furious beyond imagining. *If there is any justice in this world*, the old lady said – Beatrice was an expert at mimicking her – *that man's ship will sink to the bottom of the ocean.*

'The funeral, of course,' pronounced the Duchess in her grandest manner, 'will proceed without Lord Ashley's presence.' Still Lord Ashley – never the Duke.

'Of course, Your Grace.'

'Your Grace.'

More house guests arrived for the funeral with their valets and ladies' maids in tow. The lower servants had to wait on them in addition to their usual work, and all half-days off were cancelled. Betsey, Harriet and the others grumbled increasingly about their workload, but they knew very well the Duchess would dismiss them – just like *that* – if they complained, and without a reference they would never find anything else.

I kept my distance. I had become colder and harder, I knew; Beatrice had offered me the chance of getting away from here and starting a new life, and I wasn't going to throw that chance away. The day before the funeral, she and I had dressed up in some new lingerie that had just been delivered from London. 'Mourning attire,' Beatrice had explained sadly to the Duchess when the trunks arrived, but once the footmen had hauled them up to Beatrice's rooms we opened them together, exclaiming with joy over the contents. We dressed up – well, rather we *undressed* each other, then put on the exquisite slips of nothingness, the little satin brassieres and Milanese silk vests, the short chemises with flounces of lace, and then we danced.

She was teaching me more tango steps, I remember, but her gramophone was turned low, so low. 'Not suitable for funerals,' she winked at me, while the Latin pulse faintly throbbed, stirring my blood as we stalked arm in arm up and down her room to the hypnotic beat of 'My Tango Girl'.

We kissed, of course, and ended up on her bed, entwined naked in each other's arms on the silken coverlet. But I think by then that I was aching in my bones for a man's love, and I guessed she saw it.

★ ★ ★

The funeral was a day of great state and solemnity. I dressed Lady Beatrice in her black mourning clothes; she seemed agitated and was smoking more than usual. The new Duke's transatlantic crossing, Mr Peters had heard on the telegraph, had been delayed by easterly gales; Mr Peters, like the Duchess, still referred to him as 'Lord Ashley'. I also knew, because Beatrice had told me, that the new Duke would be faced with enormous taxes – death duties – on his inheritance, and the old Duchess was cackling with glee.

'But I will not permit him to sell any more land!' We all heard the Duchess's imperious voice ringing down the corridors. 'I will not allow him to betray my dead husband's sacred heritage!'

'As if she'll have any say in the matter,' Beatrice muttered to me.

All the servants walked to the church for the funeral, and it was so crowded that many of the tenants and villagers had to stand outside. We maids were in a pew right at the back, with the footmen in front. Robert turned round to whisper to us that the Duchess was praying not for her dead husband's soul, but that the ship the new Duke was on might sink mid-Atlantic. We giggled, and Mr Peters gave us such a look over the rims of his spectacles.

The vicar addressed the old Duchess in his final summing-up. 'To lose a son, an heir and a husband in a few short years is a tragedy indeed, but the Lord God Almighty is wonderful in his ways. Let us all pray for Her Grace in her grief.'

Though we, the servants, knew it wasn't grief but

sheer fury at the thought of the upstart Lord Ashley inheriting the estate that so contorted the Duchess's face.

After the funeral several guests stayed on at the Duchess's invitation, and Mrs Burdett was so short-staffed that Lady Beatrice agreed to let me go for two or three hours each day to help the other maids. 'You can listen for gossip, Sophie,' Beatrice instructed. 'I know they're all Ash's enemies and I want to hear what they say.'

I took my place below stairs again with trepidation. Only Nell was in any way my friend, and my dismay became acute when I realised that Will Baxter had taken a job here as a footman – Nell whispered to me that there wasn't enough work at the mill for him now that autumn had set in. Occasionally our paths would cross and I was aware of him watching me, a silent reproach on my secret life, my secret ambitions.

Nevertheless Beatrice had been wise to ask me to listen for gossip, since most of the conversation below stairs revolved around the new Duke. The Duchess, they said, was in despair and existing on smelling salts, but all the maids were terribly excited about Lord Ashley's arrival. He was cold-hearted, they whispered, and rich and ruthless.

'When he was a child in France, his parents found him simply a nuisance – so they sent him off to an English boarding school as soon as he was six.' This was another of Cook's scraps of information, offered up when a few of us were gathered in the servants' hall.

'And one summer,' she went on, 'when little Lord Ashley had just turned eleven, no one at all came to collect him for the holidays. Imagine! It turned out his mother had run off somewhere with a Frenchman – and his father had gone painting in Switzerland. *Painting.*' She made a sound of disgust. 'Neither of them could be bothered in the slightest with their little lad. And so, for that one summer, he came here to stay – *here.*'

'Here?' gasped Betsey, peering around as if he might suddenly appear.

'Yes,' said Cook, thoroughly enjoying the rapt attention, 'for the school holidays, though of course it was before I worked here – in fact I think Mrs Burdett and Mr Peters are the only ones who would remember it. The Duke and Duchess had as little as possible to do with him – Lord Charlwood too. After all, Lord Charlwood was ten years older than him, and far superior in rank.'

I could see Nell's eyes filling – she was always easily moved to tears. 'Oh, poor, poor Lord Ashley! Did he never see his parents again?'

'Certainly not his mother, and his father didn't want much to do with him either, I gather,' said Cook briskly. 'But the lad knew how to get on in life. After his schooldays were done he went on to Oxford – they say he's terribly clever, terribly sharp-witted. Look at all the money he's got – most of it made during the war, while other men were fighting; though he doesn't throw it away on high living, oh no. Why, he doesn't touch a drop of alcohol, they say. And he must have had mistresses in plenty, but he's mighty discreet about it, and he's never been in any hurry to marry.'

'I wouldn't be either,' chuckled Robert as he polished the glasses, 'with all those rich lasses eager to bed me.'

After that I returned upstairs to find Beatrice pacing her room with 'Alexander's Ragtime Band' playing on her gramophone. She wore a silk kimono patterned with pink flowers; she often said she found it too depressing for words to see black all around.

'Well?' she demanded. 'What's the servants' gossip today?'

'They're saying he's been here before,' I told her.

She turned on me, suddenly guarded. 'Are they?'

'Yes. When he was a child, and his parents divorced.' I couldn't help thinking of the lonely child in this vast house where nobody wanted him.

But Beatrice waved her hand dismissively. 'Ah, *that*. Now, what else did you learn?'

I searched my roaming thoughts. 'They say, my lady, that Lord Ashley won't touch any alcohol. Do you think it could be true?' I'd taken note when Cook mentioned this, because it was so rare; most of the rich men seemed to live for their fine wines and their brandy.

Beatrice wanted me to brush her hair, and I did so while she sat at her dressing table and answered me. 'I've heard the same. No wine, no spirits . . . Yes, that's lovely, Sophie, carry on, do. Though when I met him in London he used to drink as much as anyone. Perhaps he became an alcoholic and had to give it up.'

My image of a portly imbiber changed to one of a thin, unhappy man.

'Whatever,' Beatrice went on, 'we need to be ready to move quickly. It would have helped if he drank, but I'm still going to make very sure of him. My God, I've had enough of this deadly place to last me fifty years.'

'But surely, now that Lord Ashley's the Duke, he'll make Belfield Hall his permanent home?'

'You're joking, little Sophie. With the Duchess here, and all her cats?'

'Won't she move to the Dower House if she hates him so much?'

'She'd still be less than a mile away, breathing fire down his neck. Don't forget she's convinced herself he's a changeling and not the true heir at all.' She turned her head a little, touching one of her exquisite pearl earrings. 'Sophie, I know – I'm *sure* – that a place like this, for a man like him, would be hell on earth, as it is for me. So you and I are going to make him our little offering, just as soon as possible.'

I'd stopped brushing her hair and I shivered, though she didn't notice; she was too busy studying herself in the mirror.

'As soon as possible,' she repeated softly. 'He might arrive any time. And it's best if he doesn't see you at all, Sophie – until we're ready to act.'

Would she watch? I remembered her lacquered case with that ivory wand, which I'd not seen since; I felt a storm of sudden longing, to be replaced by bitter disappointment that the man to whom she was in effect selling me was a man I'd already learned to despise.

'Perhaps he won't want me,' I said.

'My dear, there's no chance of that. No chance at all.' Beatrice rose to her feet, slipping her hand under my starched apron to gently stroke my breast through the black cotton of my maid's dress. My blood raced and a sudden dark turmoil churned in my abdomen and below. 'I have prepared you nicely,' she breathed, fingering my breast more firmly, drawing out the nipple until I was biting my lip to restrain the low moan that rose in my throat. 'He will not be disappointed with my present to him.'

Striving for calm I raised the question of pregnancy, remembering poor Nell: Lady Beatrice simply laughed and told me about the sheaths the gentlemen used, to ensure their seed did not spill inside the woman. 'Or sometimes,' she explained, 'they withdraw just before their crisis. They might ask you to help them, to hold them, at the moment of their ejaculation; to stroke them.'

I remembered seeing the thickset American naked on her bed; the way she caressed his thick arousal, the way she cupped the heavy pouch at the root of his shaft. *Oh, God, let it be over soon*, I breathed to myself. *Let it be over, and then I will be free.*

November came, and rain lashed the countryside until the trees in the great park were almost bare. And during a particularly heavy squall of rain, the new Duke arrived at last. I didn't see him, but I heard about it because I was down in the kitchen fetching some bread and butter for Lady Beatrice when Betsey flew in. 'He's here! The new Duke's here, in his motorcar!' she called out in excitement.

But then, faced with a barrage of questions, she had to admit that she hadn't been able to see his face at all, because his coat collar was turned up against the rain and his hat was pulled down low. 'I saw his chauffeur, though,' she said. 'And *he* looks a proper treat.'

'Doesn't matter anyway what the new Duke's face is like,' smirked Harriet. 'If I get the chance, I'll eat him for breakfast.'

Betsey snorted with laughter. 'From what I've heard of His Grace, he'll give as good as he gets. He's a bad man, they say.'

'God, Betsey, don't.' Harriet pointed at me. 'You'll embarrass our innocent little Sophie here.'

They chuckled and carried on whispering as I prepared Lady Beatrice's afternoon tea. 'He's had his full share of beautiful women, apparently,' Betsey went on. 'Though now he's Duke he'll have to be a bit more careful, because there'll be all sorts of marriage traps laid for him . . .'

The fine china plate rattled as I set it on my lady's tray.

'The new Duke is here,' I said as I returned to Lady Beatrice's sitting room.

'Oh, Sophie. *Sophie.*' Beatrice, ignoring her tea, did a little twirl of happiness, then pulled me to her and kissed my cheek.

When can I go to London? When will I be free? All my unspoken questions burned on my lips.

Beatrice was still holding me by the waist and we stood looking at ourselves in the mirror, she reluctantly wearing the black of mourning, me in my maid's outfit. 'You feel used, sweetheart?' she said to my reflection.

The words piled up inside me. At first I could hardly speak. Then . . . 'I must get away,' I whispered.

'Sophie,' she chided, 'there's no rush. You're still so young. And you surely realise I'd be happy to keep you on – once Ash and I are married and I'm his duchess. We would live in London – you could be my maid still . . . what do you think of *that?*'

'I've told you,' I said stubbornly to her reflection. 'I want to dance in a London theatre. You promised to help me.'

She nodded, impatient all of a sudden. 'Oh, so you keep reminding me. But first things first.' She pushed me towards the door. 'Go back downstairs and find out what's going on. Ask Mrs Burdett if she has any jobs for you.' She gazed at herself again in the mirror, frowning over a stray strand of hair. 'I'll meet the Duke tonight at dinner, of course, but I need to know who else will be there, and what they're all saying about him, and – oh, I need to know *everything.*'

She kissed me again, but this time I shrank from her touch.

I went downstairs to report to Mrs Burdett, who was very harassed. 'Her Ladyship's had enough of you, has she?' she said tartly to me. 'Or is it that she's set you to spying again? Well then. The Duchess has invited some of the local gentry to dine here tonight and meet the

All I Want Is You

new Duke, though of course she's extremely displeased at the lack of notice that His Grace has given her, and who can blame her? Now, Sophie, you can help the others prepare the dining room. Mr Peters will tell you exactly what needs doing.'

Several housemaids including Nell were already there, and the footmen would come later to set out the silverware. It was a rule that we were never supposed to work together, the men and the girls; they said it wouldn't be seemly. Well, if only they'd known what Harriet and Betsey got up to with some of the grooms in the stables at night; though now the talk was all of the new Duke, of course. 'To think,' said Harriet, 'that he hasn't even got a valet! But he told Mr Peters how that chauffeur of his – he's called James – will do everything that's required. My, my, things are going to change round here.'

The room was still dark with funeral draperies, and there were no flowers except the gloomy white lilies with their sickly scent. But all the best linen and china had been brought out for the new Duke; candles burned in the great chandeliers overhead, and fires blazed at each end of the room. We maids had been ordered to sweep the carpets then dust the furniture, but within a few minutes we were distracted by the arrival of a couple of footmen, each carrying one of a pair of heavy silver-gilt candelabra for the sideboard. One footman was Robert; the other was Will. Will looked at me once then turned away; I saw Nell glancing at me and felt my usual sad guilt.

Robert was over-familiar with me once Mr Peters had gone. 'How's Lady Beatrice?' he asked me, sidling too close. 'Is she all tarted up for His Grace yet? That paint on her face, that short hair; she's quite the flapper, isn't she?'

I tried to move away but he grabbed my wrist. 'Good God. You're wearing the stuff too, Sophie. I thought you looked different, your eyelashes are all dark – it suits you.' He gave a low whistle. 'You're beginning to look really very pretty. And I do believe you're filling out in all the right places . . .'

He was leering at my breasts beneath my apron and bodice and I tried to push him away. But suddenly Will was there between us.

'If you speak to her like that again,' Will said to Robert, 'by God, I'll thump you to kingdom come.'

Robert backed away, holding up his hands to fend Will off. 'All right, all right, big boy, keep your temper. I'm not the Boche, you know. But Sophie here is looking ripe for it, you've got to admit—'

Will knocked Robert flying. 'You bloody coward,' he shouted. 'You with your weak chest, dodging the fight-ing. I'll give you a weak chest.'

Robert struggled to his feet and threw a punch at Will; crockery smashed and chairs fell over. Other foot-men came running and – under Mr Peters's furious orders – Will and Robert were dragged out. But it took three men to hold each of them, so wild were they. Shaking, I pressed myself back against the wall behind a big folding screen.

My fault. All my fault. The other maids had all fled, and I was about to hurry out after them, but suddenly I heard more footsteps and the voice of Mr Peters, who was coming back and bringing three housemaids with him. I retreated once more behind the screen, which was there to hide the serving hatch and its pulleys from the view of the diners.

'Sweep up all this mess,' Mr Peters ordered the maids. He looked furious. 'My God, someone's going to pay for all this.'

He fussed over them until the place was tidy again, then he ordered the maids to leave and he left too. I gathered up my skirts ready to run, but with a sinking heart I realised he'd stopped just outside the door and was calling to another footman. 'George! Is that you with the drinks? About time. Come in here, and be quick about it, will you?'

Mr Peters had a list. He liked his lists. He adjusted his spectacles and turned to George, a new young footman, who bore a large tray of crystal decanters. Mr Peters started to examine the silver name-tags that hung round the neck of each decanter.

'Whisky. Gin. Sherry. Madeira. Hm, the Madeira's getting a little low. Tonic, soda water, lemon-barley water . . . Put them down here.' He pointed to the side-board. His nose had turned up as he read out the last few labels.

George said chirpily, 'Lemon-barley water? That for the ladies, is it, Mr Peters?'

'No, no. It's for Lord Ashley . . . I mean, for the new Duke.' Mr Peters could not have poured more scorn into his voice.

'His Grace doesn't touch spirits, then, sir?'

'He doesn't drink *anything* alcoholic, spirits or wine,'

emphasised Mr Peters, inspecting his pocket watch. 'That's it for now, George. Be off with you.'

I prayed for Mr Peters to leave too, so I could at last escape. But he didn't. He went and closed the door then came back towards the drinks again. My heart was hammering as though it might burst.

I'd never liked the butler, but I knew he and the Duchess were as thick as thieves, for she adored his sycophantic snobbery, and now I saw him inspect the decanters anew, then pull forward the one of lemon-barley for the new Duke who didn't drink a drop of alcohol. I saw Mr Peters ease out a small silver flask from his pocket and unscrew the top. I saw him remove the crystal stopper from the lemon-barley decanter then slowly, carefully, pour in the clear fluid from his flask.

He replaced the stopper in the decanter, looked round again and hurried out.

What had he poured in? Gin, I guessed. My first thought was that this was a trick being played on the new Duke. Surely, though, he would smell the spirit and be alerted straight away?

But what if – my mind was racing now – what if perhaps the Duchess was involved in this? Mr Peters was an ally of hers. What if maybe the Duchess were to say, in her icy-sweet tones, 'Is that lemon-barley water for you, Lord Ashley? Do you know, I fancy a little of it myself – so refreshing – you don't mind, do you?' Then the old lady would sip at it, and splutter self-righteously, and cry, 'Gin! Dear Heaven, this drink is full of gin!'

I could just picture Her Grace having hysterics at the dinner table while everyone, guests and servants alike, all watched. She wouldn't need to say much more. Everyone hated the new Duke already. To reveal him as a secret alcoholic would be a sweet victory for the Duchess. Petty and silly, but a triumph for her nonetheless. And why should I care? My one thought now was of self-preservation – to get out of that room before anyone else should enter.

But before I could move the door was opening again.

I heard a man's husky, aristocratic drawl. 'Thank you, Peters, but I don't need you with me. I just want to look round the place again.'

Something about that voice made my heart hammer.

Mr Peters was hovering anxiously outside. 'But my lord – I mean, Your Grace . . .'

A slight chill in the voice now. 'I assure you that although it's some years since I was last here, I can find my own way around. That will be all.'

I heard Mr Peters retreating, and the door closed. The man who'd just spoken was walking slowly further in, not noticing me because I was still protected by the screen. But I could see him now.

His hair was dark brown and his eyes were blue, so blue. And I, a foolish thirteen-year-old, had once raged at him: *Would you let this happen to your wife or your sister, sir? Would you?* I'd have known him anywhere.

Too late, I realised what I should have guessed long ago – that Mr Maldon, the man I'd written to, the man I'd dreamed of for years, was the new Duke of Belfield, and Beatrice's Lord Ashley.

Chapter Nine

How did I feel? I felt as if the ground would never be secure beneath my feet again. I was still hidden; I could still have waited for him to go. I gazed at him, thinking, *Oh, God. Why did I not know? How could I not have guessed?*

He was my Mr Maldon, I'd met him in Oxford on that dreadful day my mother died, and now, even in the sober attire of mourning, he set the room ablaze. Beatrice was after this man; half the women of London, Paris and New York were after this man, according to Lady Beatrice, according to the servants' gossip. And no wonder.

My memory hadn't played me false. I'd never seen a man who looked to me as beautiful as he did – neither before nor since. As I watched him, as I absorbed his . . . how to describe it? . . . his *perfect* face, the face of my dreams, I felt desperate with disappointment – yes, and with rage – at the cruel trick that fate and Lady Beatrice had played on me.

Beatrice was going to offer me to this man. She'd told me that in the kind of world the aristocrats inhabited, it was considered amusing for a lady to provide her male lover with a small gift now and then: a virginal serving maid, for example, for him to enjoy in the privacy of his bedchamber, maybe while she looked on.

I felt heat explode within me, spreading up to my face, burning at my lungs. I knew Beatrice would have hissed, *Stay out of sight, you stupid, stupid girl.* She wanted me to be a surprise for him. A novelty. But – he was my Mr Maldon.

I stepped forward from behind the screen. He looked astonished, because of course people of his class weren't meant to be obliged to acknowledge the lower orders. We weren't even supposed to exist. But his good manners prevailed. He nodded at the cloth I was still carrying. 'Last-minute dusting?' he said coolly.

My fingers were nerveless, the blood was pounding through my veins. But I said, as steadily as I could, 'Forgive me, Your Grace. But they have put gin in the lemon-barley water that is set out there for you. I saw it.'

He frowned, his blue eyes suddenly dangerous. 'Is this some kind of trick?'

'Not on my part, I swear. Please believe me,' I begged.

'Who . . . ' he began, then stopped. 'No. I won't ask you who did it.' He gazed at me, puzzled, then shook his head as if to rid himself of some half-remembered thought and turned to inspect the labels of the decanters. 'This one?' I nodded. He took out the stopper, then sniffed it. Put back the stopper and looked at me again.

He was wearing a black dinner suit. His hair was as thick and dark brown as I remembered, his mouth as finely shaped. He was older now, of course – faint lines crinkled at the corners of his eyes – but he was still the most heart-stoppingly handsome man I had ever seen.

And by presenting myself to him like this, I had ruined all Beatrice's plans. I had most likely ruined all *my* plans. I kept my eyes lowered, of course, but he was still gazing at me.

'Haven't we met before?' he asked.

This was it.

I braced myself. 'Four years ago, Your Grace, my mother was taken ill in the street in Oxford. You took her to the hospital. I . . . I was not as grateful as I should have been.'

His eyes narrowed. Blue, intense as a cornflower, with black, black lashes . . . 'My God,' he breathed. 'Sophie. It's Sophie, isn't it?'

I bowed my head in mute acknowledgement, aware of all my dreams crashing around my ears, for he knew me now not only as a grief-crazed girl in Oxford, but as an idiotic little serving maid who was in the habit of creeping around where she had no business to be and who had once ranted to him about the iniquities of the rich.

'You wrote to me,' he said, stepping closer.

I nodded blindly. Pain clawed my chest at the reality of what all this meant. I raised my eyes briefly to his and stammered, 'I did write, Your Grace. But I never guessed that you would one day be a duke. I always thought of you as just . . . Mr Maldon.'

His gaze was grave and steady. 'I *was* plain Mr Maldon then, until my father died. And you're still working here, which I think is fortunate for me.' He turned to look again at the decanter of lemon-barley water. 'Did they really think I would drink this? Did they think I wouldn't smell the gin in it the moment it was poured?'

I gazed up at him and I said, 'I think perhaps the Duchess herself intended to ask for some of your drink, Your Grace. Maybe she planned to sip it and feign shock at the gin in it, to make it look as if *you* gave orders for it to be put in. I beg your pardon if I sound disrespectful, but I think the Duchess wants to make you look like a . . . a—'

He said quietly, 'A secret drinker.'

'I think so, Your Grace.'

His lip curled. 'My God,' he said softly. 'Do they really hate me so much?'

My heart was still thumping so hard I couldn't speak. All of a sudden his blue eyes burned me.

He said, 'Sophie. You are answerable to them, not me. Why didn't you just keep quiet behind your screen just now and wait till I'd gone?'

'You helped me,' I said. There was a huge lump in my throat. 'You helped my mother. You paid for her funeral and her gravestone. You got me my job here, and I wrote to you, like you said—'

'You wrote to me because I told you to,' he interrupted. 'And I wrote back, only for a while, but all your letters were waiting for me when I . . .' He seemed to be gathering his thoughts. 'When I returned to London.'

My cheeks burned. I was desperate to say, *I lived for your letters. I read them over and over again. I imagined you speaking the words you wrote aloud to me . . .*

But I said nothing, because suddenly I saw his hands – oh, dear God, his beautiful hands. They were badly scarred, they had been burned, I thought; the skin across the backs of them was ridged with mottled white and red tissue. I tore my eyes away, but I felt sick at the thought of the pain he must have endured as they healed.

I swallowed to ease the ache of my dry throat and remembered what I wrote to him. *I don't know where you are now, and I wish I did. I wish you had written back to me. I wish you had come for me.*

He was watching me, appraising me with those unreadable blue eyes. The faint lemon scent of the soap he used brought back wave after wave of memories of the day my mother died. He was saying softly, 'I'm so very sorry I was unable to reply to all of your letters, Sophie. Have they treated you well here?'

I thought of Robert cruelly telling me my father was not my father; I thought of Beatrice's maid Margaret, showing me those pictures and teaching me pleasure. I thought blindly of Lady Beatrice herself, and of her plan to give me to this very man, and I saw it for the madness it was. I blurted out – I couldn't help it – 'They hate you here, Your Grace. All of them hate you, except Lady Beatrice . . .'

I broke off, for I'd heard footsteps approaching, I thought I heard Mr Peters's voice, and I ran. Anguish tore through me still from the sight of his scarred hands. *What had happened to him? Who had done that to him?* I wanted to hold his poor hands in mine; I wanted to soothe them with my lips. I'd hoped so much to one day see him again. But not like this. Not like this. I felt quite sick with shock, sick with loss.

Lady Beatrice was excited that night when she came upstairs at last. As I attended to her in her bath, sponging her shoulders and washing her hair, I was very quiet but she didn't notice. She told me what had happened at the evening meal.

'They hate Ash so much, Sophie! But he was utterly polite all the way through, especially to the wicked old Duchess.' She chuckled. 'And there was something rather odd. Peters offered him lemon-barley water – apparently it's what Ash drinks now – but he chose soda water instead. Old Peters looked quite shocked. The Duchess had already asked for lemon-barley, but when Ash asked for soda water, she looked absolutely furious and almost knocked her own drink over! Pour in some more of that bath oil, Sophie, will you?'

I reached for the crystal bottle and poured the expensive unguent into her water, but for once I was clumsy, I had trouble concentrating, because I didn't know what to do next. I suppose I still couldn't believe that the man who was my Mr Maldon could be the man Lady Beatrice had described – someone who had used the cruel war to make money; someone who was capable of coldly taking an innocent girl's virginity under the eyes of another woman as a casual piece of entertainment, a gift.

But I had to believe it, I had to accept I had built a fantasy of him in my mind; I had been wrong to think him honest and strong and kind.

Beatrice stretched out her smooth legs in the water as I soaped her feet. 'Then the topic of the estate's debts came up, and death duties,' she went on. 'How bored I am with death duties. Since the war ended, it's all anyone talks about. But oh, Sophie . . .'

I was passing her the sponge now so she could soap her own breasts; I saw how her nipples tightened and her eyes gleamed. 'Sophie, Ash was *magnificent.* He said that practical steps have to be taken. He pronounced that we're no longer living in the Victorian age, and that if necessary land from the estate will have to be sold. He also said that the miners ought to be given the increase in wages they're demanding. You've heard, I suppose, that the miners are on strike again? At that the Duchess said to him, "You'll sell my husband's land and support those wretched miners over my dead body." Ash said, "I sincerely hope not, ma'am, since my mind is already made up on both matters."

'The Duchess was *speechless*, Sophie! Then Ash said he would get electricity up and running throughout the house, he would install a hot-water boiler in the kitchen – "We are, after all, in the twentieth century, not the eighteenth", he said – and I thought the Duchess would quite simply faint!'

I broke in, 'What happened to his hands?'

'What?' She frowned slightly. 'How do you know about his hands?'

Oh, God, a mistake. 'I heard about them in the servants' hall,' I lied. 'Someone noticed that the backs of his hands are badly scarred.'

She reached for more soap. 'He dismisses it as some kind of accident.'

'A motorcar accident?'

Again, that sharp look in Beatrice's eyes. 'Quite likely. What does it matter? Who cares?' Still reclining in her bath, she pulled my face down to kiss me on the lips, and I shivered when I saw the hunger in her eyes. 'Oh, little Sophie. I cannot wait to see his face when I offer you to him tonight.'

Tonight. My lungs felt as if a great weight was pressing on them. I could hardly breathe.

'Yes, tonight,' she went on. She was stepping out of her bath now, wrapping herself in the thick towel I'd held out. 'He needs to return to London in a day or so; he has his own business affairs to deal with, he said, besides all the legal matters concerning the estate. So I've asked him to visit me in an hour—'

'An hour?' My heart was hammering painfully.

'Yes, I told him I have some ideas for saving the estate that I want him to hear. But we'll get that over with very quickly. I'll have you concealed in my bedroom; I'll pretend I need something from there, then we'll come out together, you and I, in our new lingerie from Paris, and I'll make a present of you to him.' She almost danced with happiness. 'Now it's time for *you* to get ready. Your turn for the bath, little Sophie . . .'

She broke off suddenly. 'Sophie? You're very quiet. Is something the matter?'

'I can't do it,' I whispered. 'I'm sorry, my lady, but I cannot do it.'

There was a long, long silence, in which all I could hear was the ticking of the ormolu clock on her mantelpiece. 'My God,' Lady Beatrice breathed at last, 'is this supposed to be a joke? I thought you were desperate to get to London and kick your legs around on stage in some stupid show . . .'

Suddenly she gave her dark smile. 'You've seen him,

haven't you? You gave yourself away with your question about his hands. You've seen him.' She'd dropped the towel and was pulling on her silk flowered kimono.

'Yes,' I whispered back, helpless.

'Does he repel you, with those scarred hands of his? Is that it?' She was reaching for me now but I shrank back from her, suddenly hating the way she smelled of cigarettes.

'He doesn't repel me,' I said. Indeed she was so, so wrong to think that. What I wanted was to hold his poor hands and kiss them and I didn't care what he'd done. I only knew now that I'd lived for him for all these years, I loved him, and I couldn't let myself be presented to him as a whore. 'He doesn't repel me but, my lady, there must be something else I can do to earn my freedom. You see, I've met him before.'

She stared at me, speechless.

I stammered on, 'I met him four and a half years ago in Oxford. He was kind to me, though I'd no idea who he was, and I can't—'

'*Be quiet.*' She was pacing the floor, as she did when agitated. She suddenly turned on me. 'Listen to me, you little fool. You're going to do *exactly* as I say. Or I'll accuse you of stealing, do you understand?'

Bewildered, I shook my head. 'You know very well that I haven't stolen anything.'

She pulled me closer, so I was face to face with her. 'Didn't you realise,' she went on in a suddenly husky voice, 'didn't you realise how easy it would be for me to ruin you, sweet Sophie? You like to secretly borrow books from the old Duke's library, don't you?'

Colour slowly flooded my face. 'Yes, but I take such care of them, and I always put them back.'

'What if some went missing, though? What if, for example, some valuable editions of old poetry somehow found their way to a bookseller in Oxford?'

I felt sick. 'No. My lady, no—'

'Your word against mine,' she interrupted calmly. 'If you don't do *exactly* as I say tonight, I'll see you accused of theft. I'll ruin you, Sophie. I mean it.'

She smiled because she thought she'd won. She talked as if nothing had changed, as if she and I were the best of friends. She insisted I bathe myself in her bath, using her perfumed oils, though that night the rich scents made me nauseous. I let her wash me and dry me – she did it with such care – then she rouged my nipples and dabbed some of her patchouli perfume at my pulse points, but all of her attentions were hateful to me.

I stood deathly cold with a towel wrapped around me while she chose garments for herself – a delicate brassiere and lacy French knickers in palest blue. She chattered on as if nothing had happened, as if she hadn't just held the threat of prison over me.

'Now I think,' Lady Beatrice mused, fastening her cream stockings to the suspenders that lay against her gleaming thighs, 'that you're frightened, because Ash is so beautiful. Isn't he?'

'Yes,' I whispered.

She smiled in satisfaction. 'Yet you were thinking – for a reason I simply *cannot* understand – of turning my present down. But I won't let you.' She thrust champagne in a crystal flute at me. It tasted odd, but her eyes were on me, all the time.

'Drink,' she said.

I did so, for I hoped in despair that it might help to numb me for all this. She began to work on me then, dressing me like her in a satin bra and knickers, only mine were in dusky pink. She helped me smooth on my stockings, and she herself eased the pink satin garters over my thighs. At last she made me sit in front of her dressing table and started applying her own make-up to my face – powder, mascara, lipstick.

I remembered the first time she'd done this, when I'd been so excited. Now I felt sick with dread. She drew me up and kissed me on the mouth and I was shivering with rage and despair.

She poured me more champagne. 'Drink up, Sophie,' she murmured. 'He'll be here any minute. Drink, I said. Drink it all.'

I swallowed the champagne, still aware of that faint, odd aftertaste. I felt shaky and strange. She was watching me. She took my glass. 'That's better,' she said. 'Go into my bedroom – yes, as you are.'

I stumbled towards her bedroom door on the high heels she'd made me wear, in the pale pink lingerie she'd made me wear, my painted nipples still tight from her caresses, my cheeks still flushed with hating her.

Yes, hating her for what she'd done to me.

Your own fault, Sophie, my inner voice whispered. *Your own fault, you little fool, for wanting more. For always thinking you were worth more.*

Oh, Mr Maldon.

I sank back on the bed, feeling light-headed and float-ing and unreal. My legs looked long and smooth in the new silk stockings, the pink garters a teasing contrast to my pale thighs. Beatrice was my enemy, yes; but even so I felt an insistent ache bloom low in my stomach, and as I ran my fingers over my most intimate place, through the satin of my underwear, I felt hot desire unfurling through every vein. I compressed my burning breasts with my palms, trying to cool them.

Oh, God, any minute now I was going to show my Mr Maldon that I'd repaid his long-ago kindness to me by becoming a whore. I stumbled to the door, which was still half open. 'I can't do it,' I called to her in despair. 'And the drink. You put something in my drink . . .'

She marched across and jabbed one finger at me. 'Those books. Remember?' she hissed. 'Now get out of sight. He'll be here any minute.'

I realised she must have heard footsteps coming along the corridor because she pushed me back into her bedroom, into the darkness there. Losing my balance, I stumbled against the side of the bed and found myself on my knees, with my arms flung out in despair across the satin bedspread.

He was here. My Mr Maldon – Lord Ashley, the new Duke of Belfield – was here. My man with the blue, sad eyes. And what had they done to him? What had they done to his hands? An accident of some kind, Beatrice had said dismissively, but I knew there was something else, something that had happened, to make him stop writing to me.

I heard Lady Beatrice go to open the door to the

corridor outside. 'Come in,' I heard her say in her seductive voice.

Though I myself was in darkness, I found that if I turned my head I could see it all, for she'd only half closed the bedroom door. I saw him enter; I saw her stand on tiptoe to kiss him on the cheek and my skin prickled with heat. Oh, God. If a man could be described as beautiful, then he had beauty. I'd seen many men, of course, I'd seen many male guests from afar, but none of them struck me to the heart as he did. All I could think of, in my pitiful naivety, were the pictures in that book of my mother's that I'd loved, the tales of King Arthur's knights, because to me he was like the drawings of those knights: proud yet somehow so sad.

He still wore his black dinner suit, of course, but he'd unfastened his black bow tie, so it hung loosely around his neck. Against the white starched linen of his shirt collar, his skin looked almost golden, but was faintly blue-black around his jaw where stubble was starting to grow. *If I get the chance, I'll eat him for breakfast,* Harriet had murmured in the kitchen. I remembered the American and what Beatrice had done to him in the dark. Shivering, I turned away with my thighs tightly pressed together; but the muscles of my belly still clenched, and my secret parts felt molten.

Sweet Jesus, I was on fire for him.

Beatrice's back was to me now and I couldn't hear quite what she was saying, though I think she was offering him a drink.

'Nothing to drink for me,' he said. He sounded curt. 'You told me you'd some ideas for saving the estate and paying off the death duties. You must realise that's the only reason I've come to you, Beatrice. Not for anything else.'

'I think I can make you change your mind about the *anything else*,' she said.

I was trapped there. I could do nothing. My satin undergarments were flimsy but still too hot, too confining. *Breathe, Sophie, you idiot. Breathe.*

'My plan is quite simple, Ash.' Beatrice drew out a cigarette and lit it, taking her time. 'I've always had a hankering to be a duchess.'

He replied almost instantly, 'A pity, then, that your plan went wrong and Lord Charlwood died.'

'Oh, I haven't given up on my desire for the title – not in the slightest.' There was a purr in Beatrice's voice. 'I've made fresh plans. My dear Ash, I think it would be an excellent notion if you and I were to get married. What do you think?'

In the deathly silence that followed I imagined I could hear Beatrice licking her red lips. Then the coals on the fire shifted and crackled and he replied calmly at last, 'I don't imagine you go round making proposals like that every day, so I suppose I should be flattered. But as it happens, I'm afraid I've not the slightest wish to be married – to anyone.'

Beatrice didn't hesitate. 'Sit down, Ash, and listen, *please*.' She settled herself on the settee and he sat on it also, keeping his distance. 'You're aware, I'm sure,' she pressed on, 'that my father is very wealthy. He was devastated when Charlwood died, so I've talked the matter over with him, and he'll give you half a million pounds if you'll marry me.'

I smothered a gasp at this truly incredible sum, but the Duke merely gave a low, lazy chuckle. 'Dear Beatrice,' he said, 'at times I confess I find you amusing, but neither that nor half a million pounds is a good enough reason to commit myself to lifelong devotion.'

'I wouldn't expect it,' she answered promptly. 'Your . . . *devotion*, I mean.'

He'd risen to go, but now he turned round slowly. 'What, precisely, do you mean?'

I despised myself for it, but I was riveted by what was unfolding before me. From the darkness of that bedroom I saw Beatrice get to her feet, sinuous as a cat, then kneel on the thick rug at his feet, softly stroking his thigh. 'Ash. Darling Ash. We'd be so well suited, you and I. I'd love to be a duchess – you'd love my money. As for devotion and commitment, I wouldn't expect it, and neither should you. I would bring you far more than that. I would *entertain* you.'

'I'm in the habit of buying all the entertainment I need,' he drawled. 'You surely know that.'

She rose to her feet, her head a little on one side. 'This is for free, my dear.'

She went to put a record on the gramophone. She started to dance slowly and let her kimono slide from her shoulders to the ground, revealing her pale blue undergarments.

He laughed softly. 'Oh, Beatrice, Beatrice. Not very original, I'm afraid.'

'No?' she breathed. 'You've not seen my little surprise yet.'

She put out all the lamps except one, while he watched

her with a slight frown on his face. Then she opened the door to the bedroom – I was on my feet by then, trembling anew – and she beckoned me into the sitting room. She whispered warningly, '*The books. No one would take your word against mine, you little fool.*'

I still didn't know if she was lying, but I knew she could have put me in prison. Slowly I walked into that room in my lingerie, with some vague hope that he wouldn't recognise me in my scanty attire, with all the face paint Lady Beatrice had applied. Of course I realised by then that she'd drugged me. My senses were hazy, but I wasn't sleepy, oh no. I wanted something – I wanted *him* – quite desperately. My breasts were heavy and aching, my lips swollen, and between my legs I burned with torment, so much so that I guessed one touch, one simple touch from his lean fingers would topple me over the edge.

I sidled towards him while she, Lady Beatrice, leaned against the wall with her arms folded, smiling to herself. When I stumbled clumsily on my high heels I saw him start; I saw him make a move towards me, then freeze as his expression turn to raw, bitter anger. And even Beatrice must have registered his exclamation of scathing astonishment.

'*You*,' he said.

How did I feel? I think, by then, I was hardly conscious of what my brain was telling me; I was only conscious of my body's demands – and my body wanted him. My heart shook with wanting him. I felt myself swaying towards him; I think I was looking up at him from under downcast lashes, a classic whore's trick. I knew all the time that I was being cheap, I was being stupid; I remember that even in the ravishing intensity of my desire I felt quite sick at heart. Oh, God, I wanted him. But there was, in his beautiful, hooded eyes, an expression of pure scorn.

I swayed so close to him, yet he didn't move a muscle. He kept his arms rigid at his sides and his gaze was on me, burning into me. I couldn't tell what he was thinking, and doubtless that was just as well. I took his left hand and lifted it up to my mouth. I kissed that ravaged scar tissue, and I felt something like a harsh sigh ripple through him. Then I placed his palm over my breast, where the silky fabric ended and my sensitive flesh was bare.

His touch was glorious. My blood pounded so heavily I thought I might faint. I remember I moved myself beneath him, so he must have felt how my nipple pressed yearningly through the silk against his palm. The sensation shot straight to my lower abdomen; I caught my lip between my teeth and breathed his name as that damned champagne throbbed through my blood.

I lifted my head to meet his blue gaze. 'I've missed you,' I whispered. 'I've waited for you, for so long. But your hands, your poor hands . . .'

Tears came to my eyes as I raised his hand to my mouth and kissed it again, feeling the scar ridges beneath my lips. I can guess well enough now what he must have been thinking: that the innocent girl he'd once done his best to help had become a painted blonde in silk underwear and high heels, drugged to do work she found repulsive.

He snatched his hand from mine and I nearly fell. He let out a low exclamation and steadied me; I leaned against him with my cheek pressed to his chest. I clung to him, murmuring endearments.

I heard him say sharply to Beatrice, 'For God's sake. What have you given her?'

Beatrice gestured at my almost-empty glass. 'She's a little too fond of champagne. There's nothing unusual about that.'

'This isn't just champagne. Her pupils are like pinpricks . . .'

'Don't leave me again, Mr Maldon,' I whispered to him. '*Please.*' I ran my hands up and down his back, over his shirt but beneath his jacket. He felt so warm, so strong, and all my years of loneliness, all my longing for this man flooded tormentingly back. 'Please don't leave. Please don't be cross with me. Books. There were some books, you see . . .'

Suddenly I was aware that Beatrice had put on another record to drown out what I was saying. It was 'Alexander's Ragtime Band', a tune that I have come to detest. She came over to take me away from Ash, holding out her hands to me, and when I didn't move she pulled me close. Away from him. 'Dance, you little fool,' she hissed at me. 'Dance.'

By then I hardly knew what I was doing. 'Of course.' I smiled at her, tripping again on the rug in my high heels. 'Of course. I'm going to be a dancer on stage in London.'

'You are,' she said between gritted teeth. 'You are.' Then she whispered, so only I could hear her: '*If you damned well do as I say.'* I could tell she was furiously angry with me.

She took my hands, and we danced together. Then I stumbled again, and Beatrice steadied me; I found myself in her arms. Suddenly she kissed me, her tongue sliding between my painted lips, and though I hated her, my body was on fire again. Hungrily I pressed my breasts against hers, feeling the silk of her brassiere and the creamy coolness of her flesh against mine.

I heard the beautiful man in the corner whisper, *'What the hell . . .'*

She was still holding me close, kissing me more slowly, more deeply, until I could hardly bear the exquisite torment any longer. I imagined it was him, imagined it was his beautiful mouth coaxing mine, his tongue teasing my lips, my inner flesh.

I reached to stroke Beatrice's short dark hair and her scent was heavy, smothering me. She started to slide off the narrow shoulder straps of my flimsy brassiere, and once more I heard the hiss of Lord Ashley's indrawn breath as he caught sight of my painted nipples. Still Beatrice and I danced in one another's arms, as she lowered her head to draw the tip of my breast into her mouth . . .

He jammed the arm of the record player. The record stuck, kept playing the same phrase over and over. *Come on and . . . Come on and . . .*

He said to Beatrice, 'What the hell is this? Are you turning into some kind of damned brothel-keeper, Beatrice?'

Come on and . . . Come on and . . .

134

Beatrice had whitened, but she smiled defiantly, keeping her hand on my arm. 'It's a gift, Ash. A surprise, my dear. I wanted to show you that life with me would never, ever be dull.'

'So you're offering me a tart?'

She flinched a little, but her smile never wavered. 'Wrong, Ash. You don't know *how* wrong. She's a virgin, a complete innocent. And I've saved her, I've prepared her, for you and you only . . .'

He'd grabbed the champagne glass I'd drunk from and swirled the dregs beneath his nostrils. 'You've given her cantharides,' he said, 'or something very similar. My God, I feel as if I've walked into the lair of the Borgias here.'

'But Ash, darling Ash—'

He looked round, snatched up Beatrice's silk kimono from the floor where she'd let it fall and wrapped it round my shoulders. I stumbled against him. Felt his arms around me. *Oh God, this was where I belonged.* But it had all gone so wrong. I was shaking badly.

Still holding me, he said to Beatrice, 'I'm taking her to my room.'

I saw her smirk with satisfaction. 'Of course. We'll both come. You'll not regret it.'

He answered flatly, 'My primary purpose is to get this girl away from you, Beatrice. And to find out – from her, not you – what the hell is going on.'

She tried to speak again, but he guided me out and shut the door in her face. He led me along the corridor to the suite that he occupied; he was practically carrying me, I think. Thank God we saw no one. I was still trembling. I was devastated that he despised me so.

He got me into his suite where, as in Beatrice's, there was a sitting room with his bedroom leading off it. He made me sit in a chair by the embers of a fire onto which he piled more coals, perhaps because he'd noticed I was shivering, though it wasn't on account of the cold. He locked the door, then walked back to me.

I can see him now, tall and lean and wide-shouldered, wearing black slim-fitting trousers that clung to his thighs; and beneath his black jacket his white shirt emphasised the power of his chest. With his rumpled dark brown hair he looked so beautiful, so dangerous; like one of my knights, I thought again, or like some exotic creature – a tawny lion or a panther, lithe and deadly . . .

His blue eyes blazed with danger. He said, 'Now tell me. Tell me when you and Beatrice started planning your cheap little scheme.'

Chapter Ten

The effects of the champagne and the 'cantharides', whatever it was, were wearing off and I felt heavy and tired. 'I had to do it,' I whispered at last. I clasped my hands in my lap and looked down at them in despair. 'I didn't know. I didn't realise, when she talked of Lord Ashley, that . . . it was *you.*'

His eyes narrowed, then he poured me a glass of water. 'Here. Drink this. So you've become a little tart, set up by the ever-enterprising Beatrice to somehow trap me. Is that it?'

I gazed at him, quite agonised. Suddenly I thought, *He might be beautiful. But perhaps he is just as hateful as everyone has said.* I moistened my dry lips, wishing my brain would work properly again, guessing that if I explained about my dream of being a dancer and how Beatrice had promised she would help me; if I explained how she'd threatened me with prison over the old Duke's books, he would just think I was lying.

I lifted my head, looking steadily into those beautiful, sad blue eyes I'd remembered always in my dreams and I said, 'I'll go now if you want.'

He just stood there a moment, gazing at me. Then he reached out and slowly drew me into his arms.

Deliberately he slid the silk kimono from my shoulders.

My body jumped; my pulse rate accelerated again. *Oh, my.* I realised his hand was resting at the base of my spine, half on my skin and half on the silk of my knickers. His palm glided up my ribs and I gasped as sensation spiralled through my body; it took a conscious effort to hold myself still and to meet his dark eyes.

Get out now, you little fool, Sophie. Get out while you can.

But I didn't. I didn't listen to that lonely voice of sense – and, anyway, where could I go, dressed – *undressed* – as I was? Back to Lady Beatrice's room?

'Show me your tricks,' he said almost bleakly. 'Before I send you back to her. You're damnably sweet and pretty for a whore.'

'No,' I whispered. Beatrice had told him I was a virgin but he hadn't believed a word – this was all going so horribly wrong. 'No, you don't understand . . .'

Suddenly I realised I could hear faint music in the distance. Was Beatrice playing her gramophone again? Was it a trick of my imagination? Then I saw that he could hear it too, and he said, 'Come and dance with me.'

I must have backed away in shock. He repeated more harshly, 'Dance with me. And do something to earn the money Beatrice has promised you.'

He shed his jacket; he pulled me close, so I could feel the muscular heat of his body warming mine. He began softly singing the song we could hear; it was 'Jazz Baby, Be Mine' and he had, I realised, an adorable, melting voice. My bones became liquid and ripples of need started to unfurl deep inside me. I was still mute with misery and shame, but he was already moving with me in time to the music while humming in my ear, his body hard and blissful against my fragile underwear, against my skin.

What could I do?

I knew he was mocking me. I knew he must despise me. I should have pushed him away, I should have fled. It was so simple. Except that dancing with this man was sublime, for he was calm and in control, yet I couldn't help but be conscious of the restrained power of him, of the strength of his thighs brushing against mine. He was still singing softly and I sang with him, I couldn't help it.

Jazz baby, I love the things you do to me,
Jazz baby, you drive me wild ...

His hand lingered at my hip and I shivered as his thumb brushed a rhythmic pattern over my sensitised skin, until I felt a piercing hunger for something I'd never had, never been able to imagine even. Inside, my heart was breaking.

I stopped suddenly. 'Cantharides. What is it?'

He was still holding me, but his body had tensed. 'Do you really not know?'

'How could I?' There was pain in my voice, I remember. He looked down at me gravely and ran his thumb over my lips. I shivered badly.

'It's an erotic stimulant,' he said at last. 'Popular with women like Lady Beatrice. Spanish Fly is its other name. Were you truly not aware that she'd put some in your drink?'

'No,' I whispered. 'No.'

I wanted to add, *I don't need it, with you.* I think I realised then that all I'd ever wanted was to be with him, like the song said. Despair overwhelmed me.

He stroked my hair. He pressed my cheek against his crisp white shirt. He was still humming softly under his breath as we moved; his voice was divine, it tore at my ragged senses. Then he was tipping up my chin with his fingers to brush my lips with his, while his other hand slipped beneath my satin brassiere to skim the warm skin as he traced a path to my nipple. He deliberately fingered the tender tip until it hardened to his touch, sending shafts of liquid need to my belly.

My body started shaking again.

He frowned, holding me close, pressing his cool forehead to mine. He was muttering, '*Oh, Sophie . . .*'

Being so near to him tipped me over the edge. His fingers still stroked and tugged at my nipple so skilfully; his strong thigh was pressing against me just at the juncture of my legs, where I was wet and burning. Gasping, I ground myself helplessly against him, while thrusting my breast harder against his fingers. I shuddered as my climax shook me.

'I'm sorry,' I whispered at last. 'I'm so sorry.'

'My God, Sophie,' he said.

I clung to him, shaking as tremors of exquisite pleasure washed through me. My cheek was still pressed to his white shirt, my eyes were closed in shame.

'You really *are* an innocent, aren't you?' His voice was quiet but urgent. 'Damn Beatrice and her tricks.'

'You don't like me. I thought you might not. I told her so.'

'Don't like you,' he echoed. 'Don't like you . . . Sophie, why the hell did you *do* this?'

'I . . . it was part of a plan.'

'Tell me about it.'

By now my voice was raw with torment. 'I wanted to dance,' I breathed, 'I wanted to be on stage, and dance and sing.'

I'd thought I wanted freedom. Independence. But now my world had changed completely. All I wanted was him – and he despised me.

He was silent for a while, rubbing his temple. Then – 'Sing for me,' he said. 'Sing.' His harsh voice lashed me, sensitive and aroused as I was. I half closed my eyes, took a deep breath and sang. I didn't smile or lick my lips or do the silly things I knew whores did, I just clasped my hands in front of me and sang. To him.

'*My man with the blue sad eyes,*
I want to make you smile.
But what does it take for you to realise
I've given you my heart, for such a long while?
Oh, yes, it's true. All I want is you . . .'

I could only whisper the last words. I put my hands to my cheeks and the tears burned at the back of my eyes. *All I want. All I want . . .* 'Please don't leave me this time,' I said. 'Please.'

He moved suddenly. He held me. He kissed me hard on my lips.

I wasn't prepared. My knees gave way; I was battling fresh floods of sensation. He swung me up so easily and carried me into the adjoining bedroom, where he laid me on the big bed, then he flung off his jacket and gathered me once more in his arms; I could hear his breath rasping in his throat. *Oh.* I was spellbound. I was terrified. I was quivering with excitement.

He kissed my lips again and kissed my breasts, slipping them out of my flimsy brassiere and drawing them into his mouth. His kiss was not like Beatrice's, it wasn't like anything I'd ever known. The weight of him, the strength of him, made my body leap with raw hunger.

Then, suddenly, I realised what he was doing.

He was already pinning me to the bed with his body, so my legs were splayed and I was helpless. My underwear had gone already, now he was peeling off one of my stockings – and he was doing it for a reason. He was using it – to tie both my wrists behind me, to the bedrail. *What on earth . . . ?*

'Gently,' he murmured.

I squirmed, my eyes full of anxious questions; I could see him above me, his face dark and so intent. But as I opened my mouth to speak he kissed me; more than that, he ravished my soft mouth with his tongue, and as he withdrew I found my protests had vanished into thin air.

'*Jazz baby, you drive me wild,*' he whispered, and smiled.

Then I realised that he was fastening a piece of fabric around my head, covering my eyes, and I didn't understand. I was frightened. *Tying me? Blindfolding me?* Beatrice had said nothing about all this! 'No,' I protested, trying to wriggle free. My heart was thumping in fear. 'Please. I want to see you.'

'I can't let you,' he said. 'I'm sorry.'

'But . . . why?' His tender apology reassured me, but I was still dismayed.

His voice, when it came next, was grave. 'Sophie. Do you want me to stop?'

I couldn't bear him to leave me and that was the truth of it. 'No,' I breathed. 'No. Do what you want, but don't stop. Please.'

'Are you quite sure?'

As sure as I've been of anything in my life. 'Yes. Yes, Your Grace—'

'Don't call me that. Call me Ash,' he broke in roughly. '*Ash.*'

The blindfold was black. He'd caressed my cheek after he put it on, and I remember how in a strange way not being able to see him heightened all my other senses: for example, I was acutely aware of the pull of the silk stocking at my wrists, the sounds of him unbuttoning his clothes; the male scent of him, his soap and the hint of fresh body sweat, powerful and arousing.

I felt him run his hands – his dreadfully scarred hands – up over my legs towards my naked skin and my pulsing core. I arched my hips, trembling helplessly, longing for him; I remember how my thighs fell shamefully apart, welcoming him.

I felt the pressure of his strong legs as he eased himself over me and between me. God help me, I felt the brush of something hot – like velvet, like steel – quivering against my belly. I realised it was him, and excitement roared through me.

Jazz baby, I love the things you do to me,
Jazz baby, you drive me wild . . .

He was still humming as he caressed my silken wet folds knowingly with his fingers. I quivered again, pulling at my bonds, and I called out his name.

He thrust his hips, hard. He filled me. There was a moment of shock, a moment of brief pain; I cried out.

He stopped moving. 'I'm hurting you,' he said.

I lay very still under his weight, feeling something shatter inside me, feeling heat suddenly consume me at his possession. A bone-deep longing surged through me like a rising tide.

'If you leave me now,' I whispered, 'I think I will die.'

He kissed me. I groaned as he drove his tongue between my lips and deep into my mouth. My breasts throbbed and tingled almost unbearably. Blindly I drew up my legs, longing to feel him, to let him know what *I* felt.

He raised himself on his arms. With a sort of sigh he thrust into me again, then put his lips to one breast and sucked the nipple deep into his mouth.

I remember I burned and ached all at the same time. Torrents of pleasure shot up and down my spine and all across my sensitised skin. I moaned and moved as he moved, pulling at my bonds, lifting my hips and clenching him to me with my inner muscles. I soared; I possessed him; I loved him. He was driving himself into me, deep and hard, and I shattered in his arms.

Molten delight unfurled slowly through my whole body. I shook, I called out his name – *Ash* – as he continued slowly, deeply to ravish me. Only when I was sated, drifting in the rippling after-waves, did he pull out of me, shudder and then lie very still. I remembered

Beatrice saying: *Sometimes they withdraw just before their crisis . . .*

I hardly dared breathe. A few moments later I heard him fastening his clothes, then he unbound my eyes and released my wrists. He kissed the skin where those bonds had been, then wrapped me in the silk kimono. He said, 'I must call Beatrice in.'

No. I shrank into his arms. I said, 'I don't want to see her. I don't want to have anything more to do with her, ever.'

He didn't reply at first but led me to sit on the settee in the other room. Then he stroked my cheek and said, 'You don't have to say a word. Let me do the talking.'

He went quickly for her while I sat there with my hands covering my face, still breathing in the scent of his skin, my most secret places still throbbing from his caresses. This must be the end, I thought wretchedly. This *has* to be the end. She would tell him everything that she and I had planned; she'd tell him how I'd agreed to it all.

He came in with Beatrice following. She was fully dressed, and she looked at me with near hatred. She must have known full well what we'd been doing, for my body and my face must have screamed it.

He said to her, 'Beatrice, I've found you amusing in the past. But I don't like the way you've tricked me and used this girl.' She licked her lips, looking at me then at him. She said huskily, 'Tricked you, Ash? I thought you'd enjoy her. But if you'd prefer someone with more experience . . .'

She tried to lift her hand to his shoulder, but he

pushed it away. 'I don't want a single damned thing from you, Beatrice. I want you to be very sure of that. I also want to remind you that I'm leaving for London tomorrow. Whether or not you decide to stay here at the Hall is entirely up to you.'

Beatrice looked very pale but she was still trying to be in charge. 'Thanks, but London will suit me just fine. I'll come too, and I'll bring Sophie.'

'No you won't,' he said. 'Because I'm taking her with me.'

I saw Beatrice's face, and I knew I'd made an enemy for life.

'You little cow,' she said to me softly, heedless now of Ash at her side. 'You've been scheming behind my back, haven't you?' I think she made some threatening move towards me, because I jumped to my feet away from her, and the next thing I remember was the sight of Ash – my Mr Maldon – gripping her by the arms and pushing her unceremoniously out through the door.

He locked it. Then he came back to me, his eyes burning into me. 'I meant what I said, Sophie. I have business in London, and I want you to come with me.'

I didn't understand. Why, in God's name, should he want me with him? 'You and me – it's not possible. You know it's not possible.'

He moved closer. He put his arms around me; he held me very close and he said, 'You promised me devotion in your letters. Didn't you mean it?'

Oh, more than ever. 'Yes,' I breathed. 'I meant it, every word.'

'Then come with me. Stay with me.'

He still looked troubled, and so sad I wanted to hold him and comfort him. But instead I stood very still, with a sense of terrible dread starting to permeate my whole being. 'You told me once,' I said steadily, 'that people would judge me by the value I placed on myself.'

He lifted my fingers to his lips, and again I saw the terribly scarred skin of his hand. 'Believe me, I value you, Sophie.' His eyes were dark once more, the cornflower blue deepening almost to black. 'You've given me something precious tonight, and I don't take that lightly.'

'But you can't promise me for ever.' There was something desperate in my voice by then. 'I *know* you can't.'

He let my hand fall and rubbed his palm across his temples, looking tired suddenly. 'No. Of course not. You must realise that.'

Yes, I'd realised it, from the moment I'd seen him in the dining hall and realised who he was. Raw emotion was pouring through me. I loved him, I wanted him, I would have given anything to be with him, on any terms, whatever the price.

But . . .

'You couldn't bear me to look at you,' I breathed. 'Or even to touch you. When we were intimate just now, you had to do *that* to me. Tie me up and blindfold me.'

He went very still, then he drew air into his lungs and his face grew harsh – as harsh as when he'd spoken to Beatrice. 'Those are my terms,' he said. 'I'm afraid you'll have to take them or leave them.'

I shook my head, remembering with terrible bitterness how one of the first things I had been told on becoming a servant was that I was invisible. I'd been instructed to turn aside and pretend not to be there if any of my superiors should come across me in a corridor. This man wouldn't even let me look at him when he was making love to me.

I gazed into his fathomless blue eyes. 'I can't accept your terms,' I said. 'I'm sorry.'

And I felt my heart breaking, all over again.

'At least stay with me tonight,' he said. He trailed one finger down my cheek; he lowered his mouth to mine and caressed my lips with light butterfly touches. He must have felt me tremble with need, because only then did he put his arms around me to draw me close and properly fasten his beautiful mouth over mine.

I placed my palms against his chest, feeling beneath his shirt the steady rhythm of his heart. His body was warm; the citrus-masculine scent of him filled my senses. As his kiss deepened, as his tongue cherished my lips, I felt heavy with needing him again. His hands had slid down to my hips and I felt myself swaying gently beneath his warm touch. His mouth moved to my cheek, to the hollow beneath my ear and the curve of my neck.

'Stay,' he said again. He was gazing down at me, but the expression on his face was impossible to read. 'Please stay. I want to sleep tonight with you in my arms, Sophie.'

He had the most beautiful face I had ever seen, and those were the most beautiful words I'd ever heard, but a huge lump hurt my throat. 'I have to go,' I whispered.

'Go where?' His voice was harsher now. 'Back to Beatrice? Up to the servants' attic?'

I shivered with dismay. He was right – I had nowhere.

'Come with me,' he said hoarsely. 'Come with me to London. I need you.'

I was in the arms of the man with whom I'd fallen in love before I knew what love was. I thought of my future stretching bleakly ahead of me without him, and I felt a long, deep shiver of despair run through me. But I still somehow pulled myself away from his embrace. Oh God, I can't remember if he tried to stop me, but I do remember how cold I felt.

'No.' I was shaking with the force of my emotion. 'I can't come to London with you. I can't *be* with you. I'm sorry.'

He said, 'Is it because of what they say about me?'

I was confused now, and terribly distressed. I remembered what Cook had said – *Look at all the money he's got, most of it made during the war while other men were fighting.* I thought of Beatrice saying: *Men like him have their pick of the most beautiful, most sophisticated women in the world.*

'It's what you yourself said.' I gazed up at him, begging him to tell me that he'd been lying – that everyone else was lying. 'You said you're in the habit of buying all the entertainment you need. And there are so many stories . . .'

My voice trailed away. His face was hard suddenly, his eyes cold. 'I'm sure there are,' he said.

I remember I stepped backwards away from him, the ground suddenly uncertain beneath my feet. 'I don't listen to them,' I whispered. 'I *won't* listen to them.'

'Then perhaps you should,' he said.

And so my world changed again. He meant it. He

really meant it. And how long before he tired of me? A year? A couple of months?

Tonight I'd been a novelty for him – I was a virgin, an innocent. Perhaps he'd felt a vague tenderness towards me because of our meeting in Oxford, and because of my childish letters to him. But he'd still tied me up and blindfolded me, so I couldn't see him or even touch him in those moments of intimacy.

He said again, 'Stay.'

Something squeezed my heart till it hurt, so badly. I could hardly bear to look at him as I whispered my fare-well and turned towards the door.

This man would only tear my world apart. Surely he knew it too, because he didn't try to stop me. But I would never forget the expression on his face as I left him.

I was still wearing Beatrice's silk kimono, but I needed clothes if I was to leave. I didn't know what to do, but as I passed Beatrice's rooms I saw that she had put my things outside her door, in an overnight bag – my one dress, my shoes, my few books and my old coat. I picked the bag up – silently, I'd thought, but suddenly the door opened and Beatrice was there.

'Had enough of you already, has he?'

I didn't know what to say. She wore some patterned satin pyjamas and she was smoking.

'I've been thinking, Sophie.' Her lip curled. 'I've worked it all out. You said to me earlier that you met him four and a half years ago in Oxford. It was around then – in the spring – that Ash came from London for an appointment with the old Duke in Oxford, and the two of them had the most tremendous row. Quite simply, Ash wanted money and the Duke refused. That must have been the day you met him.'

'I don't see—' I began.

She interrupted. 'One of the maids told me you wrote regularly to someone in London soon after you started work here, and it was him, wasn't it? Ash was already laying his plans, and meeting you in Oxford that day must have seemed a heaven-sent opportunity for him. He would have known there was a chance he might some day inherit the dukedom – he was third in line, after all – so he got you your job here and he asked you to write to him. Didn't he?'

Suddenly the light from the lamp in her room seemed to spin around her and I couldn't answer; she gave her curt laugh and went on, 'Well, well. What did Ash want? He decided he needed a spy below stairs. Someone who would have no idea, in her foolish innocence, of his interest in the estate, but would answer all his questions and babble in her letters about everything that went on – Lord Edwin's death, the Duke's illness, my visits, everything. You know what they say? If you want to know all the secrets of a great house, ask the servants.'

'No,' I said. I'd clenched my fists. *Damn you, no.*

She was relentless. 'How does it feel to be used, Sophie? Oh, dear – I can see from your face that you actually thought he *cared*.'

I whirled to pick up my things, hurrying away down the corridor, away from her, but I could still hear her mocking laugh. Downstairs in the darkness I pulled my drab maid's dress over the silky lingerie she'd bestowed on me. I curled up on a couch in the kitchen and tried to sleep, my thoughts whirling. But well before the young scullery maid arrived to scrub out the range, I was up and knocking at the door of Mrs Burdett's rooms to tell her I was leaving. I knew she always rose early, but it took her a moment to register what I was saying, though then she nodded, her lips tight. 'Well, you've worked hard, I'll say that for you, Sophie. It's customary to give notice – I don't suppose you can give me a reason for this sudden departure?'

'I can't,' I said steadily. 'I'm sorry.'

She asked me to let her know my new address, because some wages would be due to me, she said. After that I picked up my bag and went out into the near dark of the courtyard. Then I set off down the drive to the main road, where I would catch the early bus into Oxford.

I was going to London. My new life was about to begin. But oh, God, I felt I'd left all my dreams and my hopes behind me that day.

Chapter Eleven

London, February 1921

'Girls, girls, you must remember to move with grace and elegance. Light as a feather. Light as a feather ...' Rupert Calladine rapped his cane on the stage for emphasis, then gestured to the pianist to play 'Ragtime Blues' again.

His sharp ears must have caught some muffled complaints, because he stepped closer to us all and raised his voice. 'Why do I ask you to do this over and over, you ask? I'll tell you why, my darling girls. It's because at the moment, you dance like a *herd of giraffes*. Have none of you any sense of rhythm? Who the hell hired you? Ah, now I remember, *I* did – fool that I am.'

We all exchanged wary glances; he was often like this. For more than four hours we'd been rehearsing. For more than four hours this inspired little man with the brilliantined black hair, whom I'd seen from afar at Belfield Hall last autumn, had made us practise our routines till our feet and bodies ached. 'He's a slave driver,' the girl at my side, Cora, muttered. But we smiled too, because his incredible energy made his theatre what it was – a success. I was on the London stage, which had been my dream for so long.

That morning I'd received a letter from Nell at the Hall – she'd written to me regularly, ever since I'd sent Mrs Burdett my address as she'd asked. *The new Duke is sweeping round here like a whirlwind,* Nell wrote. Her handwriting was plain but clear – they taught them well at the workhouse, she'd once told me, so they could be of use to their betters as soon as they were old enough. *He put old Peters firmly in his place, hoorah! He went to London just after you left but he was back before Christmas, and he let us hold a servants' party. Harriet is for ever mooning around because she's so, so in love with him. He's going to pull the whole Belfield estate into the modern age, he says. The old Duchess keeps flying into a towering temper at all this and would move to the Dower House – except, of course, she knows he'd count the hours to her departure . . .*

'You! The new girl, Sophie – come to the front!' Mr Calladine was curtly beckoning to me.

I was in my practice costume, a pink dress with a short flared skirt – we all wore them. My dancing shoes were of kid, with ankle-straps and one-inch heels. Nervously I took a few steps forward, while Mr Calladine watched me and barked, 'How long have you been here?'

Had I done something wrong? 'About . . . about two months, Mr Calladine.'

Rupert Calladine nodded at me then turned to the others. 'This girl isn't eighteen yet,' he pronounced. 'And already she puts the rest of you to shame. Cut out your late nights and boyfriends, you slappers, and put some effort in – we've a new show opening in a week!'

His praise gained me a few dark looks from Pauline

Moran and her friends – they were experienced dancers several years older than me and saw any newcomers, especially young ones, as a threat. But Cora next to me squeezed my hand and murmured, 'Oh, well done! Pauline and her crew are livid – hoorah!'

And afterwards, when we were back in the changing rooms, Cora came to me again. 'Sophie, there's a spare room where I live. The house is a bit small, but – well, would you be interested in sharing it with me?' My face must have lit up. 'You *would!*' she cried. 'Oh, bliss!'

I'd come to London in November on the train, having never been further than Oxford in my life. At first I was overwhelmed. But by looking at the signs in the windows of the lodging houses near Paddington, I'd found a tiny room to rent and then I'd set off the next morning to buy some clothes in Oxford Street, with the money Margaret had given me.

London was a new world to me, with its tall, crowded buildings and thronged pavements, and traffic passing by relentlessly. But within a week I'd had my long fair hair cut fashionably short, and the hairdresser told me where Mr Calladine's theatre was, just off Leicester Square; so the next day I called there and a young woman with painted lips and fingernails like Lady Beatrice's looked me up and down then said sharply, 'Have you danced before? Had lessons?'

'Yes,' I lied.

She'd already picked up the internal telephone. 'New girl here, Mr Calladine. Yes, she's young – oh, eighteen or so. She's pretty, yes. Says she's had lessons . . .' She nodded at me. 'He'll see you now.'

Mr Calladine's office was almost filled by an enormous desk, and the walls were covered with bright posters that proclaimed, *You've not seen London until you've seen Calladine's Chorus Girls!* After taking a swift look at me, Mr Calladine went over to a gramophone cabinet and put on a record.

'Right, let's see you dance,' he instructed. 'Doesn't matter what steps – just go with the music.'

The tune was . . . 'Jazz Baby, Be Mine'. Raw emotion poured through me as I remembered dancing to it in Ash's arms. *Jazz baby, the things you do to me* . . . I'd closed my eyes for a moment, feeling helpless and vulnerable, but then the rhythm of the music swept through my veins and I began to dance. I thought I danced well, but when the music stopped I wasn't sure, for Mr Calladine sat silently, his finger pressed to his lips.

'Which theatres have you worked at?' he asked abruptly.

'I haven't,' I whispered.

He gazed at me a while longer, his bright eyes narrowed. He said at last, 'So no one's even seen you on stage before. That's good. It means you'll make all the more impact when you start working for me.'

My breath hitched in my throat. 'When I . . .'

'When you start appearing in my shows,' he said, getting to his feet and shaking my hand briskly. 'I think you've rather exaggerated your experience, young lady, but you've got a good sense of rhythm and you move well. It should only take a few weeks for you to pick up all our basic routines.' He was already sitting again at his desk, drawing out some paperwork. 'You can start tomorrow – I'll get my secretary to draw up a contract. Your name is . . . ?'

At Belfield Hall, I had always been known as Sophie Smith. One of the first things I'd been told there was that I must on no account use my correct surname – Davis – because my poor mother had been one of Lord Charlwood's many conquests so long ago. But now I was free of the Hall and its rules. 'It's Davis,' I said clearly to Mr Calladine. 'Miss Sophie Davis.'

There were twenty of us in Mr Calladine's Chorus Line, and though I was too late to perform in the December show, I was allowed to take a small part in the rehearsals. I spent Christmas Day on my own in my lodgings, but rehearsals started the morning after and Mr Calladine worked us harder than ever.

Each morning I hurried to the theatre off Leicester Square, marvelling anew at all the people filling the streets, but once inside my mind was focused on one thing: the dancing. Precision was vital, and we needed energy as well, because even between our numbers, while solo singers or comic turns diverted the audience, we had no time to rest; we had to rush to get changed for the next act.

But I was eager to learn, and it was a turning point when Cora asked me to share her house. Cora had black curly hair and her hazel eyes were always merry; she was four years older than me, and was one of Mr

Calladine's most experienced dancers. After the show, many of the older girls, like Pauline Moran, would meet up with rich men then drive off in their cars to restaurants and clubs. But I'd noticed that Cora always seemed to go straight home.

'It'll be such fun to have you here!' she'd beamed when she first showed me round the terraced house she rented in Bayswater. It was small, as she'd warned me, and noisy too; the milkman's cart went by at five in the morning, and often at night a musician next door would practise his saxophone till the early hours. A ginger tomcat yowled regularly on the doorstep to be let in, and Cora, who had a soft heart, called him Fred and gave him tinned sardines.

I didn't mind any of this at all. After my years at Belfield Hall I had a sense of the most incredible freedom. No longer did I have to get up in the pre-dawn darkness to put on my maid's gown. I was free not only from the long hours of drudgery, but also from the sense of not even being allowed to use my own name.

But sometimes I woke in the night feeling that perhaps I'd made the most terrible mistake, because I'd turned my back on the only thing I wanted – Mr Maldon. *You know what they say?* Beatrice's final words still trickled through my veins like poison. *If you want to know all the secrets of a great house, ask the servants. How does it feel to be used, Sophie? Oh dear – I can see from your face that you actually thought he cared.*

It was as well my new life kept me so occupied: indeed, I was constantly absorbed with the business of finding my way round London, and of getting to the

158

theatre in time for the various rehearsals and shows. Though if Cora and I were working different shifts – she might do the matinées and I the evenings, for example, I had to travel to the theatre on my own, and sometimes I made mistakes.

One evening, as I was taking the trolleybus home after a show, it broke down; rather than wait for another, I decided to walk. But I took a wrong turning and before I knew it I was in a narrow street where the gutter down the middle ran with filth and some women in rough clothes pointed and laughed at me. I turned and hurried back the way I'd come, my heart pounding, afraid because I was in a place I shouldn't be, but it wasn't just that. For I'd felt someone was watching me.

I dismissed it as my foolish imagination. But after that, the feeling that I was being watched never left me. And every evening I gazed round the theatre with its rows and rows of packed seats; I looked up at the ornate boxes swagged with satin where the rich people sat and, fool that I was, I never stopped thinking: What if Ash were there? What if he were to come for me?

I want to sleep tonight with you in my arms, Sophie. I couldn't forget those words of his, nor the look in his eyes when I left him.

I continued to be surprised that Cora, who was so pretty, had no followers. One night, when we were in the sitting room of our tiny house drinking cocoa, she told me she'd been involved for a while with a man called Danny, and though she laughed about him and said he was a no-good two-faced cheat, I guessed that she'd been really, really hurt by him.

She wanted, of course, to know about my life, and so I told her about being a scullery maid at Belfield Hall. After she'd put some more coal on the fire – outside it was raw, with a thick London fog filling the streets, she slipped off her shoes, sat next to me on our rickety sofa with Fred the cat on her lap and said, 'You don't fool me, sweetie. There's more. Isn't there?'

Suddenly a huge ache almost blocked my throat. I tried to speak but couldn't.

She sighed, her eyes full of pity. 'A man. There's always some wretched man. Is he a cheat, like Danny? Married, then? Religious?' I shook my head to each. 'A gambler?' she pressed on. 'A bankrupt? A drunk?'

'Stop. Stop.' I was almost laughing. 'He's not married, he doesn't drink – or gamble, as far as I know. He's also handsome and he's very, very rich . . .'

My voice broke and she leaned across to hug me. 'Oh, Sophie! Where on earth did you meet him?'

'He owns the Hall where I used to work.'

She whistled. 'My, my, handsome *and* rich. Attagirl. Was it – you know – your first time?'

Just then our neighbour began practising his saxophone and Cora broke off to throw one of her shoes at the wall. 'Dratted man . . .' She turned back to me. 'Look, Sophie, you can tell me all about it even if it was a let-down – losing your virginity's a complete bore. I remember my first boyfriend fumbled away for a few minutes, and it was over before I realised it had begun.

Most of the other men in my life have been the same, except for bloody Danny . . .'

For a moment I saw tears sparkle in her eyes, but she dashed them away and laughed. 'Go on,' she urged, 'tell Auntie Cora what went wrong. No, let me guess. Did you find out that he preferred men, like our Cally?'

Cally was what the girls called Mr Calladine, and I'd already realised I was quite safe with him. 'Prefer men? No. I was only with him for one night, but it – *he* – was quite wonderful.'

'Wonderful in what way? Spill the beans, girl. Did you reach – ' Cora rolled her eyes – 'the pinnacle of bliss with him, Sophie?'

I hesitated. 'Twice.'

'In one evening?'

'In an hour.'

'Oh, my goodness. And . . . your first time.' Slowly she tucked her knees up under her – Fred the cat had jumped off her in disgust – and gazed at me in awe. 'You lucky, lucky thing. I so often feel as if – you know, as if I'm almost there. But then the blessed man comes too early, or pulls out, or something disastrous. Only Danny, blasted Danny gave me the full works. But this bastard of yours didn't want any more? Sweetie, that must have been awful for you.'

'But he *did* want more.' I tried so hard to be light-hearted. 'He asked me to be his mistress.'

'And you said no?' Her hazel eyes were solemn. 'Sophie, how can any girl refuse an offer from a man who is gorgeous, rich and fantastic in bed as well? What would you do if he turned up again?'

'I'd say no again.'

'But why? Were you worried about getting pregnant? You can deal with it, you know – make him use a sheath, or make sure he pulls out in time. Though of course,' she added, 'if you go on top of him, you can be so much more in control.'

'If I go on top?' Then my cheeks burned because I'd suddenly remembered the picture Margaret had shown me in Lady Beatrice's book.

'Oh my, you're such an innocent!' marvelled Cora. 'Ride him, girl, or take him in your mouth – they all love *that*.' Once more I blushed hotly, remembering Beatrice and her American. 'In other words,' went on Cora blithely, 'if your man turns up again, don't lose him this time. You must have made quite an impression on him – you were a virgin, you clearly had no idea what you were doing, yet you had him desperate for more.'

I felt so young and so stupid. The other maids had never talked to me like this, not even Nell. 'I thought it was like that for everybody, Cora.'

'My God, no.' She leaned closer. 'I've told you about *my* first time. And you should just try asking some of Cally's girls about their ghastly experiences. Mindy – you know poor Mindy? Her stepfather used to rape her regularly till she ran away. As for little Jeannie, she was put on the game in Soho by her dear mother when she was scarcely out of school. London's a big, dark place, Sophie, once you lose your way. So your first-time experience was . . . *unusual*.'

I was silent a moment. 'You can say that again,' I replied at last. 'He tied me up.'

'Oh.' She sat back a little. 'Oh, my goodness. One of *those*.' Then she brightened. 'Well, you know – if that's all . . .'

'He tied me up and blindfolded me,' I said, 'before we did it.' *Did it.* How cold, how clinical, but how else could I describe what Ash and I did? *Making love* just wasn't right at all, though he showed desire, oh, yes – harsh, furious desire. But not love. Never love. 'He didn't want me to see him, Cora. Or touch him, even. It made me feel . . . it made me feel so far beneath him.'

Fred had leaped onto her lap again; she stroked him thoughtfully and said, 'That's really strange. But Sophie, lots of rich men are a bit odd you know – I blame their upbringing. They have strict governesses when they're little, then there are peculiar masters at those boarding schools of theirs. They get beaten and God knows what else. You hear such stories.'

I remembered the servants' gossip about Ash as a boy, and how his artist father and his French mother once forgot to collect him from school at the beginning of the summer holidays. I shivered.

'Tying you up,' Cora went on, clearly intrigued. 'Do you think he does that to all his women?'

The thought made me feel even bleaker. 'I don't know. Apparently – ' I tried to steady myself – 'apparently he pays his mistresses well; in fact he said that he prefers to pay for his entertainment.'

'Makes sense. Money pretty much guarantees a woman's silence, since she'll tend to keep quiet about a man's funny habits in the hope that he'll come back and pay her for more.'

I nodded. 'He despises women, I think.'

'Sounds like it, sweetie. Have you – you know, been with anyone else since?'

'No!' I must have gone rigid at the thought. 'Oh, no. How could I?'

Cora tickled Fred's tummy. 'Might be the only answer,' she said thoughtfully. 'The only cure. But there's no rush. Your man – was he in the fighting?'

'I don't think so. Why?'

'Hmm. I've heard that men who've been in the trenches can have very strange habits once you get their clothes off, to make up for what they've been through – bombing, shell-shock and the rest of it.' She reached for her cocoa. 'Then again, some are just born peculiar. *Men.*'

'Men.' I made an effort to smile back. Just then a particularly piercing saxophone melody wafted through the wall from next door. 'He's good,' I said.

'What?' I think I'd startled Cora out of a Danny-reverie.

'The man next door. On the saxophone.'

'Benedict? He plays in a band. He's rather sweet. But after midnight – too much!' She threw her other shoe at the wall and we rose to go to bed, but first Cora hugged me. 'It's bliss, isn't it, Sophie?' she whispered. 'Being young, being in London and being free to do what we like?'

But that night I heard her weeping her heart out into her pillow.

I couldn't sleep either. For the first time since leaving Belfield Hall I drew out Ash's letters, looking for the last one written early in 1917. *I have to go away. I want you to still write to me, though, Sophie. I want you to still think of me, and to think well of me.*

I thrust it away, remembering Beatrice's sneer. *He must have decided he needed a spy below stairs.* But where had he gone to, early in 1917, in the midst of that terrible war? Everyone said he'd used the war to make money; but I thought of his dreadfully burned hands, and when I fell asleep at last, it was to dream of flames engulfing him, while I tried desperately to save him, calling out his name.

I woke with a dry throat in the middle of the night. After tiptoeing downstairs for a glass of water, I happened to glance out of the front window, where the tattered curtains didn't quite meet – and on the other side of the street a shadow moved. I was being watched. I was sure of it now. I was being watched.

Have I mentioned that I had, by then, an admirer? He'd been an airman in the war; his full name, which he hated, was Algernon Stewart-Lynton, but he preferred to be called simply Lynton, and he asked me out, so sweetly, every week. Poor Lynton was twenty-four years old and his right leg had been badly broken during a German bombing raid over Kent. He had to walk with a stick, which he hated.

A few nights after my conversation with Cora, Lynton came backstage after the show to bring me a bouquet of flowers. His stick clattered to the floor as he tried to present them to me, and I heard him swear under his breath.

'Bloody stick,' he said. 'Sometimes I wish I could hurl it to kingdom come, but then I'd never get anywhere, would I? Come out with me tonight, Sophie, do!'

I was putting his flowers in a vase but I turned to him with a smile. 'Lynton, I never go out after the show.' I didn't want him to think it was because of his injury.

He sighed, then gave his sweet grin. 'I won't stop asking you, you know. We could dine at Claridge's, the Ritz – anywhere you fancy. I'll be in again tomorrow in case you change your mind, Sophie!'

I knew I wouldn't, but I didn't want to be cruel to him. How was he to know that I still dreamed of only one man?

Chapter Twelve

Around then a spell of cold, grey February weather closed in on the city, which coincided with the time that I started to have my first doubts about having joined Mr Calladine's show.

Fashions in entertainment had changed since the end of the war, and the rich set were now starting to abandon theatres like ours in favour of restaurants and nightclubs like the Embassy in Old Bond Street and the Café Royal in Regent Street. Meanwhile Mr Calladine's rent had almost doubled in the last year, his pianist Miss Ronald informed us, and in his attempt to pull in customers, Cally was changing our routines almost weekly and our costumes as well, making them flimsier and more revealing, which I hated, especially as it meant more men started hanging around the theatre afterwards to proposition us.

Another way Cally was trying to boost custom was by offering reduced ticket rates for large groups, and since fancy-dress parties were all the rage then amongst the young, we would see them piling into the theatre dressed up as anything you could think of – ancient Greeks or Hawaiians, Victorians or even cowboys and Indians, because of the Tom Mix films that were so popular.

One night twenty or so young men and women came in wearing soldiers' uniforms, calling themselves 'The Injured Heroes'. They wore bandages stained with red dye and used false crutches to hobble into their seats, then in the interval they shrieked with laughter at each other's outfits and fake war wounds. As ill-luck would have it, I'd seen that Lynton was in his box that night – he'd waved cheerfully to me at the start of the show as usual. But after the interval I noticed he'd gone.

'They shouldn't do it,' I muttered fiercely to myself at the end of our final number, in which we marched around the stage to the tune of 'Keep the Home Fires Burning', while the fancy-dress party stood and made ridiculous army salutes. 'They shouldn't be allowed to do it.'

Pauline heard, and mocked me. 'You *are* a little fool, aren't you?'

Ignoring her, I went to find Cora. Last night after the show she'd told me she was going out for a meal with someone – I'd waited expectantly for her to tell me more, but to my surprise she hadn't uttered another word. I'd heard her come in very late, after a motorcar stopped in the street outside, and the next morning, though I'd had to wake her up, she still said nothing about where she'd been, and with whom.

But that evening she'd stumbled through our numbers as if she was ill, and on our way home on the trolleybus she suddenly became so drained of colour that I feared she might faint. I got her to our usual stop, but she made for the gutter at the side of the road, then she leaned over and was violently sick.

'Oh, Cora.' I tried to steady her. 'You're ill, you shouldn't have danced tonight.'

She turned to face me, looking like death. 'I saw Danny last night, Sophie. He's been begging me to go back with him. I'm sorry, sweetie, so sorry.'

I hate you, Danny, I muttered under my breath. Cora's legs were like cotton wool and I was wondering in despair how I was going to get her inside when suddenly Benedict, our neighbour, was out there. 'Gently now,' he was saying to Cora, 'gently does it.'

Half carrying her, he got her up to her bedroom and I thanked him fervently.

'She's on something, isn't she?' he said. He was only a few years older than Cora, and he had a kind face, though his expression was grave. I didn't reply; he shrugged and said, 'Just call if you need me. Or – ' and he flashed me a smile – 'you could throw something at the wall.'

I helped Cora change into her pyjamas and went to make her some tea, but I kept thinking it was like Belfield Hall, when I'd failed Nell. When I got back to her, she was trying to pull herself up against the pillow, then she looked at me and said, 'Oh, *Sophie* . . .'

Tears were running down her cheeks, making her black eyeliner run. Quickly I put down the tea-tray and rushed to her side to hug her. 'Cora. Cora, darling. It'll be all right, you'll see.'

'I know he's no good for me,' she wept. 'I know he's a no-good cheating bastard. But he keeps coming back to me, and – and *fucking up* my rotten life, and though I beg him to leave me alone, I love him, Sophie, I need him, and I know Cally will sack me soon, and then what am I going to do? I love him, so much.'

By then she'd collapsed in my arms, her body racked with sobs.

The next afternoon Cora was truly not well enough for the rehearsal, but she insisted on coming with me, and at the theatre my spirits sank even lower when I saw our latest costumes, since they consisted of short, low-necked dresses in garish colours. Later Cally produced large feather fans for each of us, which we were to use in a teasing sort of dance.

Things went from bad to worse. Just before we were due to go on for the evening performance, Cora rushed to the Ladies' room – then, with seconds to spare, came hurrying back with a big smile on her pale face and winked at me. 'Had you worried then, didn't I, Sophie? Let's hope old Cally's not on the prowl . . .'

Mr Calladine *was* on the prowl. 'Cora,' he said from behind her. Slowly, she turned to face him. He went on, in a clipped, icy voice that everyone could hear, 'This afternoon at rehearsals you might as well have been dancing in a different show to everyone else. Sort your-self out, girl, and quickly – or you're dismissed.'

He stormed away from our dressing room. 'I've got a touch of 'flu,' Cora said brightly to everyone after he'd gone. 'Cally'll soon get over his temper.'

Somehow, she got through the show and she never mentioned Danny to me again, but sometimes I would hear her creeping out of the house late at night, not to return till dawn, or she'd make some excuse not to come back with me after the show. I guessed she was getting drugs from him. I would help her to change in and out of her stage costumes, but her eyes glittered oddly, her speech began to be slurred; she was hardly eating, and how she got through those gruelling shows I just didn't know. I missed Belfield Hall. I thought I would never say it, but I missed Belfield Hall and the time before Lady Beatrice, when I'd been almost happy dreaming my dreams and writing my letters to Mr Maldon.

One night, after we'd done our first routine and were coming off stage to change our costumes for the second set, Mr Calladine had another of his surprises for us.

'Here you are, girls – French maids' outfits, with fish-net stockings,' he pronounced. 'Like they wear in Paris.'

I put the things on and looked at myself in the mirror. The short, tight-waisted black dress and little white apron barely covered the tops of my thighs – I might as well be putting myself up on that stage as a tart, I thought bitterly. Screwing up the white cap in my hand, I was silently resolving to find somewhere else to work, as soon as possible, when I realised that Pauline and her friends were talking avidly about some man in the audience.

'He's in one of the private boxes – third from the right, as you look up from the stage. Surely you saw him? My God, you'd mistake him for Rudolf Valentino, he's bloody wonderful . . .'

They often talked like that about men they'd spotted, so I hardly listened; I was more concerned about having

171

to go out there again in my French maid's costume with a bright smile plastered to my lips. But as I went out, under the lights, I looked up without thinking – *third box from the right* – and the bolt of shock that shot through me almost overwhelmed me.

My Ash. My Mr Maldon.

The music played on. I kept my usual bright smile on my face, my legs and my feet moved as ever to the rhythm – *step, kick and back; step, kick and back* – but my mind was exploding. I wondered what Pauline and her friends would say if they knew that the man up there had bedded me. Had bound my wrists and blindfolded me, but then had made incredibly passionate love to me and begged me to stay. Yet I'd been right to leave him. He was ruthless, he was damaged, and I'd left him because I'd known he would break me.

Now I told myself, *He cannot have recognised me on stage, amongst all the others.* Even if he had, he would surely turn from me in disgust on seeing me dressed in this stupid cheap mockery of what I used to be – a scullery maid. As the applause faded, I rushed from the stage to the changing rooms with Cora following me, uncertain, shaky, as she always was now. Pauline Moran came up to me as well, her mouth curved in a slight sneer.

'You looked as if you'd had a nasty shock back there on stage,' she said. 'Cally's favourite girl losing her grip – that would be something new. Anything wrong?'

I gazed at her. 'I so appreciate your concern, Pauline, but I'm fine, thanks.'

She sauntered off to join her friends, who were all

talking avidly about Ash still, though no one knew who he was, thank God. I sat gazing at the mirror pretending to clean away my make-up while shaking inside.

Mr Maldon, oh Mr Maldon, I thought I'd got you out of my life.

Lynton came backstage after the show to offer me a lift home, and I'm afraid I was more curt with him than I should have been. He'd only just departed, crestfallen, when I saw Ash coming towards the open door of the dressing room, his expression as black as thunder.

The other girls had stopped their chatter and were gazing in awe, because he was, in his evening attire, quite simply beautiful – and he looked mad, mad as hell. Without hesitating I grabbed my coat and I ran out through the door at the far end of the room. Was he coming to see *me*? But why? I was nothing to him, I never could be. I'd pulled on my long coat over my silly little French maid's costume; I flew out into the night with my make-up on, still wearing my fishnet stockings and my high heels, and I found myself in the narrow street at the rear of the theatre.

It was dark here as well as cold, with a chilly wind blowing litter around the pavements. I shivered; this was, I knew, a place where prostitutes loitered. A man with a greasy moustache was already sauntering towards me. 'Fancy a drink, darling? Fancy a bit of something else?'

I looked round for escape. Oh, God, I should have accepted a lift from poor Lynton. I should have stayed back there and faced Ash. The man started stroking my arm but I tugged myself away and snapped, 'Leave me alone.'

His face darkened. 'What's up? Hoping for a richer customer, were you, you little stuck-up bitch?'

Suddenly someone was thrusting himself forcefully between my assailant and me. The man backed away. 'Hey. I was after her first . . .'

His voice faded as Ash – for it was Ash, of course – said to him, 'Get out of here. Quickly, if you've any sense.'

The man went hurrying off. Ash turned to me. His face was so pale, and so full of rage that I sank back against the wall. He said, *'What in God's name are you doing, Sophie?'*

I moistened my lips. I tried to answer him, but couldn't.

The corner of his mouth lifted. 'Sophie? It *is* Sophie, isn't it? Underneath that whore's make-up, those whore's clothes?'

My beautiful man. My Mr Maldon, who'd made love to me with such tenderness and yet was now so furious, so incredibly hateful. I found my voice at last. 'I'm a dancer,' I breathed, white-faced with shock. 'It was what I came to London to do. I'm not a whore, you have no *right* to call me a whore.'

'Then what the hell are you doing out here?' He swept his hand round to indicate the sleazy street, where women waited for the men drawing up in their cars. Down an alleyway a girl was with a client, and oh God, I could see he was taking his pleasure of her there and then. Ash's hands were on my shoulders, pulling me towards him. 'What the hell are you doing, Sophie?'

I could hardly speak. 'I'm a dancer! I'm earning my living, my lord . . . Your Grace—'

'*Ash*,' he broke in curtly.

'*Ash*. I'm earning my living, Ash, but you wanted to make me your whore! And I'm not a whore, I'm not . . .'

He dragged me towards him. It had begun raining, but he ignored it and pushed my coat aside; his hand was plunging beneath my black short skirt, feeling for the tops of my fishnet stockings, palming the bare flesh of my thighs. He said, 'You're certainly giving a good impression of one.'

I jerked myself away and slapped his face, feeling the hardness of his jaw and the slight roughness of his evening stubble against my hand. 'Bastard,' I breathed. 'You bastard.'

He smiled then; a slow curving of his beautiful mouth that betrayed no joy, no pleasure, but simply a sardonic acknowledgement of the truth, as if he were saying, *Did I ever tell you otherwise?* His fingertips brushed my neck then moved lightly along my chin and tipped up my face so I had no choice but to look into his blue, hard eyes.

Then he was hauling me towards him, he was kissing me, and his mouth was moving harshly over mine. Oh, God, there was nothing tender about his kiss; nothing tender about the way his tongue delved and thrust against my teeth. I wanted to cry out my defiance, but instead I found myself clutching the lapels of his coat, twisting at the expensive cloth in desperation as my breasts tingled and the heat in my stomach unfurled. He tasted like cold champagne, but infinitely more intoxicating; he was hateful, but his embrace and his kiss ignited the core of my existence.

'Stop,' I breathed, pulling away. 'Stop. You have no right to do this.'

I beat with my fists against the hard wall of his chest. He moved away a little, his face harsh, his dark eyes unreadable. 'No right?' He reached in his pocket, pulled out some coins and, without even looking at them, he pushed them into the pocket of my cheap coat. 'No right? Well, I do now.'

That made me want to cry. But then he kissed me again and he lifted my skirt again to find my panties; he stroked me there with his strong fingers, feeling my heat, the wetness between my thighs. Shame coursed through me; it felt wicked and, at the same time, sublime.

He breathed rawly, 'Do you still want me to stop?'

There was nowhere to hide from him. Nowhere for me to hide from the savage force of the feelings he aroused in me. And as if reading my mind he rasped out, 'You're mine, Sophie. You're mine. No one else's. Ever.'

In that moment, on that grimy London street, with the rain seeping down on us and the darkness all around, he turned me roughly so I was facing a brick wall and I had to throw my hands flat against it to keep my balance. From behind he was ripping my panties aside, diving his fingers into my wetness, kissing the nape of my neck while I gasped for air.

'You are to stop dancing,' he grated in my ear. 'I will not let you dance in public, do you hear me? You will not whore yourself.'

His hands were driving up me, his hips were pressed

against my bottom and I could feel the upthrust of his erection, even through the thickness of his clothes. A shiver of desperate need ran through me as his fingers dipped then circled, dipped then circled inside me.

I was trembling uncontrollably, I was moaning with despair and desire. All I could see was that brick wall; his presence obliterated my other senses. His other hand was suddenly round my body, covering my breast and pulling at my nipple through my flimsy bodice; I felt myself helplessly tilt my hips back towards him, meeting his strong hand, matching his rhythm. His fingers were still stroking me, driving into me, and I climaxed wildly, calling out his name.

Almost instantly he spun me round and held me close, protecting me from the rain, sheltering me in his arms, warming me with his body, kissing the top of my head while I wept. He repeated softly, 'You left me, Sophie. You turned me down – for *this* life.'

Something twisted so hard, so deep inside me that I couldn't bear it. I really hadn't known I could hurt so badly. I cried, 'You have no right to preach at me! You asked me to be your mistress, but only for a while, and isn't that exactly the same as making me a whore? You wouldn't let me see you, you wouldn't let me touch you at Belfield Hall!'

And it was the same just now, I thought bleakly. Oh, God, it was the same just now; he'd pushed me against that wall and relished my helpless longing for him, but he hadn't even let me see him. He'd been aroused – hadn't I felt his acute need for me? – but he'd kept himself coldly, disdainfully aloof.

And now he said, 'You promised me devotion.' His eyes were without expression.

'You didn't *want* devotion,' I retorted bitterly. 'You told me, quite plainly, that you wanted to be able to discard me as soon as you'd had enough of me, didn't you? Didn't you? You only got me that job at Belfield Hall and asked me to write to you, because you wondered even then if some day you might become duke and you wanted me to tell you what was happening there—'

'What?' he broke in. '*What?*' His expression was so bleak I felt almost frightened. 'Oh, God,' he said. He dragged his hand through his hair. 'So you thought that your letters . . . What nonsense. What sheer, utter nonsense. Do you really believe, Sophie, that you – a scullery maid – could tell me anything I didn't already know?'

I stared at him. *Beatrice. Beatrice again.* But . . . 'I can't believe anything you say,' I breathed. 'You've set men to follow me, you – you do *this* to me . . .'

I was trembling still from the staggering climax of pleasure that he'd released in me, so coolly, so dispassionately. I felt sick with shame. He could control himself, but I couldn't. *No one. There would never be anyone like him.*

He had gripped my shoulders again. 'Set men to follow you? Is that what you said?'

'Perhaps you hoped I wouldn't notice?' I pulled myself away bitterly.

'I haven't told *anyone* to follow you. I swear it on my honour. Are you sure about this, Sophie? What do these men look like?'

It was raining quite steadily now but he didn't seem to care. I stared up at him defiantly. 'I haven't exactly had much chance to inspect them. Would they be doing their job properly if I could?'

He brushed some rain from his angular cheekbones. *Oh, his poor, poor hands.* 'Come with me, Sophie,' he said at last. 'Leave that damned theatre.' He reached out for me, but I jumped backwards.

'I was a scullery maid, remember? I had to learn to look after myself long ago. The rules for people like you and people like me aren't the same. And it's months since I left Belfield Hall – why this sudden concern for me?'

He said, 'Beatrice told me you'd gone to live with your relatives in Wiltshire.'

I broke in, '*What* relatives in Wiltshire?' but then my voice trailed away. *Beatrice's lies again.* 'I've no relatives,' I said.

He nodded curtly. 'So I realised, thanks to Nell. It was she who told me in the end that you were working in a London theatre and I found you as quickly as I could, but I've been busy at Belfield Hall as well as in London, dealing with the estate.'

I tried to sound cynical. In control. 'Counting up your wealth, I suppose?'

'No. No, actually, I've been trying to save jobs.' He still looked almost dazed. 'And now I find you here, selling yourself . . . '

I'm not. I'm not, I wanted to weep. I wanted to rage at him – but hadn't I just let him take me up against the wall, like a whore? And I was worn out with denying it – so I shrugged. 'Why not? All the other girls do.'

'*Jesus Christ,*' he breathed.

I shook with horror as soon as my words left my lips. What made me say it? I supposed I was desperate with hurt, so I tried to hurt him too; but the moment I said it, *All the other girls do*, I wished I'd bitten off my tongue, because he looked . . . devastated.

The colour drained from his face. The skin was taut across his angular, beautiful cheekbones, his high-bridged nose. His blue eyes were quite bleak.

'If you need help,' he said at last, 'come to me. Do you understand?' He was thrusting a card with an address on it at me – not Wilton Crescent, where I'd sent my letters for so long, but Hertford Street, Mayfair. 'If you need help,' he finished. 'That's all.'

I shrugged. 'I think I've learned to look after myself pretty well, thanks.' I let his card fall in the gutter.

He didn't move. 'I can't let you go, Sophie. I can't let you go back to this life you're living.' His eyes were wild; he looked distraught, and suddenly I was frightened, terribly frightened, both of him and of my feelings for him. Just then a taxicab went by so I hailed it, stumbling towards it on my high heels. Ash was not far behind, his long strides covering the ground in seconds. 'Sophie,' he was calling. '*Sophie . . .*'

I was already scrambling into the back seat. 'Bayswater, please,' I said to the driver.

I felt sick inside; I was cold and shaking and shattered from seeing Ash again, from letting him make such savage yet excruciatingly skilful love to me. Cora's awed words came back to me – *He had that effect on you? He made you come so quickly?*

Yes. Yes, he did. And – my chest clenched with pain – he still meant so much to me. He still meant *everything* to me, and that was why I had to get away.

And so I left Ash, my Mr Maldon, standing there, though I wanted to stop the cab and hurl myself into his arms. I wanted to say, *Please, please keep me with you. I will be your servant, your slave, anything – I don't care what you do to me, or how, or why . . .*

Whatever he'd done – made money from the war, hired women then paid them to keep his dark secrets – I didn't care. There would never be anyone else, ever, yet I'd let him think . . . Oh, you fool Sophie, you stupid, stupid fool. The cab driver said over his shoulder, 'Are you all right, miss?'

'Yes,' I said. 'Yes, thank you, I'm perfectly all right.'

But I wasn't. And as I climbed from the cab outside our pitiful little house, I thought again – if Ash wasn't watching me, then who was?

Cora was inside. 'I've left Danny,' she whispered to me. She was huddled by the fire. 'I told him tonight that it's all over, Sophie. All over.'

She cried and cried.

Cora swore to me she'd finished both with Danny and with the cocaine he gave her, so for the next few days I struggled to get her to bed early and to make her eat properly, and when she told me she couldn't sleep at night, I took her to the chemist to get her some pills, but they made her feel low, she said. My days were taken up with Cora; but at least it took my mind off Ash, and my heartbreak.

Only you, I'd wanted to whisper to him. *There's always only been you.* But oh God, I'd let him think I was a whore.

And then one day, Cora disappeared, just like that. I'd gone as usual to the two o'clock rehearsal and returned home at five expecting to find her waiting for me, perhaps having prepared some tea for us both, but instead she had packed her few pathetic things and left. Our friendly saxophonist had moved on as well, to go touring with his band, and even Fred the cat no longer turned up at our door. I felt lonelier than I'd ever felt in my life.

Chapter Thirteen

Since I'd now started looking for a new job rather desperately, I'm afraid I didn't have much time for Lynton when he came backstage a few nights later with his usual flowers for me.

'Been meaning to mention to you, Sophie,' he said with his shy smile. 'That chap who was here looking for you the other night – do you know, he looked rather like someone who was in the RFC for the first year or two of the war, and gave us younger fellows a few training sessions.'

I'd turned round to him, at a loss. 'The RFC?'

'The Royal Flying Corps,' Lynton explained. 'That's the outfit I was in. The man I'm talking about was an absolutely ace flyer.'

'No,' I said. 'It's quite impossible. He wasn't in the war.' Clearly Lynton didn't know that Ash was now the Duke of Belfield; their social paths couldn't yet have crossed.

Lynton shrugged. 'My mistake – must have confused him with someone else. Anyway,' he gave his endearing grin, 'I've come to ask you if you'll go on a date with me, Sophie. There's a bash at the Dorchester next week and I'd be pleased as punch if you'd let me take you.'

Elizabeth Anthony

'Lynton, I'm a chorus girl! You'd be a laughing stock!'

'No I wouldn't,' he protested. 'You're damned beautiful, and kind as well – that's what matters to me.'

I shook my head and he sighed resignedly. 'Maybe someday you'll change your mind?'

'I won't,' I said gently. 'I'm sorry, Lynton, but I won't.'

The theatre kept me too busy to think much, although at night, now that I didn't have Cora to talk to, I would remember Ash again, obsess about Ash again, until my emotions were raw from going over that last, harrowing evening with him.

Tell me, he'd urged, *tell me you haven't been selling yourself.*

Why not? I'd replied. *All the other girls do.*

If I'd thought I could help Cora in any way, I'd have searched all of London for her, but I guessed she was beyond my help now. I even asked Pauline Moran if she'd heard anything of her, but Pauline shook her head and said, 'She'll be in bad company. Leave her to it – there's nothing you can do.'

And I was in trouble myself, because I couldn't afford the rent of the house on my own. I'd got an interview coming up with a new dance troupe called the Sandy Bay Girls, who were based in a Covent Garden theatre, and I was due to meet their manager there at half past four. Our rehearsals usually ended at four but, as luck would have it, on the day of my interview, Cally was late. My heart sank – no doubt we would overrun – but to my relief our pianist Gaye Ronald began the rehearsal without him.

184

We were preparing a new number and, as I grew more confident with the steps, I found myself humming the words. Gaye Ronald must have heard, because she clicked her fingers and said, 'Come to the front and sing the song, will you, Sophie?'

So I did, and for just a moment I felt confident and happy in my talent. For a few minutes I even forgot Ash. But then Rupert Calladine came in. 'Sophie. My office, please.'

I'd not wanted to tell him yet about my interview, not until I got a definite offer, but as I followed him I was afraid he'd already heard.

But it was worse than that. He told me I could not work for him any more.

I stared at him. 'I don't understand. Why?'

'Because you've been stealing.'

'No. No.' I almost laughed. 'That's ridiculous—'

He broke in impatiently. 'Items have been disappearing from my office for a while – pens, some cufflinks of mine, a leather bag of coins for the till. I was reluctant to have the police anywhere near, but now it turns out I don't have to, because that bag of coins – empty, needless to say – has been found in your locker.'

'My locker?' I was incredulous. I never used it; I preferred to take all my clothes and belongings home with me each night. 'No . . .'

'Let's keep this simple, shall we? I want you off the premises now, Miss Davis.'

'No! Please, Mr Calladine!' I was desperate. I'd intended to leave, yes, but not to be cast off like this, without a reference.

'It's not something I can discuss,' he said.

My thoughts flew wildly to Ash. Could *he* somehow have arranged this? He'd told me he didn't want me dancing in public, but surely he wouldn't stoop to such a low trick? In complete despair I got all my things together and left without saying a word to anyone, but the sound of Miss Gaye's piano and the rhythmic tapping of the girls' dancing feet echoed in my mind all the way home.

No point in going to my interview, not without a reference. The first thing any theatre manager would do would be to contact Cally about me, and that would be it – no job. I remember it was typical March weather, blustery and wet, and I tidied round the little house, made myself a meal I could scarcely eat, then searched through the London newspaper for a job as a shop assistant, a cleaner, anything. I went to bed feeling tired and depressed, and when I awoke an hour or two later, I imagined I'd been disturbed by more rain beating against my window.

But then I heard someone pounding at the door and a voice calling rather desperately, 'Sophie. Are you there? Sophie, please let me in!'

Cora. My heart thudding, I pulled on my dressing gown and ran downstairs. She stood there in the pouring rain wearing only a thin, cheap coat, her wet hair clinging to her face, and she flung herself into my arms, shaking with cold. 'Sophie, it was my fault you got sacked from Cally's. I know what happened. I-I met Pauline by chance in a bar tonight. It was me who stole that money and the other things, and I used your locker, and I'm so desperately sorry! And now there are people after me . . .'

I realised that as well as being terribly distressed, she'd taken something, because her pupils were dilated, her breathing shallow. I tried to make her come through to the parlour – our door was wide open, with the rain blowing in – but she was still clinging to me wildly. 'Oh, I wish it was like the old days, Sophie! You and I coming back here after the show and talking into the night. With Fred . . .'

She swallowed a sob, then began to dance in our hallway and sing in a broken voice one of our old routines from Cally's – 'I'm Always Chasing Rainbows'. I suddenly realised that underneath her coat she wore nothing but a black brassiere with holes for her nipples, black panties and a garter belt to hold up her stockings. 'Cora.' I grabbed at her arm to make her stop. 'Oh, God, Cora. Come inside and get changed into something warm.'

I glanced at my watch – it was well after eleven. Somehow I got her in and peeled off her wet coat, but then I heard the sound of a car coming to a halt at the end of our road. Running to the window I saw that some men had jumped out of it and were looking up and down the street. Cora was beside me, just in that scanty underwear. 'Danny's men,' she breathed. She clung to me, suddenly trembling again.

I felt quite cold with shock. 'Why are they after you, Cora?'

She didn't answer, but she wouldn't let go of me. 'All I wanted was love, Sophie,' she whispered. 'Please, please help me . . .'

Tight with fear by now, I managed to pull a warm coat of mine over her and scrambled into some clothes myself. I could already hear someone banging at our front door. 'We've got to get out the back way, Cora. We've got to run. Can you make it?'

She pulled my coat around her. 'Yes. I'm sorry, Sophie, so sorry.'

'It's all right.' I hugged her swiftly. 'Now, follow me. *Hurry.*'

There was a small yard at the back of the house and I helped Cora to climb the high brick wall into the lane beyond, though she kicked my ribs unintentionally with one sharp heel as she heaved herself over it. Once out on the narrow lane, we ran. I was very afraid we would still be followed on foot, and I knew those men would be much faster and stronger than us. But where could we go, for safety?

Then Cora leaned against a wall. 'I can't go any further, Sophie. I can't. You go on without me. Please.'

'I'm not leaving you,' I said, but inside I was panicking. Somehow we got to Westbourne Street, where I saw an approaching taxicab and desperately hailed the driver, but he went on by – I wasn't surprised. Another car was drawing steadily nearer and slowing up as it approached us. I grabbed Cora's hand and swung her round to run again, but the car – a Daimler – was already pulling to a halt. The driver stepped out and gave a slight nod. 'You might remember me,' he said in a calm voice. 'My name is James, I'm the Duke of Belfield's chauffeur. Would you please get in?'

Where ... how ... ? I bundled Cora inside; he closed

the door on us and drove off steadily into the night, while Cora clung to me, terrified.

So we were brought to Hertford Street in Mayfair in the middle of the night, and as Ash's chauffeur helped Cora out I simply stood there, gazing up at the massive, cream-stuccoed mansion. This was Ash's house, his London house – and his chauffeur must have been following us. Cora, still drugged or drunk or both, was gazing up at the house too, her gaudy eye make-up running down her cheeks in the rain.

'My, but you know some rich people, Sophie.' She began to giggle, poor, exhausted Cora, then she started to sing, in her faltering voice. 'I'm Always Chasing Rainbows . . .' She tottered up the steps before I could stop her and was banging the knocker.

'Cora, no . . .'

Just then the door opened and a woman in a smart grey dress and apron stood there, looking startled at first, but when she saw James behind us her face brightened. 'It's you,' she said to Cora and me. 'His Grace said you would be here shortly.'

She beckoned us into a place that might as well have been a palace, with its massive entrance hall hung with gilt-framed paintings and a huge sweeping staircase at the far end.

And my heart stopped because a man was coming steadily down that staircase towards us: Ash, the Duke of Belfield, my Mr Maldon. Something inside me twisted so hard I had to drive my fingernails into my palms.

He looked so beautiful, you see, in a black evening suit with his tie unfastened but still hanging round his neck. So impossibly beautiful, whereas we looked what we were – two girls picked up from the streets and drenched with rain. Cora was transfixed by the sight of him, watching him with her eyes opened very wide, and then to my horror she started tottering towards him. 'My, oh my, but aren't you a beautiful man? Do you know, I might let you fuck me for free . . . Sophie, don't you think we should let him fuck us for free? Both of us together?'

Her coat had fallen apart to display that shocking underwear and I felt sick. '*Cora . . .*'

I saw a range of emotions flash across his expressive face; then he said to the woman in grey who'd opened the door, 'Mrs Lambert. Take this one, will you?' He pointed to Cora. 'Get her dry and warm. James?'

The chauffeur went up to him and the two of them conferred, swiftly and in low voices. Then James set off after Mrs Lambert and Cora and, as soon as he'd gone, Ash turned to me.

I was aware that my short hair clung in damp, ungainly strands to my face, and by now the pain in my ribs where Cora had unintentionally kicked me throbbed like hell. I said, 'You were having me followed. You had no right to have me followed.'

He answered curtly, 'From what James has told me, you should be on your knees thanking me for it. What the hell have you both been up to?'

His expression was filled with pure, stark anger. I hugged my coat around me, knowing full well that I

looked as cheap and as desperate as Cora, but somehow I made myself meet his beautiful blue eyes. 'Cora
shares my house,' I said with defiance. 'Some men
were . . . pursuing her, I don't know why.' His eyes
were unreadable; I shivered in the draught from the
still-open front door, and I shivered even more as he
came towards me.

Cora is safe and I can go, I kept telling myself. *Cora is
safe and I can go.* I wrapped my coat more tightly around
myself; I was about to hurry outside again, but then his
fingers brushed my hands. They were warm, too warm
on my bare skin, and a dark, dangerous heat rose deep
within me. Helplessly I remembered the savagery with
which he'd pleasured me, in that back street outside the
theatre.

Dear God, I didn't want this. I hadn't wanted to see
this man ever again. I couldn't afford to see this man
ever again. I remembered the girls at Cally's, all agog
that night he'd been in the audience, almost licking their
lips as they watched him – and he thought me a whore.
No doubt he assumed that beneath my coat I was clad
in underwear just like Cora's, a peephole black brassiere
and scanty knickers, both of us dreaming of a rich client
like him.

I dragged myself away while he stood motionless. I
backed towards the door, saying, 'If you will look after
Cora – find her somewhere – I will be grateful.' I turned
to walk out into the night again, away from him. But
he'd moved far more quickly than me and was gripping
me roughly by the shoulders.

He said, his voice flaying me, 'Did it occur to you that

by associating with your friend Cora, you were putting yourself in considerable danger too?'

I didn't know whether to laugh or cry. *I'm in danger from you, Ash, because you haunt me. Being near to you again, like this; I cannot forget, I cannot, what it was like that night at Belfield Hall, when you took me to your bed and made sweet, sweet love to me ...*

I dragged myself again from his arms and pushed my damp hair back from my face. 'You underestimate me,' I said with cool finality. 'I've been in London for some time now. I can look after myself.'

'That's why you were both fleeing for your lives at almost midnight?'

My breath hitched. 'It's Cora who needs help – I don't. I told you before not to think me some naïve innocent—'

He broke in, his voice dangerous again. 'My God, yes; I remember you boasted that you'd become a tart last time we met, in that street outside your theatre where men pick up women for a shilling a time.'

'I'm going,' I said flatly. 'If you'll just look after poor Cora for the night, I'll come for her in the morning.'

I swung round towards the door, but once more he grabbed me, and when he pulled me back to face him there was no tenderness in his eyes. 'You're mine, Sophie,' he said bitterly. 'I told you. You're mine.'

'*No.*' I was shaking so badly.

'You told me you're a whore.' His arm clamped round my waist. 'So be it. You will be mine, for tonight at least – consider it payment, for shelter for you and your friend. You say you're no longer some naïve innocent;

very well, you can show me what tricks you've learned.'

I wanted to throw myself into his arms. I wanted to say, *I was lying about being a whore. You've got everything so wrong – I've loved no one but you, ever.* But he was looking at me with such terrible, such raging scorn.

'If I'm a whore, then you showed me how,' I breathed. 'At Belfield Hall.'

'Enough,' he grated almost savagely. 'Enough.'

What next? Did he take me in his arms, or did I fall into them? Sweet Jesus, he must have known what he did to me; he held me so close I felt flame and heat, and soft, soft warmth flooding my cheeks. I glimpsed his faint, bitter smile; then he lowered his head and he brushed his mouth against mine. He kissed me.

I felt the teasing sweep of his tongue as he caressed the curves of my trembling mouth in a kiss that tore the damned breath from my shaking body. His arms were strong around my ugly, damp old coat, and everything about him reminded me of the devastating pleasure he'd bestowed on me before: his touch, the heat of his powerful body, his very scent melted me; the faint citrus of the soap he used, the clean fragrance of a rich man's fresh linen.

I tried to push at the hard wall of his chest, my futile tears pouring down my cheeks. 'Bastard,' I whispered, 'you bastard.' But oh, God, my body was melting, my tongue was matching his, meeting him stroke for stroke; I could hear a soft moan rising in my throat.

'Stay the night with me, Sophie,' he urged in my ear. 'Be mine, if only for a short while.'

His tenderness. That was what undid me. The

sudden gentleness of his voice. For a moment, I could only gaze up at him, my whole being in turmoil as I saw something in his bleak, sad eyes that shook me to my very core.

I was lying, I wanted to say. *I was lying, about being a whore. There's never been anyone, Ash. No one except you. There never will be.*

Chapter Fourteen

He swung me up in his strong arms and carried me towards the sweeping staircase. He climbed up and up with effortless ease, kicked open a door and walked through with me still in his arms.

I saw we were in a luxurious private sitting room, with easy chairs, a low-burning fire and a big desk. There were wide doors, leading onto a balcony; the curtains hadn't yet been drawn, and the lights of the city outside glittered in the wet night. He set me on my feet and went to close those curtains, then he gestured me through to another beautiful room dominated by a big bed draped with a cream satin counterpane and pillows. He shut the door from the sitting room and came to where I stood.

From the night I'd left him at Belfield Hall, I'd carefully erected my defences. I'd taught myself to remember, whenever my thoughts turned to him, that I was absolutely nothing to him. But the look in his eyes as he carefully removed my wet coat shook my resistance into a thousand pieces.

He took off his black jacket and in just his shirt and slim-fitting trousers he was so beautiful. I lay there shivering although the room was warm, and I watched the fluid movements of his lovely body beneath his clothes. *That kiss just now.* It was as if he cared, but of course he didn't – he was furious with me. *Sophie, don't you think we should let him fuck us for free? Both of us together?*

You little fool, Sophie, I whispered to myself. You bloody little fool.

He laid me on the bed and pulled off my cheap gown almost roughly. He gazed at my silken brassiere and flimsy French knickers and stockings – yes, I too liked pretty things now – and I heard him suck in his breath harshly as he cupped my breast, his thumb circling my nipple where it pressed against the pale silk. Sensation curled deep inside me; desire spiralled through me until I was begging with my body for more, even though he thought me a whore, he thought me a whore.

Suddenly he pulled away, his face sombre, his eyes brooding. 'Please,' I whispered. 'Ash, don't leave me. Not now.'

His finger was curling against my panties, making me shiver with delicious need. He said, 'You know my conditions. Stay there.'

I knew. I knew what was going to happen. Perhaps this would cure me of him – if there was any cure. I felt sick with sadness and despair but I lay there while he walked purposefully towards a chest of drawers and came back with a black cord looped in his hands.

'Lift your hands up,' he commanded.

I did so, and his face was without expression as he

went about his work, binding my wrists to the bedposts, testing the bonds so my whole body became taut in a way that sent shivers rioting through me. 'Please,' I begged, my hips squirming. 'Please . . .'

'This first,' he said. And he drew out a long, dark piece of cloth from his pocket, and blindfolded me.

Oh, God. I strained against my bonds, but I yearned for him, sightless as I was. I rubbed my legs together, trying to relieve my need like an animal on heat. I felt the bed move a little and knew he was sitting there beside me, then with one fluid movement he cupped my bottom to lift my hips and, pushing my knickers aside, he guided his fingers into the moist heart of my being. My legs fell apart; I cried aloud with wanting.

He was kissing my breasts, after pulling my brassiere down beneath them so they were both upthrust and swollen; he was drawing the peak of one nipple into his mouth, and at the same time his strong fingers were driving deep inside me until I felt my vaginal muscles contract around him as his skill sent me spiralling into sweet, wanton need.

There was no tenderness here. But the physical pleasure – oh, God, I moaned for him in despair. But by then his fingers were urging me on in their oh-so-skilful work, my breast was in his mouth again, his tongue and lips were tugging at my nipple until I could bear no more. As his fingers drove into me in a deeper, more vigorous rhythm, I climbed high, so high, and fell, crying out his name again and again as my senses shattered.

I slumped in my bonds, aware that he was still beside me, but I felt cold, so cold because I knew his eyes would be shuttered, his face impassive. He was taking his revenge, that was all this was. This was a game, his private game of power and domination, in which he was the winner always.

With meticulous care he removed the bonds from my wrists and the blindfold from my eyes. He sat on the edge of the bed watching me as I pulled myself up against the pillows; was I cured? No, but I was terribly ashamed, because my body was still bared to his gaze, still heated from his lovemaking. I would never be cured of this man whose eyes were dark and so impenetrable that I had to turn away, shivering. Then suddenly—

'My God. Sophie. *Sophie?*'

I realised he'd seen the purple-red bruise on my ribs from where Cora had accidentally kicked me while climbing that wall behind our house. He was swearing softly under his breath. 'This must have happened *tonight*. Why in God's name didn't you say?' He reached to a bell-pull then went swiftly to a wardrobe and pulled out a man's dressing robe of heavy silk paisley. 'Here. Put this on.'

Within a few moments there was a knock at the outer door to his sitting room, and when he went through to open it I heard the calm voice of his housekeeper, Mrs Lambert. He must have left with her, because I heard the door closing, and I was all alone again. Racked with despair I curled myself up in his dressing robe on the bed, breathing in the lovely, all-male scent of his skin and body that lingered there. *Oh, God.* He was so beautiful, but perhaps Cora was right. *Lots of rich men are a bit fucked-up, you know*, she'd said. *I blame their upbringing ...*

Then I heard him coming back and I could hear his housekeeper asking, 'Are you sure the young lady doesn't need anything else, my lord?' She sounded kind and anxious.

'I think we're all right for now, Mrs Lambert.' He was coming towards the bedroom now and I tried desperately to compose myself. 'I'll let you know,' he added to his housekeeper, 'if I require anything.'

Handcuffs? I thought bitterly. *A whip?* Then the door was opening, and he stood there with a large water jug that steamed lightly and some folded towels. What? I pulled the dressing robe even tighter around me and swiftly shut my eyes, pretending to be asleep. But I heard him come up to the bed and put the jug on a small table there.

'I know you're awake. Please let me see to that bruise,' he said.

'Leave me alone.' I shrank away.

'Do as I say, Sophie.' With dawning disbelief I saw him dip a towel in the water, then he squeezed it out, eased my robe aside and held the towel like a compress against my bruise. The water was warm, it was scented faintly with lavender oil, and after a few moments he dipped the cloth in water again, squeezed it out and pressed once more. Still I refused to move or say anything.

At last he broke the silence. 'How did this happen?'

Oh, God, questions. To make matters worse, there'd been a hint of tenderness in his voice that if I listened to it would simply rip me apart. 'It was a stupid accident,' I said. 'I tripped, that was all.'

'While you were being pursued.'

This time I said nothing; he too was silent a moment, still sitting beside me, still dipping, squeezing, pressing. Then: 'I've been talking to Cora,' he said.

I closed my eyes in despair – what had she said this time? I swallowed and nodded. 'Is she all right?'

'She's relatively sober now, if that's what you mean. She's capable, at least, of a certain amount of rational speech. She told me that you helped her. That you've *always* helped her, even though she's rarely returned the favour. She confirmed what you told me earlier – that you helped her escape from some men who were after her tonight. Were they drug-dealers?'

Interrogation time. I pulled myself up against the pillows and I stared down at my hands. 'I would imagine so, yes.'

'She also told me,' he went on, 'that you've never slept with a single man since you came to London. Not one, despite all the offers you must have had from the men who watch you on stage night after night . . . Jesus, Sophie. *Jesus.*' Suddenly on his feet, he swung around and went to pace the length of the room, then turned back to me, his face haggard. 'Why, in the name of God, did you tell me you'd been living as a whore?'

My throat was quite raw with emotion. 'Well, let me see,' I said. 'Could it be because someone – *you*, let's say – simply assumed I was a whore? Maybe I didn't like to disillusion you.'

He closed his eyes. 'Oh, Sophie.' He drew his scarred hands through his hair. 'Oh, Sophie.'

I'd tried to sound haughty and sophisticated like

Pauline Moran, but I was shaking inside. Oh, God. I should have left Cora here and run like hell, run anywhere; instead of which I'd let him see, yet again, how utterly powerless I was to resist his merest touch. Nothing had changed.

Does he know how very beautiful he is? He must know. That night when he was in the audience at Cally's, the other girls hadn't been able to stop talking about him. He was always beautiful, even at his most hateful, even that night in the dirty street behind Cally's theatre, when he'd shoved coins into my pocket and brought me to an excruciating climax. *All I want is you.*

And I was in his power once more. What a mess. I swallowed and said, 'I didn't mean to play games with you. I came to London to earn my own living – to be a dancer. Cora is my friend, but she's so vulnerable.'

He nodded, pacing again with his hands in his pockets, concentrating on every word. 'You said you felt you were being watched. That was why I told James to look out for you. Why are those men after her? Who are they?'

I hesitated.

'Tell me,' he said.

'There's a man called Danny. He's no good for Cora – he gives her drugs, Ash, but she loves him, so much—'

'Sounds like he's her pimp,' he broke in harshly. 'You'll have to face up to the fact that there's no hope for her if she's in the grip of a rogue like that.'

My heart turned over in despair. 'I can't leave her. I've got to help her.'

'Do you really, truly think she wants to get away from him?'

'Yes!' I cried. 'Of course she does!'

His mouth thinned a little in scepticism, but after a while he said, 'Then I've a suggestion, though it's an idea I don't expect you'll like. I think she should go into service, somewhere as far as possible from London and from this . . . Danny. She could even work at Belfield Hall.'

'*No.*' My outburst was instinctive. 'No, she's a dancer, a talented dancer!'

'She's also a cocaine addict and a whore.'

My mind whirled desperately. *She's Cora. She's lovely and she's my friend.* 'Ash,' I begged. 'Please listen. If she could get back her old job at Mr Calladine's, but perhaps find somewhere safer to stay . . .'

I'd heard there were charity homes for girls in London, but already he was shaking his head. 'She'd still be within his damned reach if she was anywhere in London.'

'Please, Ash. She loves dancing. Being a servant would destroy her!'

'I just don't understand you.' He looked perplexed and almost angry. 'Why show such concern for a girl you can't have known for long, and who seems to be marked from the start for trouble?'

I didn't say anything for a moment. Then – 'She reminds me of my mother,' I breathed. I hadn't even thought of it before, but it was true. Cora was sweet and loving and hence so terribly vulnerable, just like my mother, whom I'd been unable to help.

He was silent a moment before replying quietly, 'I'll see what I can do.'

Suddenly he caught hold of my hand and threaded his fingers through mine. I was immediately aware of my betraying pulse as it raced at the faint slide of his thumb over the veins at my wrist. 'Don't,' I breathed wretchedly. 'Please.'

'You hate me so much, Sophie?'

I tried to pull my hand free and failed. *Mr Maldon, Mr Maldon.* 'Please don't do this,' I whispered.

He loosened his hold but still didn't release me, and oh God, I'd have been devastated if he had. I scanned his beautiful big bedroom with a sense of utter desperation. What had Ash done in the past? What had scarred his mind as well as his hands so very badly? There was nothing I longed for more than being in his arms again; nothing I wanted more than to feel his lips, his exquisite body against mine. But it wouldn't do. I was no good for him, he was no good for me.

He looked at the clock on the mantelpiece. 'Clearly you can't go back home,' he said, 'so I suggest you spend the night here.' He was getting up and folding the damp towel. 'I hope you're not going to object.'

'But—'

His face betrayed tension; anger even. 'Has it occurred to you,' he broke in, 'that you might be a target yourself, after helping Cora to escape from that man of hers this evening?'

Suddenly a wave of fragility swept over me; I fought it down. 'I need to be on my own,' I whispered. My body felt cold even as I said it.

His face was bleak. 'Of course.'

★ ★ ★

203

He took me to a guest suite, and oh, my, it was beautiful. To my amazement the calm housekeeper, Mrs Lambert, was there for me, even though it was two in the morning. I was a mess, my hair was wild and as for my state of undress, *God, what she must think?*, but then I remembered how at Belfield Hall the most important lesson we servants had to learn was to act as if we'd seen nothing and heard nothing of the goings-on above stairs, and to be invisible. That was what Mrs Lambert was doing. Being invisible; while I, instead of being a scullery maid and the lowest of the low, was – however briefly – the Duke of Belfield's whore.

I sat on the edge of the perfectly made bed while Mrs Lambert – didn't the poor woman sleep? – fussed gently around me, all the while being so motherly, so sensible that I really, really wanted to cry. She'd even filled the sunken marble bath in the adjoining bathroom with hot, scented water for me, so I dipped myself in it quickly, well aware of how late it was, but she appeared untroubled by the hour, simply busying herself around the place while I bathed.

Then she came to me with warm towels, smiling. 'Is your injury a little better now, Miss Davis?' She also handed me some slippers and lovely pyjamas in pale cream silk after I'd dried myself. *Pyjamas – exactly my size. Did he keep clothes here, for his mistresses?*

'Your bruise,' she added.

Of course, she knew all about it – she'd provided Ash with the warm water and towels. 'Thank you, much better,' I said quickly. 'And I'm really sorry to have kept you up so late. But before you go, could you tell me how my friend Cora is?'

'She's sound asleep,' Mrs Lambert soothed. 'I gave her a warm bath, poor girl, then a little supper and put her to bed. You mustn't worry about her. His Grace will make sure she's well taken care of.'

She was about to leave, but I barred her way. 'Please. He told me you've worked for him for many years. Will you tell me what happened to his hands?'

Mrs Lambert's face was suddenly shadowed, her lips pressed together.

'I really need to know,' I floundered on. 'But all I've been told is that he might have been in a car accident . . .'

'A car accident? So you don't know about the war?'

What? 'No.' I felt as if iron clamps were squeezing my lungs. 'No. I don't know anything about the war. Please tell me!'

But she had already opened the bedroom door to leave, and she hesitated only briefly, though I saw that all manner of emotions were crossing her intelligent face. 'I think,' she said quietly at last, 'that you ought to ask him yourself, my dear. Now, try to get some sleep.'

Then she left me.

Chapter Fifteen

That night I dreamed my old dream: that Ash was in pain, and crying out to me for help. I wanted to get to him but I couldn't move and when I awoke I was shaking, because, oh God, it had all been so real, so terribly real. *I'd left him alone, the man I loved. I'd left him alone, and in my dream he'd said he needed me.*

Swiftly I pulled the dressing robe he'd given me over my pyjamas, then tiptoed along the corridor to his room – I was good at remembering directions, it was something that Belfield Hall had prepared me for. I knocked on his door then waited. Nothing. Silence. But a light was on, I could see it under his door. Perhaps he was asleep. What on earth was I doing here? What would he think I was doing here, calling on him in the middle of the night?

Coming to him for more, he'd no doubt think. But he was in pain; I somehow knew from the depths of my being that he was in such pain. I opened the door and went in to find the elegant sitting room empty, although a single lamp burned on his desk. On it were stacks of correspondence; I could see he'd clearly been working, even after I'd left him. At the far end of the big room the curtains across the doors to the balcony billowed in a current of air. I padded quickly across the luxuriously carpeted floor to see that those doors were half open; the balcony was bare to the elements. I slipped outside.

A chill wind blew across the rooftops and a lone car went by in the street below. I looked around, and when I couldn't see him, I began to fear the most terrible things in my mind. Gripping the cold iron railings I saw how far it was down to the pavement; then I realised that a few yards away from me a spiral metal staircase rose to another, smaller balcony on the next level. I hurried over to it. The rain had started again but I hardly noticed; I climbed the staircase with fear in my heart, but he was there at the far end, with his hands thrust in the pockets of his jacket, and an expression of the greatest despair on his face that I had seen, before or since.

I stood there, at the top of the steps. 'My God,' I breathed. 'My God, Ash.'

He whipped round and saw me. 'Sophie.'

I was already stumbling towards him. 'Ash, what are you doing out here?' I must have been frozen, but I don't remember even thinking about it. 'It's three in the morning, you're soaking wet . . .' I must have sounded like a stupid, coaxing nurse or governess, but I didn't know what else I could say or do.

'I often don't sleep.' His expression was still harsh but he didn't move as I drew nearer.

'So instead you come out *here*? In the cold and the rain?' I was babbling now in my distress, because I couldn't bear to see him like this, alone and in such agony of spirit. Whatever had befallen him since the day I met him in Oxford all those years ago, whatever sins could be laid at his door, every fibre of him spoke to me of raw courage and silent honour and terrible mental torment. 'You hate yourself so much,' I whispered. 'Oh, Ash. Why?'

'Go inside, Sophie.' He had suddenly realised, I think, that my dressing robe and pyjamas were getting soaked through, my short hair was plastered to my face. 'Do you hear me?'

'No,' I said steadily. I'd thought, with sudden lacerating perception, that he wanted to die out here. Not by leaping from the balcony – nothing as showy, or as childishly *look-at-me* as that – but by simply staying out here in the elements all night, trusting, *hoping* that the wind and cold rain would somehow reduce him to elemental parts also and bear him away on the night for ever. Away from his pain. Oh, God.

'I'm not going back in there,' I went on, 'unless you come inside with me.' My teeth were chattering, and I knew that *I* was no temptation; I must by then have looked more like a bedraggled street beggar than a siren of the night. But I had to try. I didn't know what else to do, you see.

'Sophie—' he began.

'I'm not going in, Ash,' I repeated. 'Not until you do too.' Fresh gusts of rain were battering both of us now, and below us London, with its spires and steeples and skeins of twinkling lights, was made murky by the downpour.

He was slowly coming towards me, then stopped. 'I thought you might leave me. After tonight.'

I shook my head. 'I shall never leave you. Not unless you tell me to.'

'I thought you would be . . . afraid of me.'

'No,' I said, quite calm now, seeing him with fresh clarity for what he was – a proud, suffering, honourable man. 'I trust you, you see.'

Gently, almost wonderingly, he lifted his hands and pushed my wet hair back from my cheek. He too was soaked, but it made him gloriously, primevally male, with his thick hair turned jet black by the rain and clinging to his high forehead and cheekbones, while the stubble of his beard darkened his lean jaw. His scarred knuckles had brushed my skin, and though I was shivering with cold, I felt weak with wanting him.

'You trust me,' he echoed quietly. 'God knows I've done nothing at all to earn it, but you trust me.'

'You're Mr Maldon again,' I breathed, realising the miracle of it, feeling my heart revel in it. 'Seeing you here tonight, realising your concern for poor Cora, it reminds me of when you were Mr Maldon. You want to look after her, just as all those years ago in Oxford you wanted to take care of me.'

He shook his head almost violently. 'Take care of you. Is *that* what you call it? At Belfield Hall I seduced you. Then I was abominable to you that night in London outside your damned theatre, and I've behaved no better tonight. You're a fool to trust me.'

I stood my ground. I said softly but clearly, 'Listen to me. I dream of you every night. I dream of you making love to me. There will never be anyone else.'

'Then think again,' he said flatly. 'I beg you, for your own sake, Sophie, to think again. You cared for Mr Maldon, who was a figment of your imagination.'

I moved towards him, but he held up his hands as if to ward me off. 'Sophie. Sophie, my God, however you look at me, I'm damaged. I've got to warn you, I've no right to ask anything of you or to expect your trust in any way. But those letters you wrote to me, they . . .'

My heart was pounding painfully against my ribs. 'What? Please tell me.'

'They helped me to survive,' he said very quietly, 'after I'd been in a dark, dark place.'

They did what? My foolish, girlish letters, how could they have meant so much to him? 'So you got them?'

'Eventually.'

Even as my thoughts whirled, even as I tried to summon the courage to ask more, I saw him drawing in a deep breath. 'It was the same that night at Belfield Hall,' he went on, 'when you gave me the gift of your innocence. Your devotion. Time and time again I've thought that I did not deserve either.'

Moving towards him, I wrapped my arms around his waist and lifted my rainsoaked face to his. 'I gave you everything freely. But why won't you let me see you, or touch you, when you're making love to me? Why, Ash?'

'It's because I need to be in control,' he answered. 'Of those around me, and of myself.'

In control. Understanding blazed through me. 'Is that why you refuse to drink alcohol?'

'Perhaps,' he said.

I was shivering again; I felt like a foolish intruder into the darkness of his past. 'I shouldn't have disturbed you out here.' I started moving away. 'I'll go back down to my room . . .'

'No. *Sophie*. Stay out here a while – please.'

And suddenly his arm was around me again. I tried to smile and said, 'It's a little cold out here, you know. My brain works better when I'm not freezing to death.'

'Let me warm you,' he said softly.

And he pulled me close in a way that almost made me stop breathing. His body heated me; I felt his arms round me and inhaled the intoxicating man-scent of his skin and hair. We could have been standing on an iceberg and I wouldn't have complained; I said nothing, not wanting to break the spell, but I was aware that though he still held me, he was looking somewhere beyond me, his perfect profile pale against the night sky with its ragged rain clouds.

'I need space, Sophie,' he said. 'I need freedom, and I only fully realised it when I was a boy, and confined to Belfield Hall one summer.'

'I know. I heard.'

'Of course you would,' he said. 'I should have remembered, how servants talk. I was eleven, and often that summer I used to climb out on the roof at night and watch the stars, telling myself, *This will pass. All this will pass.*'

My heart turned over. 'Was it so very bad?'

He looked down at me. 'Not really, no. But you've no doubt heard that my parents had separated and so for all that summer I had to stay with the Duke and Duchess, who didn't want a thing to do with me.' He gave his faint smile. 'Actually that quite suited me – I was fed well, I had my own rooms, and there were a couple of friendly grooms who used to let me ride the Duke's horses whenever he wasn't around. I had my tutor for company, and he was a kindly old soul who taught me Latin and Greek as if his life depended on it. In the afternoons I'd go roaming.'

'So that's how you knew the grounds so well! And all about the Duchess's cats, and Mr Peters!' I was remembering his letters, finding a sudden, surprising happiness in this feeling of being close to him, however briefly.

'I knew about the Duchess's cats and Mr Peters indeed,' he nodded. 'At night I'd climb on the roof and lay plans to be rich and powerful when I grew up. As you'll have gathered, I felt no gratitude towards the Duke and Duchess and their son.'

'Lord Charlwood was there?' Remembering his brief affair with my mother when I was a child, I felt fresh bitterness at his name.

'Unfortunately, yes. Charlwood was twenty-one years old and a bully. He'd invited friends to stay for a couple of weeks, and for a while I was part of the entertainment.'

My breath caught. 'What do you mean?'

He looked at me quizzically. 'One afternoon,' he said at last, 'when he and his friends were drunk, they all decided to go fox-hunting – with me as the quarry. They gave me ten minutes' start. I ran like hell, and thanks to that start I managed to keep ahead of their horses until I got to the river close by, where I swam downstream so the dogs lost my scent.'

'*Dogs* . . . Oh, Ash.'

'Don't feel sorry for me.' His low laughter warmed me; he was still holding me close and I hardly dared breathe in case I broke the spell. 'I got back well before they did,' he went on. 'They were scouring the grounds on horseback for over an hour – so in the meantime I went to Lord Charlwood's room and emptied his full chamber pot over all his clothes that were laid out for the evening. He whipped me for it, of course, but I didn't care. His friends found it amusing, the servants too – the news of it was all over the place. He was made to look an absolute fool.'

'I'm glad,' I said fervently, thinking again of my mother. 'You don't know how glad.'

But I must have shivered slightly, because suddenly he wrapped his arms around me even more tightly. 'God,' he said, 'my God, Sophie, you're frozen, and I've kept you out here in the cold; I'm a brute. Come inside.' Quickly he led me back to his rooms, where he put more coals on the fire while I stood in my soaked dressing robe and pyjamas.

'Take them off,' he exclaimed, 'take them off – here.' He'd handed me another of his dressing gowns; then he removed his own wet jacket while I stripped myself and put on the quilted silk dressing gown, which was miles too big for me, but I loved it, because it was his, and I wrapped it tightly round me.

Then he came back to me.

Ridiculously, I found I was shaking harder now than I had been out on the balcony, but I was clinging to him. His lips were cool and sweet on my forehead, on my eyelids; then he was tilting my face up to his and he was looking at me, his gaze penetrating and so sad.

'Ash,' I whispered. 'Ash.'

Suddenly he eased me away and went towards the door. I thought he was going to leave me here in this room, cold and alone; I felt as if I was standing on the edge of that damned balcony again and about to fall into the blackness below.

But he'd only gone across the room to lock the door. He came back and I remember I was excruciatingly aware of the rise and fall of my chest with each and every breath I took. I knew that this was madness, utter madness, to stay with him and surrender myself to him, but I loved him so much, you see.

He held my gaze, almost daring me to look away. Then he slowly came nearer to me, his eyes never leaving mine as he held out his hand. 'Come to me, Sophie.' His gaze was so penetrating and so sad that even more intense emotions clawed at me. 'Look at me,' he instructed.

I did. His hands – oh, his badly scarred hands – moved to my cheek, then slid to cup my chin. Then, with his forefinger, he traced the curve of my upper lip and lowered his exquisite head to mine.

The brush of his lips was scarcely a touch, yet it had me wanting more, so much more.

I lifted my eyes to his, drinking in his face, because I knew already what was going to happen next. *Not yet. Please, Ash, don't blindfold me just yet. Let me see your glorious face, your glorious body for just a while . . .* But already he was drawing a soft black blindfold from a nearby drawer, and I stood very still as he tied it round my eyes, then knotted it at the back of my head.

'Why?' I whispered. 'Oh, why? Can't you . . . can't you just turn out the light, Ash, if you don't want me to see you?'

I felt him ease a tendril of my hair behind my ear, then his lips were tracing teasing kisses down the sensitive column of my throat. 'But I want to see you, Sophie,' he said.

I nodded, swallowing. One of his hands was under my dressing gown, sliding down my spine, sending delicious shivers through me, before gliding to my hips and caressing me there. I drank in the feel of him, the male scent of him, realising anew that his touch was heaven, but it wasn't enough. I wanted to touch him back, to stroke his skin, to kiss him everywhere. I lifted my hand to his stubbled jaw . . .

'*Stop*,' he ordered.

I let my hands drop to my side. My heart thudded sickly in disappointment. He cupped my face with his hands again and turned my face upwards so I could almost feel his gaze burning into me. 'Sophie,' he said quietly, 'I thought I explained that I don't like you to touch me at times like this.'

Bitterness etched my reply. 'I know you find it difficult to be intimate with someone as . . . as lowly as me.'

He let me go, and swore. 'You think that? You really think that?'

I felt powerless, I felt almost afraid of him now, blindfolded as I was. I tilted my head in his direction. 'What else am I supposed to think?'

'That the fault lies with me, not with you. Please believe me.' I could hear him breathing hard. 'Let me

215

spell out my terms. I cannot let you see my face or touch my unclothed body with your hands while we're making love. Can you accept those conditions? *Will* you accept them?'

I realised I would do anything, *anything* for this man, and the thought terrified me. To leave him now would break me. He was my master, I was his possession; I was his, and he knew it.

'Yes,' I breathed. 'Yes, yes.'

He began to kiss me again. He lifted me onto the bed completely, then eased the dressing gown from me; it was warm in the bedroom now with the fire burning, and I felt flushed with heat. He turned me over carefully, so I was arched on all fours on the bed, on my knees, while he gently spread my forearms apart . . . *what was he doing?*

'That's it,' he was murmuring. 'Put your hands here, lift your shoulders a little more.' He was kissing me all the time, kissing my upper arms and shoulders, and stroking me, soothing me. Then I heard him move away again but soon he was coming back.

And this time – this time, he was lifting up my wrists one after the other and binding them to separate bedposts with something – my stockings, I guessed – *oh, God*. I was afraid again, but he steadied me with his hands as I crouched there, naked, and he kissed the nape of my neck tenderly.

He lifted my bottom higher in the air, so my elbows and knees were on the bed, my forearms taut, while my cheek rested on the pillow. My world rocked with sensations. I felt wicked, I felt wanton, I was burning with need. All the time his lips were pressing kisses to my body but avoiding that tender bruise; kissing my back, my hips. I squirmed in my bonds, longing for him desperately.

'Slowly,' he breathed. I heard him climb off the bed again and tried, despite my blindfold, to visualise him; I heard his trousers dropping to the floor, I heard him unbutton his white shirt and ease it off; I visualised his naked body and I waited with longing for him, with heartache too. *He must be so beautiful. Why won't he let me see him? Why?*

I must have wriggled with anticipation as I felt him kneel behind me on the bed. I think I moved immediately and shamelessly towards his sleek, hard body, gasping as I felt the full power of his steel-hard erection nudging against the tender skin of my buttocks.

'Cold?' he whispered.

'No,' I said. 'No.'

He brushed light fingers under my ribs to my breasts then teased one tender crest while I squirmed, a captive with my hands tied. *Oh, Ash. I want to see you.* I saw him instead in my mind's eye, my beautiful man; imagined him watching me with his dark, dark gaze; then I heard him moving again. He was behind me on the bed, his breathing was ragged, and he was arching himself over me, stroking my bottom – *What next? Oh, God, what next?*

I was hot and shamefully wet down there; I blushed with embarrassment. Soon he would realise it, for his fingers were slipping between my thighs and I heard a faint gasp – *mine* – as he parted the delicate folds there

217

and began a rhythmic stroking that had me lifting my hips and pressing desperately against his hand, wanting, needing more.

He kissed me. 'Oh, Sophie. How ready you are. How delicious you are.'

My bottom was in the air, my arms outspread and tied to the bedposts; my blindfolded face was pressed sideways against the pillow. I could feel his strong thighs now, parting my own legs, pushing them wider apart as he positioned himself over me and gripped my waist with his hands. Then the blunt tip of his phallus was prodding hungrily at me, and I heard Ash's low growl of satisfaction as he eased himself inside me. I felt the incredible invasion, the moist tightness as I stretched to accommodate him; the hard, pulsing surge as he filled me with his thickness, and acute pleasure rolled through me once more.

I must have cried out, I think, because he stopped abruptly. 'Sophie. Am I hurting you?'

'No. No, you're not . . .' *Far from it. Oh, far from it. So deep – so incredibly deep . . .* 'Please don't stop,' I whispered.

He kept his hips still for another moment, but I think I must have groaned aloud, shifting myself against him, desperate for more, because he began to pleasure me again, slowly at first and carefully; but as I begged with my body his strokes lengthened and intensified as I caught his rhythm and matched it. *Surely I couldn't . . . not again . . .*

'Let yourself go, Sophie,' he whispered. 'Come again, for me.'

Then I realised he was kneeling upright behind me, gripping my hips firmly. The intensity of his penetration thrilled me. He was thrusting harder now, and I revelled in the feel of him, in his possession of me, the pleasure he took in me, as I in him. My hips moved too, more and more frantically; the steady spiral of pleasure gripped my body as he drove deep, deeper than I could have believed, inside me – then held me as I exploded with pleasure.

And I realised he was close to his own extremity. Calling out my name savagely, he pumped twice, hard, then pulled out, shuddering, to spill his seed. His breathing rasped in his throat. Afterwards he untied my wrists, and though I was still blindfolded, he lay and drew me close, cradling me against his beautifully muscular body. I was motionless, I was sated. Then he pressed a swift kiss to my forehead before easing himself away, and I heard him swiftly going about the business of getting dressed.

When he came back to me, to sit beside me and untie the blindfold with care, I lay very still, curled up facing away from him, naked and vulnerable. I was overwhelmed by this man. There would never be anybody else for me. 'Sophie,' he said. 'Sophie – you're *crying?*'

'No.' I lifted my face to him steadily. 'Of course I'm not!'

Quickly he gathered me to him, rocking me in his lovely strong arms. 'Oh, Sophie. What is it?'

'You know what,' I whispered, my voice breaking slightly, though I fought, I fought so hard for control. I gave no explanation in words – I simply picked up the blindfold and let it fall.

He touched my cheek where just one tear had trick-led. 'Oh, God. You don't still think it's because I don't feel you worthy to look at me?'

I gazed up at him, my Mr Maldon; so beautiful, so bestowing of delicious pleasure, but he was breaking my heart all over again. I said, 'What else am I supposed to think?'

He held me. He cradled me, still naked, on his lap; he kissed me and I flung my arms round his shoulders, but my tears were damp on his white shirt.

'No,' he was breathing, 'no, it's not like that.'

I pulled myself away a little. 'But it *is* like that,' I answered bitterly. 'Don't worry, I learned my lesson at Belfield Hall. All the nobility are the same. None of them will acknowledge that we're in the same room as them, that we even exist . . .'

He held me tight, kissing my cheek over and over. 'You mustn't think it's because of that, Sophie,' he said urgently. 'But I *must* be obeyed in this. I'm damaged, I told you that. Badly damaged – but I want you to stay with me. Does it matter to you so very much not to see me, not to touch me when I'm making love to you?'

I was silent, thinking, *At least he's letting me touch him now.* Indeed, my arms were still round his shoulders, and my fingertips could feel his warm skin through his shirt, could sense his muscles and sinews flexing under my touch. I gazed up at him and said at last, very stead-ily, 'I think it would be the most magical moment in my life to see your face, and your expression when you move inside me, Ash. To see if it . . . if it means as much to you as it does to me.'

'Oh, Sophie.' His eyes were sad, so sad. He drew his hand across his face. 'Oh, Sophie. You don't know what you mean to me.'

Then tell me, I wanted to cry out. *Tell me your secrets.*

But he was silent, merely holding out the silk dressing gown again.

When I'd put it on, he drew me to the bed again beside him, in his arms, and my heart ached desperately for him. My poor Mr Maldon, with his dreadfully scarred hands – oh, what had happened to him since first I met him?

He pressed his forehead against mine. 'You're my good angel, Sophie. Do you know that?'

I lifted my eyes to his in surprise. 'Your . . . ?'

He smiled and stroked my cheek. 'My good angel,' he repeated. 'You believe in me whatever I do, don't you?'

His eyes were still bleak despite his smile, and I flung my arms around his neck once more. 'Of course,' I breathed. 'Of course I believe in you. You must stop hating yourself. I still think you're good and brave and true—'

'Do you?' he broke in. His eyes were sardonic now.

'Yes! Yes, I do! You took on the dukedom because you cared about ordinary working people, the miners and all the men who work on your estate—'

He broke in. 'I took the dukedom for revenge, Sophie. Nothing more, nothing less.'

My heart was plummeting suddenly but I thought I understood. 'Of course. You hated the Duke and Duchess – and Lord Charlwood – for the way they treated you during the summer you had to stay there.'

I remembered too Beatrice telling me, before I left Belfield Hall, how around the time I'd first met him, Ash and the Duke had had some fierce argument over money, and had never spoken since. 'Ash,' I went on, 'they never acknowledged your existence, they were cruel to you. No one can blame you for how you felt, no one.'

He kissed my fingers one by one, but there was no tenderness in his eyes. He said, 'It's bigger than that, Sophie. I learned to cope with their rejection quickly enough because they were nothing to me. No, I took the dukedom because I wanted revenge, on all the upper-class aristocrats who believe their birth makes them superior to everyone else on earth.'

I was silent, because now his bitterness was frightening me. This proud man was scarred to his very soul. *Oh, my poor, sad Mr Maldon.* I shivered inside for him, and for myself.

'Will you still stay with me, Sophie?' he asked me quietly at last.

As if there was ever any doubt now about that. A week? A month? It didn't matter – nothing mattered except being with him. 'Yes.' My voice was a soft sigh as I curled myself into him and yawned sleepily. 'But oh, Ash, what time is it?'

He touched the tip of my nose. 'Time for you to get some sleep. I must just attend to some correspondence before morning.'

I snuggled against him again, remembering the orderly heaps of papers on his desk. 'Don't you ever sleep?'

'I've got estates to manage, remember?' he smiled, tucking my loose hair behind my ears. 'Lots of farmland. Factories and mines as well.'

'So you *do* care! You do!'

'I like to make money,' he said. 'And that's enough talking for tonight, sleepyhead.'

I was deliciously tired. He found me one of his crisp white shirts to sleep in – it was far too big for me, and I remember we laughed about it together, then he tucked me into his bed and said he'd join me very soon.

I fell asleep almost straight away, merely turning and blinking sleepily when he eased himself into the bed and held me in his arms. But I woke suddenly just before dawn, feeling frightened, imagining – *had* I imagined it? – that he'd cried out sharply in his dreams. My spirits were low as I gazed at his exquisite profile. How long could this last? Not long, I feared. Surely he had too many dark secrets to ever give himself fully to anyone, let alone me.

But oh, he was beautiful; and I'd agreed to stay, God help me, I'd agreed to stay.

Chapter Sixteen

I awoke the next morning, suddenly aware that the place in the bed where he'd lain next to me was cold and empty. Then I realised that the sound of the bedroom door opening had disturbed me – Mrs Lambert was coming in, with a tea-tray. Remembering I was wearing one of Ash's shirts, I pulled the sheet over myself, but she looked as calm as ever, as if she was used to finding some semi-clad woman in her master's bed. No doubt she was, I thought, suddenly bleak.

'His Grace has had to go out on business,' she told me as she set the tray down on the bedside table. 'But he said you weren't to rush. Breakfast will be served downstairs when you're ready.' She smiled her kind smile. 'Your friend Cora is in the breakfast room now, and she's eating well. Shall I run you a bath, Miss Davis? Or there's the shower.'

Cora. Oh, God, I'd almost forgotten about Cora. 'Thank you, I'll take a shower.'

She started to turn, then hesitated. 'I realise that you arrived without your luggage, so I've put some clothes in the dressing room for you.' She pointed to a door I'd noticed earlier – it opened into a room that I'd seen could be accessed from the sitting room also. 'I do hope,' she went on, 'that they're suitable.'

Clothes too. Another chill settled round my heart. His house was so well equipped that even a new and unexpected mistress was almost instantly provided for. When she'd gone I lay there a moment or two, wondering. Then I jumped out of bed and hurried to the bathroom.

Last night I'd only seen Ash's rooms by lamplight, but now I realised that the bathroom here was on a scale to match his other private rooms, with a huge marble bath adorned with gilt taps. And the shower! Swiftly I pulled off Ash's shirt and experimented with the handles, until streams of lovely hot water flooded down over me from the ceiling above – bliss. There was lavender soap there, and shampoo; I washed myself all over, pausing as I smoothed my hands over my legs and discovered how deliciously tender I was between my thighs. *Last night. Oh, last night my man was wonderful.*

I dried myself thoroughly on one of the big fluffy towels. My hair was still damp, but I combed it out, knowing it was short enough to dry quickly in this beautiful, warm house. Swiftly I looked through the clothes in the dressing room that Mrs Lambert had mentioned; some were still in tissue paper, like the frocks Beatrice used to give me to wear. *Oh, my.* These were of equally exquisite quality. I eased on one of the simplest – an apricot-patterned chiffon day gown with a swirling skirt – and looked at myself in the mirror. I looked different: sleek and assured, and fresh from the arms of a man who – last night at least – had loved me as I'd loved him.

I hurried downstairs to find Cora, who was at the

breakfast table hungrily tucking into scrambled eggs and toast.

'Well,' she said. Her hazel eyes twinkled as she looked me up and down. 'What a pretty dress. And you look as though you slept rather well. This man. This amazing, rich man who owns this dream of a place – I gather you know him?'

'Yes.' My voice was scarcely a whisper.

Her eyes widened. 'Oh, Sophie. Oh no. It's *him*, isn't it? The one you told me about, who wouldn't let you see him or touch him – who did all kinds of . . . oh, my God. Is he still – you know, the same?'

I nodded, my throat suddenly tight as I sat down beside her; she leaned closer and murmured, because a housemaid was hovering, 'And is it still bloody marvellous with him? The sex, I mean. Does he still make you come and come until you don't know if you're on your head or your heels?'

'Something like that. Oh, Cora . . .' My voice broke in a little sob; her arms flew round me and she hugged me, rocking me. 'Oh, sweetie. And he's a duke, I hear, an actual, blue-blooded duke . . . Sophie, what are you going to do?'

I pulled myself away a little and gazed at her. 'I'll cope,' I said. I poured myself coffee.

'Are you sure you can?'

'No.' I tried to smile. 'No, I'm not sure at all. But what about you, Cora?'

'What about me? I'm a bloody hopeless case, I am.' With a bleak laugh she started to spread more toast with marmalade.

'We'll sort something, Cora!' I urged. 'You see, I've spoken to Ash about you . . .'

'Ash, eh?' She carried on eating.

I pressed on, 'Yes. We were thinking – you might be able to get your old job back at Cally's. You were such a lovely dancer, Cora! And Ash thinks he can find you somewhere better to live—'

'Not with you?' she whispered. 'Like before?'

I felt cold. 'I'm staying here. Just for a while. You can stay too, I'm sure Ash won't mind; for as long as you like, until you find something—'

'I can't stay,' she cut in. She poured herself more coffee and drank it almost defiantly. 'I'd ruin everything for you. No.'

'You *will* stay,' I insisted. 'Ash has said you'll be fine here, for oh, at least a week or two, you see how big this place is! And Cora, we can easily walk to the shops on Oxford Street from here – why don't we do that, this morning?'

She stood up, a half-smile on her face. 'Oxford Street, why not? Eat your breakfast, Sophie, you'll need to keep up your strength for that gorgeous man of yours. I'll go to my room and put some lipstick on, then I'll meet you in the hall in half an hour, shall I?'

I rose to hug her. 'Everything will be all right, Cora, you'll see.'

She clasped me very close. 'Attagirl. Don't let him break you, Sophie.'

I was ready and waiting in that vast hallway in half an hour, but Cora wasn't. With a sudden feeling of panic I hurried up to her room – Mrs Lambert had explained to me where it was.

Her perfume still hung on the air, but there was no Cora. There was just a note, lying on the dressing table. *Love you, sweetie. But I'm better out of your life.*

Ash told me there was nothing more I could have done for her, and in my sadness for her I accepted it. Looking back now, knowing what I know now, I should have tramped the streets to find my poor, damaged friend. But you see I was with my Mr Maldon, and selfishly nothing except him mattered to me.

The next few days – and nights – were like a dream to me, one of the kind where you snuggle deliciously into your pillow never wanting to wake up, and if Ash's dreams were darker, as they had been on the night I first slept with him, I wasn't aware of them. I was so happy, even though Ash was out most days at meetings with his lawyers and other businessmen. 'You could go shopping,' he told me one morning in his bedroom as he was preparing to go out. 'I'll tell James to take you wherever you want, in the car.'

He was tying his tie, and how I loved to watch him getting dressed. I was sitting up in his bed, wearing his silk dressing gown and still warm from his morning lovemaking. He still bound my wrists, he still blindfolded me before we were intimate, which I secretly hated, but now that he was up and preparing for his day, I was allowed to feast my eyes on him.

I rose from the pillows and tiptoed over to him; he caught sight of me in the mirror and smiled as I wrapped my arms round him from behind and leaned my cheek against his broad back, feeling the muscular warmth of him through his crisp shirt. Shopping? 'I'd rather stay here and wait in bed for you,' I teased. 'Do you always have so many meetings?'

He turned round to hold me, pressing his lips to my forehead. 'It's what happens when you're a duke.'

'Do you enjoy them?'

'They bore me extremely,' he answered with a light smile.

But I knew he took his duties seriously, despite what he'd said. I went back to sit cross-legged on the big bed and cupped my chin in my hand, watching him as he shrugged on his beautifully tailored dark coat. 'Is the old Duchess still trying to prove you're not the heir?' I asked, curious.

He gave me his grave smile as he casually ran a silver-backed brush through his thick brown hair. 'I believe it's her life's ambition.'

'They used to call her the old witch, you know – all the staff below stairs.'

'Appropriate,' he grinned. 'She's been heard to say she can die happy if she can only get rid of me, so let's hope her spells don't work. Stop worrying, though, sweetheart. I'm enjoying the contest thoroughly. And most of all – ' he swung me into his arms – 'I'm enjoying *you*.' Softly he whispered, '*Jazz baby, you drive me wild.*' I was breathless with desire and sheer joy.

Apart from our hours in bed together, I was happiest in the evenings after dinner, when Ash was home and it was just the two of us in his beautiful library. He would study the latest newspapers or write letters, while I would perhaps choose a record to put on his gramophone in there, then curl up with one of the many wonderful poetry books he had on his shelves. But often, while I was reading, I would look up at him, and sometimes he would catch my eye and smile.

'Little scholar,' he would tease.

Sometimes he would tell me just a little about what he was doing, and I loved that because it meant I had more idea of his responsibilities, and of what went on in his busy life. For example, one night he was writing a letter in a foreign language; I noticed it as I was passing his desk to choose another book.

He must have seen my wondering expression, because he put his pen aside and drew me onto his lap. 'It's in French,' he explained. 'I used to be fluent because of my mother, of course. But I'm a little out of practice these days. I have a ward in Paris; she's my mother's brother's granddaughter. Both her parents have died, and legally she's in my care.'

'Even though she lives in France?'

'Even though she lives in France. You see, I'm her nearest living relative.' He eased me from his lap, murmuring, 'And you're a minx, to distract me so. Back to your books.' He let his hand drift over my hip. 'Later, I'll be able to give you *all* my attention.'

I fluttered my eyelashes at him, my blood tingling in anticipation, but I obediently returned to my book by the fire, though I still watched him writing his letters at his desk, seeing how his dark hair fell in that endearing way over his forehead. Every so often he looked up from his work to smile at me, and my heart turned over.

But it distressed me so much still that when we were in bed together and making love, he would not let me see him or touch him. He was tender with me, he whispered endearments that made my blood tingle, but still he bound me and blindfolded me and, though his lovemaking enthralled me, sometimes I was almost frightened at the near savagery of his possession of me.

But always the surging of bliss that engulfed me at my climax was so intense as to make me think I might die of it, and when at last we lay sated in one another's arms in the warm darkness, I pondered on his brave, lonely life, my Ash; the only son to a couple who were so indifferent to their child that he spent his boyhood in unloved solitude.

So I resolved not to ask him any more about his obsessive need not to be watched or touched during intimacy. But I did ask some other questions.

'Who was the first girl you ever slept with, Ash?' We were in bed one night; we'd made love earlier, and I was in the shirt I'd adopted as my own, while he wore some charcoal-grey silk pyjamas that clung enticingly to the sleek length of his body.

His mouth twisted in a grin. '*Slept with* wouldn't quite be correct. She was a governess, as it happens.'

'A governess!' I exclaimed.

'A very . . . experienced governess.'

Leaning on my elbow so my face was just above his, I caressed the dark stubble of his jawline, because I knew his rules and now I could touch him again. 'Young? Old?' I tried to sound nonchalant.

'She was twenty-six and knew a lot of tricks,' he breathed, trying to catch my fingertip with his lips.

'And you, Ash?'

His eyes glinted with mischief. 'I was fourteen.'

'*Fourteen!* So she was twelve years older than you!' This time I couldn't help but sound scandalised, and he laughed at me.

'Yes.' He caught my finger at last with his hand and kissed it. 'After that one disastrous summer at Belfield Hall, I always spent the holidays with a schoolfriend of mine whose father was a marquis. My friend had a younger sister, and her governess – whose name, I remember, was Rosa – took it upon herself to . . . enlarge my education.'

I wanted to ask, *Did you let her see you? Did you let her touch you when you were in bed with her?* But he hated it if I raised that subject, so I tried to look severe. 'Any more governesses since then – Your Grace?'

'Chorus girls now take precedence,' he said lightly.

You'll realise that I had no other man to compare him with, but I knew that he must be incredibly virile, incredibly skilled to give me such intense pleasure. The night before, he'd kept me waiting for my release; I'd been sobbing aloud in pleasure and desperation, straining at my bound wrists, but each time I was on the brink he would pull out of me and say, 'Patience, Sophie.'

In the end, he'd driven into me with such fierce, tender passion that I'd climaxed over and over again. I was melting, I was overflowing with loving him, and I even dared to think that perhaps he felt some emotion for me also. One April night, when there was warmth enough still for us to sit out on the private terrace at the rear of this beautiful mansion and gaze up at the stars, he suddenly reached for my hand and held it to his lips.

'You think you know me,' he said. 'You don't at all. But I want you to realise that I need you, Sophie. I need you with me, right now.'

'For as long as you want me, Ash,' I whispered, 'I'm here for you.'

Even in the extremity of his pleasure he took care not to get me pregnant. Sometimes he would pull out of me to spill his seed and, though I couldn't see, I loved to feel the silky fluid spurt over my breasts while he groaned out his desire. Sometimes he used a sheath, so I could sense him pulsing deep inside me with each heavy burst of semen. Always he blindfolded and bound me with such care, tying my wrists to the bedposts or behind my back.

One night I impulsively knelt on the floor before him, when I was bound and blindfolded, and I took his erection in my mouth. 'Sophie.' He was standing; he put his hand to the top of my head. 'Sophie, you don't have to . . .'

'I want to,' I said simply. 'I want to.'

I heard him hiss out air between his teeth as I stroked my tongue along his strongly veined, pulsing member. I was a little afraid – of doing it wrong, of hurting him even, and he was so thick, so powerful. But he guided my movements, he soothed me with murmurs of approval, he stroked my sleek hair. Remembering Beatrice's avid face as she leaned over her American, I sheathed my teeth with my lips and began to slide up and down, swirling my tongue around the tip of his phallus, and I glowed with pleasure when he reached forward with a sigh and stroked my cheek, encouraging me. 'So good, Sophie. So good.'

I felt I was adoring him like this, my beautiful scarred man, and when he suddenly went still, his powerful body tight with tension, I felt that tension too. Then his hips began to pump strongly into my mouth, so I drew him as far in as I could, sucking hard. The sudden flood of salty ejaculate took me by surprise, but I let it spurt freely and I swallowed, I licked him adoringly.

Then he'd untied my hands and drawn me, still blind-folded, onto his lap. He'd told me he couldn't ever offer me love, but I still knew that I would take anything.

Then he'd made love to me. Always he roused me to such heights that I was delirious with need. Each time, when he drove into me at last, I would think, *Now. Now is a time I will remember always.*

My powerful, beautiful man, pleasuring me until the world tilted above and around me and the stars were flying and whirling in the sky as astronomers tell us they do; spinning, spinning always away from us.

Even while wrapped in my blissful idyll, I began to real-ise that Ash was more preoccupied than usual and his business advisers called frequently at the house. 'It's the coal mines again,' he told me as we prepared for bed.

I was already in my dressing gown and brushing my hair. I turned to him questioningly.

'The government, in its generosity,' he went on, 'has passed all the coalfields back to their former owners, but that's chiefly because the pits are making huge losses. During the war, coal was taken out with no thought to the future, no investment in safety or new machinery. And now the export market has all but vanished.'

I put down my hairbrush carefully. 'What will you do, Ash?'

'I can tell you what many owners are doing – either shutting their pits down or slashing the miners' pay.' I said nothing; he was gazing at me with that glint of iron determination I knew so well. 'I'm different, Sophie. I'm going to invest. I think those mines have a future – though I can't do anything for a while because the miners are going on a nationwide strike.'

I knew all this troubled him, but he said no more.

The next evening James drove us out to dine, at a restaurant in Kensington that was far from his usual Mayfair milieu. I guessed Ash chose it because he didn't want us to be the subject of public speculation, and that was a small sadness that I tried to push aside, but my spirits lightened anyway as soon as the jazz trio there began to play. They were good. Already some couples were on the small dance floor, and my feet were tapping.

'Let's show them what you can do,' Ash said, once we'd finished our main course. His eyes sparkled. 'A shame to waste your training. Let's dance.'

He led me towards the music. As I should have guessed, he was a marvellous dancer, not showy but naturally graceful. *He wasn't ashamed of me.* I loved being with him. I felt my happiness glowing through me.

But then a party of men and women came noisily into

the restaurant and started pushing their way towards the best tables, including ours. Our plates had been cleared but our glasses, half full with the mineral water we'd both chosen to drink, were still there. From where we danced I saw one of the newcomers move those glasses brusquely aside. 'We'll take this table,' he ordered the waiter.

I recognised his voice then, and with a sinking heart I realised it was Lord Sydhurst, the arrogant government minister who'd visited Belfield Hall and was friendly with Lady Beatrice. 'Please, can we go?' I asked Ash quickly. I was afraid Lord Sydhurst would recognise me as Beatrice's maid.

Ash was steely-eyed. 'Not yet,' he said. 'Not until Sydhurst's friends have removed themselves from our table.'

So I wasn't the only one to know Lord Sydhurst. As Ash marched towards him, Sydhurst looked up quickly; instantly I realised that the two men hated one another. Ash said, 'We'll have our table back, Sydhurst.'

'Belfield.' Lord Sydhurst's lip curled. 'Was this your place? Of course, if I'd known . . .'

'If you'd known I was here, you'd never have set foot in this restaurant, I hope.' Ash was already pulling out my chair for me.

Lord Sydhurst let his glance flicker casually over me, then moved his companions to another part of the room, but his pale eyes were full of loathing. Apprehension prickled down my spine. I touched Ash's hand and said, 'I'm really quite ready to go now.'

Ash had made himself comfortable in his chair. 'Well,

I'm not. Finish your water and we'll have coffee as well. Take no notice of him.'

But I could see Lord Sydhurst still watching me and I had a terrible feeling that recognition was beginning to dawn in his eyes. He waited for the band to finish its number, then he leaned back in his chair.

'Good God,' he drawled loudly so everyone could hear. 'Just fancy. I knew I'd seen her somewhere. The little floozy Belfield's with is a maid, a common housemaid—'

He didn't get any further because Ash was on him, hauling him out of his chair and shoving him against the wall. James was there too, almost instantly; I'd realised long ago that Ash's loyal chauffeur hardly let his master out of his sight whenever we were out anywhere, but was always at a discreet distance in case he was needed.

He was needed. Sydhurst was struggling in Ash's strong grip, but all his half-drunk friends were about to join in. 'Take Sophie outside,' Ash ordered James over his shoulder. James hurried me to the car and Ash followed soon afterwards – had he hit Sydhurst? I wondered desperately. Whatever had happened, I guessed he wouldn't tell me. Instead he sat in the back and put his arm round my shoulders. 'Drive on, James.' I could feel how very tense he was as the big Daimler moved away, but he was still gentle as he cupped my face and turned it to his. 'So you know Lord Sydhurst, Sophie?'

I nodded – I think I was shivering. 'He . . . he visited Belfield Hall a few times, when Lady Beatrice was there. Ash, I'm so sorry—'

237

'No need for *you* to apologise,' he cut in. 'He's a snake – did you know he was in the Ministry of Munitions?'

'Yes.' I hesitated. 'Lady Beatrice told me.'

'I'll wager she didn't tell you the whole story – that Sydhurst and his business friends made absolute fortunes from the war by getting government money to build munitions factories that either didn't produce the armaments required, or delivered arms and explosives so faulty they killed more of our own soldiers than they did the enemy.'

I was horrified. 'Why didn't someone *say* something?'

He said with scorn, 'Oh, Sydhurst had too many ministers in his pocket, and the Press as well. The Ministry's recently been disbanded, but Sydhurst's got his money safely salted away.'

A powerful man, then, who clearly hated Ash. And he'd recognised me. 'I'm afraid,' I said quietly, 'that soon it will be all around London that I'm from Belfield Hall, and I'm with you.'

He put his arm round my shoulder more tightly and looked into my eyes so I could see the intensity of his gaze. 'Does it matter to you, Sophie? Because it doesn't to me. Believe me, it doesn't matter to me at all.'

The next day Ash had morning appointments as usual, and I resolved to make a secret shopping trip because I wanted to buy the man I loved a gift. Though I'd refused to accept any money from him, I'd saved some of my pay from Cally's, and I was considering eagerly what I might buy him as I set off in the spring sunshine towards Regent Street.

I don't know when exactly I started to realise it, but the feeling, when it came, was unmistakeable. I was being watched. My steps slowed, my pulse raced. Could it be James? Yes, of course, that would be it! But then, with spine-chilling clarity, I remembered that James had driven Ash to a meeting in the City.

I tried to thrust aside my misgivings. Our house in Bayswater had been watched for a while, I knew, but that was by Danny's men, and they'd been after poor Cora, not me. The pavements were busy with shoppers, and I told myself I was being foolish. But I hadn't gone far down Regent Street when I realised that a sleek car was slowly overtaking me, then pulling to a stop. Prickles of alarm travelled through my veins. The chauffeur, young and black-uniformed, was opening the door for his passenger, and out stepped . . . Lady Beatrice. She wore a fur coat, and her familiar scent overwhelmed me with memories I would have given anything to forget.

'Sophie,' she breathed, 'oh, my dear Sophie, I made such a mistake in letting you go. I know you're with Ash now, but trouble lies ahead for him, such trouble. And I thought you of all people must be forewarned because we used to be such friends, you and I!'

She put her gloved hand to my cheek and I couldn't help but recoil. *Had she been following me? What did she mean – trouble lies ahead?*

Chapter Seventeen

'You look thin,' Lady Beatrice announced as the waiters fussed over us with the menus and napkins half an hour later. 'You look tired. I've been so very worried about you.'

She'd insisted on taking me for lunch in Selfridge's department store and I agreed, because I needed to know why she had followed me and what she intended. I certainly knew she was no friend of mine. I hardly remember what I ate, but I do remember everything she said and did.

I said, 'Worried about me? I don't believe you. At Belfield Hall you were simply using me; you had no concern for me at all.'

Beatrice sighed. 'I was only doing what I thought best for you – and Ash.' She lowered her voice as she spoke his name and reached across to touch my hand. 'I fear, my dear, that you've wandered out of your depth with Ash, though I thought you'd had your warning at Belfield Hall. Those letters he made you write to him long ago, the way he used you—'

'He wasn't using me to spy,' I broke in. 'I was a fool to believe you. And surely – *surely* you can't still be hoping to marry him?'

A year ago I'd never have dared to speak to her in such a way. She sipped her wine and regarded me carefully. 'My, you've grown up, Sophie. Do I still want to marry him? Oh my goodness, no – both Ash and I have moved on from there, I should hope. He'll be planning on finding some innocent heiress for a bride.'

My heart bumped to a stop, I couldn't speak.

'Though I don't consider,' she went on, 'that such a girl would really suit Ash at all, do you? In fact, I imagine she'd be fleeing home to her mama within days of her wedding night.'

I was wondering with a sudden chill if she'd guessed at his sexual secrets. Had she heard somehow that he would only make love if his partner could not see him or touch him? I didn't answer.

'You've hardly eaten a thing,' she went on. 'I'm so sorry you're involved with him, Sophie. You know, if I'd had any idea how badly his experiences had *scarred* him . . .'

'What do you mean?' I pushed my plate aside. 'Are you talking about his hands?'

'Oh, my dear.' She leaned across to me, a look of pity on her face. 'Hasn't he told you yet? About the war?'

My heart bumped to a stop.

'He was a pilot,' she went on, 'in the Royal Flying Corps. Forgive me, I really didn't want to be the one to tell you.'

I swallowed, my throat dry. 'He flew planes? In the war?'

She nodded, and I remembered with a dreadful rush of clarity what Lynton had said, what Mrs Lambert had said – *So you don't know, about the war?* Oh God, I should have asked him myself; oh, God, to have Beatrice, of all people, reveal this . . .

'Why didn't you tell me?' I breathed. I was sick of these secrets of hers. 'If you knew all this, why on earth didn't you tell me at Belfield Hall?'

'Because he resigned,' she said calmly. 'When the fighting was at its fiercest, halfway through the war, he resigned from the Flying Corps and disappeared from public view. And I'm afraid it's inevitable that ever since then, the rumours have spread that he got out because he was afraid.' Beatrice was still watching me, looking concerned. 'Oh, my dear. You *have* got it badly.'

I was thinking, she must have known this all along. And he must already have been a pilot when I met him in Oxford, during all the months that he wrote to me. *I have to go away. But I want you to still think of me, and to think well of me . . .* My heart was pounding. 'What happened to his hands?' I whispered.

Her lips thinned. 'That was a shock to me, I admit, when he arrived at Belfield Hall. I don't know how that happened to him.' She was still watching me carefully. 'Though it wasn't when he was in the Royal Flying Corps, that's for sure.'

'You say he "disappeared from public view" some time during the war. Where, then, did he go?' I was gripping my knife and fork so hard they were hurting me.

'He went abroad,' she said, 'that's all I know, early in 1917. But he simply refuses to talk about what happened to him next. Nor does it help his reputation that he made so much money out of his business interests round about the same time.'

So did many people, I wanted to say. I was thinking what Ash had said about Sydhurst and his cronies: *He and his business friends made absolute fortunes from the war.* The waiter was hovering to see if I wanted coffee, but I brushed him away. 'You hate him,' I said flatly to Beatrice. 'You hate him – don't you? – because he refused to take you to his bed at Belfield Hall that night.'

She put her head on one side. 'You must admit,' she drawled, 'that the two of you played a pretty trick on me that night. But, contrary to what you think, I'm one of the few people to be actually on Ash's side – simply because I think he's the best chance the Belfield estate has got of good governance. The Duchess, however, still loathes him, and is clinging with desperate obstinacy to her story that he's not really the heir.'

She sipped her wine again and ran her eyes over my face and figure. 'You surely realise, Sophie, that your association with him could ruin him? You really will have to pray that the Press don't get hold of the story. The public are always hungry for any scandal about the private lives of the upper classes.'

I did my damnedest not to let her see how much that hurt. 'I'm quite sure Ash can look after himself,' I breathed. 'You should have told me at Belfield Hall that he was in the war, and a pilot.'

'And you, my dear – ' she touched my cheek lightly with her finger and I flinched – 'should have told me at Belfield Hall that you'd corresponded with him and formed your rather absurd . . . *infatuation* for him.' She sighed. 'A pity – we used to have such fun those days at the Hall, Sophie, you and I. You know, when Ash has had enough of you, which cannot be long now, you could always be my maid again . . .'

'Never.' I started folding my napkin. 'I'm going now.'

'I suppose you're returning to his house in Hertford Street, are you? But you won't have that option, my dear, once Ash is done with you.' Calmly she began putting her cigarettes and lighter into her bag. 'I'm at Claridge's Hotel in Brook Street for the next few weeks, should you need me.'

'I really won't.'

As if I'd not spoken, she glanced again at my scarcely touched food. 'Oh, Sophie, you should have eaten more. You really look quite pale – you're not pregnant, are you? No, of *course* Ash would know better than to get someone of your class with child. All the same, you will let Christopher drive you home, I insist.'

Beatrice sat in the front next to her chauffeur as he drove me back to Hertford Street, and I didn't say a word. I realised at some point that her hand was on his crotch, and though her eyes were straight ahead she was fondling him, caressing him deliberately into arousal in front of me.

When we got to Ash's house Christopher stopped the car then came to open the door for me, his face impassive beneath his peaked cap. Beatrice climbed from the car too. 'Don't forget,' she said with her secret smile, 'that you can always share Christopher with me at my hotel whenever you wish – once you've done the right thing and let Ash get on with his life.' She stroked her chauffeur's hip, to draw attention to the thickness of his erection beneath his uniform. When I drew back in revulsion, her smile increased.

I ran into the house, halting when I saw the maid coming towards me. 'Is the Duke at home?' I asked quickly.

'His Grace is in his study, ma'am. Will you be joining him?'

'Very soon, yes. But please don't tell him I'm home – not just yet.'

'Ma'am.' She bobbed her head and I hurried on.

I went upstairs to the bedroom I'd shared with him since that first night, then I sat on his bed. *You surely realise, Sophie, that your association with him could ruin him?* I tried desperately to refute what Beatrice had said. Didn't some of the most powerful men in the land manage to keep their mistresses in London houses, while their wives dwelt far away in the country? I resolved: *This will end when Ash and I decide it will end, not when Beatrice tries to wreck our happiness.*

I thought I heard the sound of a motorcar pulling away below the window, and swiftly I went to look, wondering if Ash was perhaps leaving in his Daimler, but it was only a taxicab disappearing down the street. I dressed myself quickly in one of the gowns he most liked; it was a frivolous thing of beaded turquoise, short with thin shoulder straps and a low neckline. When he'd first seen me in it he'd said I looked like a flapper, a delicious little flapper. I buckled on some high-heeled silver shoes, painted more kohl on my eyelids and hurried

down the grand staircase, already consigning Lady
Beatrice and her malice to the very back of my thoughts
– only to realise that Ash wasn't in his study after all.

He was in the hallway, and he wasn't alone. There was
a girl with him, who was talking to Ash with great vivac-
ity, partly in English and partly in another language
– French I guessed. Mrs Lambert was by the door, looking a little bemused; I guessed she'd let the visitor in,
and was now wondering what kind of whirlwind she'd
released in the house.

Ash had his back to me, and didn't see me at first –
none of them did. The girl had eyes only for Ash. She
was younger than me, and exquisitely dressed in a flared
green velvet coat with a matching green cloche hat
perched on her black curls. She had the sweetest, most
mischievous face, and I gathered she was making some
kind of appeal to him, for she was gesticulating with her
hands, but then she saw me on the stairs in my flighty
turquoise dress, and her mouth fell open with a little
'oh!' of surprise.

Ash turned to me quickly then. 'Sophie, this is my
ward, Madeline. Will you wait for me upstairs, please?'

I got dressed – *properly* dressed – and waited for him in
his sitting room. I gazed at myself in the mirror, and my
eyes betrayed my despair that he'd sent me away. *His
ward.* She belonged in his world – I didn't.

When the door opened I was already on my feet.

'Sophie,' he began, 'her name is Madeline Dumouriez;
I think I mentioned before that she has been my ward
since her parents died. I thought she was staying with

her godmother in Paris, but she's run away and wants to stay with me. I've told her it's not possible, of course. She's only seventeen, and she needs a chaperone—'

'Ash,' I interrupted, 'Ash, please listen to me.' I think my voice must have conveyed my desperation, because he went very still.

He said, 'Is now the time for this, Sophie?'

I moistened my lips; my heart was thudding sickeningly against my ribs. 'Yes. I think it is. Ash, I don't feel it's right, that I'm living here, with you.'

He sat down facing me, looking almost haggard. 'I don't want you to leave,' he said. 'I'm sorry I had to send you away just then. Madeline won't be staying here with me, she can't. I'll start making some other arrangement for her straight away . . .'

I put my hand on his arm. 'No! I don't mean that you and I shouldn't be together! I just thought that . . . sometimes I'm an embarrassment to you, as I was with Lord Sydhurst the other night. And your ward's seen me here, coming down from your bedroom – your ward! So I wondered if it might be better if I lived nearby, in an apartment, perhaps . . .' He took me in his arms, he cradled me, he kissed the top of my head. 'I don't want you to go anywhere,' he said.

I pressed my cheek to his warm shirt. 'Oh, Ash. Do you think I want to be apart from you? But—'

'Wait,' he interrupted. 'Listen to me.' He touched my lips, so tenderly, with his fingers. 'Soon, Sophie, I have to go to Belfield Hall. And I want you to come with me.'

'*What?*' Slowly I lifted my face to his; I almost laughed

in my despair. 'How can I return there? I left without notice – they'll never take me back!'

'You misunderstand,' he said quietly. 'I want you there with me, close to me like *this*, if only for a few days.'

'But why? No, this is impossible. And the Duchess—'

'The Duchess has finally moved to the Dower House. I want you with me at the Hall,' he repeated steadily. 'And after that, Sophie, I will tell you things about my past that will make you turn your back on me with the contempt I deserve.'

I was as frightened by the look in his eyes as I was by the words he spoke. 'No. Never. Ash, never.'

He drew me tighter into his arms and cradled me close. 'You know so little about me. Come with me to Belfield, Sophie – *please* – before you make any decisions. Any promises that you cannot keep.'

I didn't understand. I was afraid. But I said yes, because I loved him.

Should I have asked him then, about the war? Indeed I should; but Beatrice's warning had frightened me, and besides I felt – from his own ominous words – that he would tell me everything, all too soon. A week later we set off from London and by nine in the evening we were approaching Oxford, with the full moon casting its silvery light over the familiar countryside.

James was driving the big Daimler and Ash was in the back with me, his arm around me, but even so I felt a growing sense of dread as we passed by the road that led to Belfield Hall. Simply the nearness of the place where he was the Duke and I had been a lowly servant made the gulf between us, to my mind, gape ever wider.

I wondered if Ash guessed my distress, because he too was silent, until at last he took my hand and said softly, 'You told me you wanted to visit your mother's grave.'

'Yes, I do.'

'And you're meeting Nell there in the churchyard tomorrow?'

I nodded. It was Ash who'd suggested to me, as he'd outlined our journey a week before, that I should write to Nell to tell her I was intending to visit the Hall. I'd not written to her for a while, and I'd felt guilty about her eager and prompt reply.

'She wrote to say that tomorrow is her afternoon off,' I told him, 'and I'm to visit the servants' hall with her afterwards to see the others. But Ash, I don't understand how—'

'It will be all right,' he interrupted. 'You'll see.'

I said nothing more, but to me this subterfuge only emphasised what Beatrice had warned – that I could bring Ash nothing but shame. The car rolled on. Ash was still holding my hand steadily. 'Tonight,' he said, 'we'll stay at an Oxford inn. Tomorrow afternoon James will drop you off in the village, so you can walk on to the churchyard. And your story for Nell will be . . . ?'

I recited it obediently. 'I'll tell her I came on the morning train to Oxford and took the bus to the village.'

'And then?' he prompted gently.

'Then I'll say goodbye to Nell in the servants' hall and tell her I'm catching the night train back to London.

But really – I'll be coming up to your rooms . . . Oh, Ash!' I wrenched myself round to face him. 'If anyone should see me with you, if you're recognised with me in Oxford, with Sophie the scullery maid, you will be a laughing stock!'

He gathered me in his arms on the back seat of the big car and as ever I was helpless, because I loved him.

'After saying goodbye to Nell, you'll come to me in my rooms at Belfield Hall,' he repeated with quiet emphasis, 'and no one except James will know you're there. No one but James will have access to my private rooms for the whole of our stay. Then we can go round the Hall by night, you and I. Looking for secrets.'

He'd said this before we set off, with his strange half-smile. 'I need you to help me find my way round all the parts of the Hall I'd normally never have access to, Sophie,' he'd told me calmly. 'You once thought I was asking you to be my spy, remember? I wasn't. But I am now.'

I went over and over all this as the big car purred along the country roads, which were so quiet, so empty after London. 'Ash,' I said quietly. 'Please won't you tell me exactly what you're looking for?'

He fondled my hand with his own badly scarred one. 'Perhaps I'm not quite sure,' he mused. 'But I'll know when I find it. Oh, yes, I'll know.'

He drew me closer, nuzzling his cheek against my hair, and I wondered again, with a sudden twisting of my heart, what could have possibly happened to him in the war to scar him so badly both mentally and physically.

'I really do think you're crazy,' I said, snuggling against him and tapping his arm in mock rebuke. 'Hiding a scullery maid in your rooms.'

And I love you, I love you, Mr Maldon. I didn't see what he could possibly tell me that would stop me loving him. He held me tightly in his arms, and I stored every hour, every minute in my heart. All too soon we were in Oxford, where we were booked into a small hotel near the railway station. What name he used I wasn't sure, but despite my fears no one recognised him, and he fell asleep holding me very tight, while I lay awake, watching him as the moonlight stole through the window.

The next afternoon James drove me to Belfield village as we'd arranged. The sun shone, wisps of white cirrus clouds floated high in the blue spring sky, and I walked on to the churchyard in my old coat and bonnet while James drove back to Oxford to take Ash to Belfield Hall. I tidied my mother's grave beneath the yews and tended some primroses I'd planted there years ago; a robin hopped nearby and the breeze sighed softly through the trees. Then I saw two figures walking towards me, hand in hand. Nell, with Will.

Nell hurried to hug me. 'Sophie. Sophie!' Despite her slight lameness she was practically dancing up and down. 'We've got something wonderful to tell you – Will and I are getting married!'

I hugged her back, and I smiled up at Will. 'I'm so glad,' I said. 'So very glad.'

Nell was chattering on. 'So much has changed at the Hall. The new Duke has had electricity put in, so we've no more dirty oil lamps to clean, you can't imagine the joy. But the main thing is – the Duke is arriving today! He's been staying in London – he had lots of business there, apparently. But let's walk back to the Hall, Sophie, and you can tell us everything – we've got so much to talk about.'

That winding drive – oh, the memories. Those tall beech trees, coming into leaf now, lining the driveway. The Hall itself, with its mellow stone and windows gleaming in the sunshine. Those wide steps, leading to the great main doors – I'd scrubbed them many mornings for years, and I remembered how my hands used to be sore, but my head was always filled with dreams of being on stage, of being with Mr Maldon.

He was the Duke of Belfield. I think it only properly sank in then, as I gazed anew at this massive place. He was lord and master of thousands of acres of land, of factories and mines also, scattered around England; he even had business investments abroad. And I dared to love him. What a fool I was.

The three of us went in by the servants' door, of course, and down to the servants' hall. I'd said to Ash that I still thought it madness to be so blatant about my presence there, but he'd shaken his head. 'On the contrary it's a well-known tactic – if you're about to do something secret, keep out in the open for as long as possible.'

They were all expecting me there thanks to Nell, but I was surprised by everyone's warm welcome. Even Harriet and Betsey were pleasant to me. 'Tell us about

London!' they cried. 'Is it as exciting as people say? Have you really danced on stage?' Robert said, 'My, Sophie, you've grown into quite a smasher.' Mrs Burdett was a little stern, but I think she was pleased to see me. As for Nell, she held Will's hand all the time; I noticed Will didn't say much, but I hoped that he would be happy.

They'd all have their usual jobs waiting, I knew, so when I'd had my tea with them I said I would have to go and catch the bus back to Oxford. But Nell caught my hand just as I was leaving. 'I haven't told you about the Duchess yet, have I, Sophie?' she whispered. 'The old witch has moved to the Dower House – she can't stand having the new Duke in charge here! She's barely begun to move all her stuff out, there's so much of it, but at least she's not living here any more, neither her nor old Miss Stanforth, and the sooner we're completely rid of her the better. The new Duke is so much kinder to us all.'

Nell came to the servants' door to wave me goodbye and I waved back as I set off down the drive. But a few minutes later, after turning a corner that hid me from view of the Hall, I hurried in amongst the rhododendrons that filled a section of the park and was soon half running back to the east wing of the house through the cover of a dense shrubbery. Breathlessly I let myself in a small side entrance that I knew was scarcely ever used and raced up the deserted servants' staircase to knock on the door of Ash's apartment.

He let me in and I think I simply threw myself into his arms, I was so delighted to see him, and to have reached him without being discovered. He laughed. He said, 'I've heard of people being dragged through a hedge backwards. Seeing it is something else.'

Only then did I realise that my old coat and bonnet seemed to have half the garden stuck to them – spiders' webs and twigs and dead leaves. 'Oh!' I stared down at myself in utter dismay, but then I began to laugh too. 'It was your idea,' I said, steadily advancing on him. 'Your idea that I run back here through the shrubbery, you impossible, impossible man!'

He started picking twigs from my coat with mock solemnity; I pulled off some spiders' webs and suddenly, impishly smeared them over his cheek. He picked me up bodily and flung me on his bed. 'Minx,' he said. 'Minx, I can see I'll have to chastise you.'

'Oh, God,' I said, 'my boots, I've got mud all over your bedspread. Oh, Ash . . .'

'What, sweetheart?'

'Oh, Ash, I was a scullery maid. I shouldn't be here,' I whispered, the enormity of it all suddenly hitting me as I gazed around his majestic apartment.

'No?' he mused. Suddenly I realised that smile was on his face, that look was in his eyes, and my heart missed a beat. He was stroking his chin thoughtfully with his forefinger. 'A scullery maid,' he said. 'A scullery maid. Do you know, I find the idea of you as a scullery maid rather delightful, Sophie.' His voice changed. 'Lift your skirt for me.'

I gasped. 'But someone—'

'No one will come in. I've locked the door.' He held up the key, and my heart pounded as he started walking slowly towards me with that predatory look in his eyes. *My man. My beautiful man.* 'Ah,' he said softly as he lifted my skirt. 'Stockings. Button boots. Long knickers. Delicious.'

I was burning for him. 'Oh, Ash. They're horrible, absolutely horrible! And surely they'll be serving your evening meal soon . . .'

'Dinner,' he announced in that gravelly voice of his, 'can wait.' He still had my skirt raised and was stroking my thighs all the time. 'Turn,' he said softly. 'Turn, and tell me what you've been doing. Whom you've seen. What they're saying below stairs – my beautiful little spy.'

He quickly stripped off my outer garments and arranged me on the bed so my folded arms rested on his pillow, then from behind he started fondling me through the opening of my knickers. *Ah.* Pleasure flooded me. I was in the Duke's apartments, with this glorious man, and he wanted me, he needed me . . .

'Nell came to meet me,' I managed somehow, 'and Will too—'

'Who is Will?'

'He's a footman here.'

'Ah. I remember now. You wrote something about him once, but crossed it out.'

'He was a friend of mine when I was small . . . oh!' My cry of delight was muffled by the pillow.

From behind he'd slipped one finger inside me, and was sliding it round and round. 'A friend? Was that all?'

My cheeks burned. 'He . . . he once thought he was in love with me. But he's marrying Nell now.'

His hand had stopped moving. I could feel him

255

reaching in his pocket for something, and I knew what it was – a blindfold. Gently he tied it round my eyes while he went on quietly, 'Did you let him kiss you when he was courting you? Did you let him touch you?'

'No! In fact we never really courted – poor Will was in the war, I didn't see him for years. I didn't even realise how he felt about me . . .'

He turned me round and gathered me in his arms, but his embrace couldn't compensate for the fact that I was in darkness again. He said, 'Do you realise how *I* feel about you, Sophie?' His voice was very soft.

No, I thought desperately. *No, I don't know at all. I only know it can't last long. Not when you can't bear me to see you.* 'I realise you've been kind to me,' I whispered.

'Kind,' he said. His voice was hard-edged now. 'Jesus. *Kind* to you.' He turned me over his knee, slid my knickers down and began to spank me, gently. 'A little chastisement,' he said softly, 'for letting Will love you.'

I was helpless. His big hand warmed me, teased me again between my legs until I was moaning with desire, then he made me kneel by the bed, my arms on the counterpane, my knees on the thick rug. He caressed my bottom, rubbing it with some sort of oil, then I heard him unbuttoning his fly, his shirt also; so indeed I was desperate for him by the time I felt his heated skin against my back. I relished his weight, I gasped as I felt the potent hardness of his erection nudging between my legs.

He teased me by several times letting his rigid penis slide tantalisingly along my moist folds then pulling back again. My hips lifted to him in despair, but from the sounds I heard I guessed he was donning a sheath. Then he was back behind me, gripping my waist as I knelt, and with one powerful move he thrust into my vagina, and I began to feel delicious tension building at my core. A light sweat sheened my skin; I raised my bottom high, causing him to slide in even deeper, and all the time his skilled hands were cupping and stroking my breasts, twisting my hardened nipples. I hated being in darkness, but at least he hadn't tied my hands . . .

Then I stopped thinking at all, because with ruthless precision he drove into me, pushing me higher, further, until I felt almost afraid at the intensity of my approaching climax. When it began, it rolled over and through me as my whole body pulsed with incredibly sweet pleasure. I felt him tense inside me and then he was there too, clutching my hips, groaning my name as he found his own release.

For a while I heard nothing but the pounding of my heart and the sound of his ragged breathing as his face rested on my shoulder. Then he eased his weight from me and gently lifted me onto the bed, while he dressed.

Afterwards he removed the blindfold and carried me over to the old armchair by the fire, where he settled me on his lap. Now I was safe to touch him, I knew, now that it was over, so I clung to him wordlessly, still dazed with the power of his lovemaking. *If only he would let me see him making love to me.* I felt suddenly bereft. It would have been easier, I thought rather desperately, if he wasn't always so tender afterwards . . . *Stop it. Stop it. Don't let him know how much you care.*

'You know,' I said, sleepily looking around, 'I was

sometimes ordered to polish the grates in here with a lump of black lead – you had to soak the black lead in water, and rub and rub. And the fire-irons as well – they were so heavy!'

'Tell me more.'

So I nestled against him, and told him about our work, and the house parties that meant yet more labour, but which I loved because I was sometimes able to watch the dancing. Then I remembered the ball to which those wounded soldiers had been invited, and I told him how sad they had looked.

Ash's hand had been stroking my hair but suddenly he was still. 'The Duke invited wounded soldiers to the Hall?'

'Yes. Yes, he did, but I think it was just for appearances – I don't think he *wanted* them there at his ball, in the slightest.'

He said softly, 'I shouldn't think he wanted them there either. The Duke was firmly of the belief that the presence of common soldiers, wounded or otherwise, would sully his ancestral home.'

I twisted in his lap to face him. 'How do you know he felt like that, Ash?'

'Because I was there when he said it.'

'You were . . .'

'Sophie.' He took my hands and he kissed them. 'Do you remember when I met you in Oxford, in 1916? I've never told you why I was there, and you've never asked. But I was there to attend an official meeting – one that the Army Medical Board had arranged with the Duke, in the town hall.'

My heart was beating very hard. *But . . . Beatrice had said that he'd come to Oxford that day to ask the Duke for money.* I nodded, my throat dry. 'What was this meeting about?'

'Some representatives of the Board wanted to ask the Duke if he would open up a wing of the Hall as a hospital for wounded soldiers – as many other landowners around the country were doing. The Duke refused. You'll be wondering,' he continued, 'why the Army Medical Board had asked me to be there, but it was partly on account of my connection to the Duke, and partly on account of the fact that I'd already had experience of the needs of injured servicemen, because—'

'You were a pilot,' I broke in.

There was a moment's silence. At last he said, 'So people have been talking, have they?'

'I heard a little,' I stammered. *From Beatrice. Oh, God, from Beatrice.*

'Servants' gossip, I suppose.' He was stroking my hand. 'I should have known . . . Yes, I was in the Royal Flying Corps. I flew planes – Sopwiths at first, then Bristol Scouts. So I was at that meeting in Oxford, and my presence there was *not* a good idea, as it turned out. The Duke and I hadn't been in touch since the summer I'd spent at the Hall as a boy. He made it plain that day in Oxford that he still couldn't stand the sight of me, and as for the hospital – well, as I've said, he was horrified by the idea of common soldiers under the hallowed roofs of Belfield Hall. I argued with him, and in front of the rather embarrassed members of the Medical Board, he ordered me never to show my face in his presence again.'

I whispered, 'I wish . . . oh, I wish you'd told me.'

He thought I meant about the meeting with the Duke; but I was talking about what he'd done in the war, as a brave fighter pilot.

I wish you hadn't left it to Beatrice to tell me. And your hands – oh, what happened to your hands? Did you really leave the Flying Corps because you were afraid, as she said?

I wanted so much to ask him all these questions, but he kissed the top of my head, then looked at his watch. 'I have to go to dinner now. But you should be comfortable.' He swept his arm around. 'There are books for you to read, and there's some cold food that James has left.' He pointed to a covered dish.

Oh, my Duke had made everything so perfect for me. I smiled up at him. 'And later, after you've come back,' I said, getting to my feet and smoothing my gown, 'it will be time for us to creep round the house in the dead of the night. Ash . . .' I hesitated. 'Are you going to tell me what we're looking for?'

'I won't be entirely sure myself until we've found it. More secrets, I'm afraid, Sophie.'

I sighed, feigning exasperation. He put his arms on my shoulders and gently pressed his forehead to mine. '*Jazz baby, you drive me wild*,' he whispered. 'By the way – did I ever tell you that on the night I came to the theatre, I thought your dancing was sublime?'

'Really?'

'Really.' His face lit up in that glorious smile of his. 'That's why I was so angry. My girl, in Cally's Chorus? I was wild with jealousy, Sophie. I didn't want anyone – anyone except me – to see you dance.'

He left and I roamed round. *My girl*, he'd said. I wandered into his palatial bathroom and his dressing room, looking at his clothes, smelling the faint, delicious scent of his soap. I lay on his bed, memorising the feel of his pillow under my cheek.

Reality returned. I was here for a purpose; everything he did had a purpose. *I want you to come with me to Belfield*, he'd told me in London. *And after that, Sophie, I will tell you things about my past that will make you turn your back on me with the contempt I deserve.*

'Never,' I whispered aloud. Never.

Chapter Eighteen

We explored the house that night when everyone was asleep, and for me it brought back vivid memories of when I was thirteen and started work here. I remembered the sheer grind of daily toil; I remembered Margaret showing me Beatrice and her American; I remembered the arrogant Lord Sydhurst, whom I hated now, because I knew he was Ash's enemy. I remembered Beatrice and her plans for me, and my devastating realisation that my Mr Maldon was the Duke, lord and master of all this.

Ash and I had slept a little, but just before one o'clock he gently woke me and we got dressed in silence. He'd explained to me earlier that he wanted to explore all the basement rooms, and so we made our way down the stairs to the lower floor with me leading the way, because this was my domain, not his.

He had a torch so we had no need to turn on any lights, and of course I knew exactly where to find everything, including – most useful of all – the full set of keys in Mr Peters's office. We went first to the records room in the basement, which was so cold that I was shivering. Ash held my hand for a moment in wordless sympathy, then he began to go through drawer after drawer of papers, quietly intent.

'I want to go up to the Duchess's apartment next,' he told me. 'Using the back stairs – the servants' stairs.'

I nodded, thinking of the Duchess at the Dower House nearly a mile away. I led him up the narrow stairs the servants used so they could scurry to and fro unseen and unheard, knowing my way instinctively in the dark to the Duchess's apartments, though I'd never, ever been inside them. Ash, too, had clearly never seen this part of the house before, but he did not waste any time in staring around as I did, but instead concentrated on an old writing desk, going through its drawers and compartments with growing frustration, and I wondered again what he could be looking for.

At last he stopped and almost slammed his hands on the desk. 'There must be something else,' he was saying half to himself. 'There must be somewhere else, where she kept everything . . .'

'I know she has another room,' I said in sudden inspiration. 'Someone once told me – it was Betsey, I think. Only the Duchess's personal maid, Miss Stanforth, was ever allowed in to clean it, never any other servants . . .'

He whirled round on me. '*Where?*'

The intensity of his expression almost frightened me. 'I've heard there's a small staircase.' I was already looking around, pulling heavy curtains aside. 'Here,' I said.

A narrow door set in the oak panelling had been half hidden by the drapery. Ash tried the handle and it was locked. But after searching through Mr Peters's keys, he found one that fitted; he told me to wait for him, and I did so, anxiously counting the minutes ticking by. But then he came back, looking triumphant. 'Sophie. Look.'

And he showed me an old dance card, and a leather-bound diary.

I didn't understand. A dance card? A diary?

He laughed at my bewilderment. 'Oh, believe me,' he said, 'I've got enough here to silence the old Duchess – for *ever* – about my claim to the dukedom.'

My eyes must have opened very wide, because he grinned and grasped my hand. 'Come on, Sophie. Let's go back to my rooms, and I'll tell you everything.'

I nestled on his big bed, while he sprawled next to me and explained. During the summer that he'd stayed here as a boy, he told me, he'd heard whispers amongst the grooms who'd befriended him that the Duchess had long ago been enamoured of another man, even while her marriage with the Duke was being arranged. 'Look at this dance card.' He held it out to me – I'd already recognised it as the kind used by ladies at formal balls, to enter their beaux's names for each dance.

'It's for the annual May ball at Winterton Abbey in Suffolk,' he went on, 'in 1882. See? The Winterton family crest is here, and the date – May the fifteenth. And there's the old Duchess's name, before she married – Lady Alison Madeley. Now, you can see – here – where the gentlemen have signed, for each dance.' He was pointing. 'The name *Belfield* crops up several times – that will be the Duke, of course, but you'll also see the initials *LT* just as often. This *LT* was clearly an admirer, but the Duke was by then her betrothed – they were due to be married in June, only a month later. Now, look at this note – folded up in her diary.'

He tipped the diary up, and out of it fell a folded sheet of expensive but faded notepaper, which he carefully spread out for me. On it was a date – 16 May 1882 – and beneath that was written, *Darling A. I will remember last night for ever.*

A for Alison, of course. Written the day after the ball – a lover's note? But, 'It could have been from the Duke,' I said. 'If they were to be married in a month.'

'It's not the Duke's handwriting,' Ash pointed out. 'Believe me, I've seen it often enough, in all the documents I've had to go through regarding the estate.'

'So this man, this *LT*, was fond of her,' I said slowly. 'It doesn't necessarily mean anything else.'

He was pushing the diary towards me. 'Look at this, Sophie. Look at the Duchess's entries for May. You'll see how she's written in all the usual social engagements, all the necessary preparations for a big society wedding – hers, to the Duke of Belfield, which must have been the wedding of the year. But look at the entry for the fifteenth of May.'

I looked closely. '*To Winterton Abbey*,' I read aloud, '*for the May ball. LT will be there, staying overnight like me. Our last chance . . .*'

That was all. I gazed up at Ash. 'You think – they spent the night together?'

'Perhaps,' he said, 'or possibly just a part of it. Long enough. It's my belief that before her marriage, the Duchess was desperately in love with this LT – so much so, that she escaped from her bedroom on the night of the May ball and went to join him, a mere month before her wedding. All right, you might say, so she had a very risky *liaison* before her marriage – does it matter?' His voice was taut with excitement. 'I would say yes; yes, it matters very much. Because Lord Charlwood was born a mere eight months after the wedding, in February 1883. An early birth, people said. But an equally likely explanation is that Charlwood was the result of that night at Winterton Abbey.'

I gazed at him. 'Ash – I always thought Lord Charlwood didn't look like the Duke!'

'Exactly. In high society there were whispers, often, while Charlwood was alive, but the rule is always discretion at all costs. And that rule won't be broken by me. Apart from having a quiet word with *her*, I'll remain silent, of course. But what I've seen here, Sophie, means I only have to mention the words *Maurice's father* for the old Duchess to keep her lips sealed for ever about my supposedly dubious claim to the dukedom.' He held those precious items tightly in his hand.

'So your inheritance is safe,' I said, nestling against him. 'I'm glad, so glad.'

But a hateful part of me was whispering, *There was just a chance, you know, that if he lost the dukedom he could have been yours. Just a chance . . .*

Then his expression changed. He went to put more coals on the slumbering fire, and then, as he came back towards me and prepared himself to speak again, I suddenly felt myself growing cold, despite the renewed warmth of the leaping flames.

'Sophie,' he said. 'I told you, back in London, that when I'd done what I needed to do here, I would tell you things about my past that would set you free from your attachment to me, for ever.'

Something caught painfully in my chest. 'No,' I said stubbornly. '*No*. Ash, you can't tell me anything that would make me consider you to be anything less than the truly brave, honourable man I know you are.' I was shivering and I hugged my arms around myself, feeling like a child terrified of the darkness beyond. *I won't ever stop loving you. Whatever you've done, not ever.*

'Listen to me,' he broke in harshly. And he told me at last, what had happened to him during the war.

'For the first two years of the conflict,' Ash said, 'I flew fighter planes, as I've told you. As you already knew, it turns out. But by 1917 I'd left the Royal Flying Corps because I'd argued with the government officials who gave us orders – amongst them Lord Sydhurst – and I've told you why: because I wasn't willing to keep quiet about ministers like Sydhurst getting their palms greased in exchange for crooked government contracts. Shortly after that, I wrote my last letter to you, then I went to join the French air force – the *Aéronautique Militaire.*'

I turned slowly to face him. I think the colour had drained from my face. 'France. But people said – people said . . .'

'That I'd fled England because I was a coward?' He smiled bitterly. 'Of course – Sydhurst and his friends were eager to blacken my name. No, I joined the French, whose air force was, incidentally, far superior to ours. And you already know that I spoke French fairly fluently.'

I was painfully tense. Why hadn't he told everyone this? Why hadn't he dispelled the vicious rumours about his cowardice?

'A few of us,' Ash went on, 'were given orders to bomb vital roads and railway junctions in Germany. But one night my plane was brought down, and I was sent to a prisoner-of-war camp called Mindhoven.'

'Was that when your hands were burnt?' I whispered. 'When you crashed?'

He nodded. 'Otherwise I was unharmed. But unfortunately the Germans were waiting for me.'

I tried to imagine what it must have been like, plunging to the earth in one of those vulnerable aeroplanes. 'So you were a prisoner.' I tried to sound as calm as he was, though the thought of him trapped in a burning plane horrified me. 'But they treated officers well, didn't they, in the camps?'

'Usually,' he answered, 'but not at Mindhoven. You see, it was run by a rogue commander, who couldn't bear the thought of defeat and was exacting revenge on all of us. We were treated badly.'

My heart lurched again. 'In what way?'

He shrugged. 'Oh, inadequate rations. Punishments. The usual.'

Punishments. Oh, my poor Ash. 'So your injuries – your burns – weren't tended as well as they should have been?'

He smiled mirthlessly. 'I won't go into details, but certain guards took pleasure in – prolonging the agony, shall we say.'

'Ash.' I leaned forward desperately. 'No one knows

anything about all this, and that's so *wrong*. At Belfield the servants used to think you'd left the country to avoid the war. They used to say that you . . . that you . . .'

'That I went off to America to make money? Believe me, it's better than the truth,' he said harshly. 'Four brave men were executed at Mindhoven – and it was my fault.'

'Four men?' I gazed at him in utter dismay. Everything was wheeling dizzyingly around me so that the room, the furniture in it, even his face were nothing but a blur as he said this. I gripped my hands together in a desperate effort to steady myself. 'But you couldn't have meant them to die. You couldn't have.'

He was gazing at me with the familiar bleak look of his that always filled me with fear for him. 'Listen to me. In my hut there were several French prisoners – pilots, like me – and they decided to begin digging a tunnel from under our hut. I couldn't help them because of my hands, but I offered to keep watch for them.'

His voice didn't change, but I noticed a chill enter his eyes. 'I betrayed them, Sophie,' he said. 'Four of them made their break for it at night. But they were stopped by the guards as they came up out of that bloody tunnel of theirs in the dark outside the camp fence. They were shot the next day, after they'd been told it was me who'd betrayed them. I was made to watch their execution. Some of them were still alive even after several bullets had hit them. One of them was only nineteen.' His voice was still steady. 'I shall never forget for as long as I live the way he looked at me before they blindfolded him. I betrayed them, and that's all you need to know.'

He spoke with such terrible finality, but it was his stillness afterwards that frightened me the most. I really thought the silence would last for ever. I wanted to say, *I believe in you, Ash. I will always believe in you.*

'I love you,' I whispered. 'I know that you are good and true.'

'No,' he breathed. 'No, you're wrong to think that, Sophie. You're wrong to waste your love on me. Because . . .'

'Because what, Ash?'

He shook his head, his eyes as dark and as savagely sad as I'd seen them. And so I simply leaned my cheek against his chest and held him tight in my arms; my poor, poor Mr Maldon, who hated himself so much; he was so beautiful, so damaged, my brave scarred man. I was half hoping, half dreading that he would tell me more, but at last, with a sigh, he moved me away a little, smiled gravely down at me, and said, 'Let's get some sleep.'

After he'd turned out the lights I lay awake in that big bed, counting the chimes that rang out every quarter-hour from the big clock down in the hallway. I'd spent so many years in this house, hearing that clock in the distance, and now here I was, in the arms of the man I loved, and I wanted that night to last for ever, so I could simply hold him.

He was sleeping, and I was glad, but once as the owls were calling outside he stirred and opened his eyes. He murmured, 'Still awake, Sophie?'

'The owls disturbed me just then, as they did you,' I

lied. 'Go back to sleep.' I smiled. 'Mr Maldon. Your Grace.'

He touched my cheek. 'I care for you, Sophie,' he said. 'You know that, don't you? Whatever happens next – you know that?'

'Yes,' I whispered, though my heart ached, because what I wanted was his love. He eased me closer to him and slept once more, and I must have fallen asleep at last, in his arms.

But suddenly he lashed out. 'Don't touch me,' he snarled. 'Don't ever touch me again, you fucking, *fucking* bitch . . .'

He jumped from the bed, wide awake now; he'd caught my cheek with his fist. I curled up away from him, shaking in the dark. His dreams. Oh, God, his dreams.

'Sophie.' He was urgently reaching for me. He gathered me up, kissing me. 'Oh, Sophie. Oh, sweetheart. Oh, God, I'm so very sorry.'

He started to tell me everything then. How at Mindhoven they'd brought in a new guard, a woman, who reported directly to the commander. Her name was Birgit and she was beautiful, in a cold sort of way, he said.

Birgit pretended at first to be on his side. 'She used to order me to come to her for questioning every day,' he told me, and I curled myself close to him with his arms around me and my face pressed close to his chest. The way he said all of this, in a flat, terrible voice in the darkness, appalled me.

'At first,' he went on, 'it was just talk. Then she would offer me coffee and cigarettes, and pretty soon came alcohol and sex. But all the time I was thinking, "If she really is on my side, perhaps I can use her to get out of here." Then one afternoon, she took me to another room behind her office and locked us both in. She'd given me vodka, lots of it, but I thought my head was clear. She handcuffed me to the wall, and I thought, "So she wants to play rough. All right, I'm stronger by far than she is. I can cope with this."'

And it was then that I felt him, my brave, strong man, start to shake. 'I couldn't cope, Sophie,' he breathed. 'She clearly enjoyed a fair amount of cruelty as far as sex was concerned – and although I wouldn't say I was eager for any of it, I could tolerate the handcuffs, and the rest of it. But that was only the start.' He closed his eyes briefly. 'I was expecting a mixture of pain and pleasure. But . . . the pain was excruciating.'

'What did she do?' I whispered.

'Look at my hands.'

'I thought you didn't like me to—'

'*Look at them.*'

With the greatest gentleness I took his right hand then his left, palms facing downwards so I could see his burns in the faint dawn light that was starting to creep through the curtains. And my stomach turned over when I saw several long silver scars cutting their way through the mottled, uneven skin.

'She did that?' I could scarcely speak.

'She did that,' he answered in a flat voice. 'I shan't go into tedious details, but she had various . . . implements in her room, amongst them a selection of whips made with thin wires. She used to whip my hands.'

But the flesh must have scarcely begun to heal from his burns. 'Oh, dear God in heaven,' I breathed.

'Then she would give me more vodka, and when I was almost on my knees, she would seduce me – if you can call it that. And the sex was intense. She could judge my limits pretty well; she knew that after a certain point an entire Turkish bordello wouldn't be able to rouse me, but she took care never to push me that far. She was damaged, badly damaged; she knew how to inflict pain, acutely so. I think in her mind the pain was inseparable from sexual pleasure; she tried, each day and night, to lower me to the same depths as her, then she would arouse me again. She relished my pain, she relished my pleasure, she bound me and then she would touch me all the time, greedy for me.'

'You mentioned day and night,' I interrupted. 'Did she keep you locked in there, Ash?'

'No, she wanted information from me about the other prisoners, so I was often back at the hut with the rest of them. But the guards would drag me again to Birgit whenever the fancy took her, you could say, and they helped her to strap me down, or suspended me in hand-cuffs from the wall. The other prisoners thought she was out to get information from me about the Royal Flying Corps.'

I closed my eyes briefly. 'You must have hated her.'

'Perhaps. But the person I truly loathed was myself, because she was still able to arouse me.'

I tried desperately to stay calm. 'What else did she do?'

'The usual. She flogged me. She put clamps on me.

273

She . . . inserted objects into me.' I heard him give a dismissive breath. 'The sort of things you'd pay for in a seedy London brothel, only ten times worse. I'm sorry, Sophie – all this must disgust you.'

I shook my head fiercely. '*No,* Ash. I'm not a child. So she did all this – and you said it was to get information from you about the other prisoners?'

'That was part of it, of course. Those were her orders – to find out about any plans for escape. But the truth was, she was simply a sadist, and I thought she might damned well kill me. I would be strapped on the leather couch she had in there, and for the first time in my life I felt completely helpless. I couldn't fight back, I couldn't control my own body. Then – ' he clenched his hands – '*then* she told me that all the other guards had been taking it in turns to watch the two of us, through a concealed window. She told me they found our sexual activities amusing. *Where is the tunnel?* she would say. She and the other guards had already got wind of the escape plan, you see. *When do they plan to break out?*'

I started to kiss him, because my heart was breaking for him and it was all I could think of, all I could offer. 'I love you, Ash,' I whispered again, 'I love you. You are beautiful and brave and good. I know you're no coward, and those poor, poor men who died must have known it too, they must have.'

'Not when they saw me led out by Birgit to watch them being shot.'

'They would realise you must have been under quite unbearable pressure,' I emphasised. 'And I would kill the woman Birgit if I could!'

He gave a sort of gasp, then he caught me up in his arms and I realised he was laughing softly. 'Oh, Sophie, sweetheart. I do believe you would. I love you, and I want you, so very very much.'

I think my heart stood still then. 'You do?'

'I do.' He was tenderly tucking my hair behind my ears. 'I do, I do. Your letters – oh, Sophie, your letters . . .'

I felt hot, remembering my childish missives. 'They were foolish,' I said quickly. 'I was so young. I was so stupid.'

'*No*. Listen, Sophie. When I was released from Mindhoven, at the end of the war, I was bitter and damaged – I'd almost ceased to believe the world had any goodness left in it. But your letters were waiting for me in London. I read them,' he went on steadily. 'I've told you that. But what I've not told you is that your sweet innocence, your loyalty, your absolute trust in me – they reminded me of better things, of a better life. I went on to America because I thought my future lay there. But I kept your letters. I never stopped thinking about you, ever.'

'All this time,' I breathed. 'All this time.'

Suddenly I twisted to face him, lifting one leg so I straddled his thighs. I kissed him, I kissed him deeply and slowly, and as I felt him slipping down the straps of my nightgown and cupping my breasts, I felt them grow heavy and their peaks tighten unbearably. I was still kissing him; I sucked on his tongue so he moaned, then I pulled away and breathed, 'I want you, Ash. I want you to make love to me now. This minute.'

I could feel his erection, rearing hard and thick against

275

my abdomen. Desperation was clawing at me. 'You can blindfold me,' I added quickly. 'You can tie me. I understand now – it's because of *her*, isn't it? – and those guards who watched you. You need to be in control, you can't bear to be looked at, and *I don't mind.*'

I waited. But he didn't make any move to cover my eyes or restrain me. Instead he tipped up my chin with his finger and kissed me, then he slowly pulled off my nightgown. *His eyes, oh, God, his eyes;* I could feel tongues of fire wherever his eyes rested, and between my legs I was desperate for his touch.

He stroked his scarred hand over my breast and my ribs. He said huskily, 'Are you wet for me, Sophie?'

I groaned in answer, my pulse racing as I sat facing him, kneeling with my legs spread over his heavily muscled thighs. He was still in his pyjamas, but I ran my hands down the sides of his powerful lean torso and started to undo the buttons of his top. A shudder ran through him, but . . . *he didn't push me away*. Gathering courage, I pushed the garment apart and pressed my mouth to his chest, kissing and soothing, finding one flat nipple and tugging it gently with my lips.

He let out a low oath, but it was a sound of need, not of horror. Still astride him, I started easing down his pyjama trousers so our naked bodies met, and his stiffened penis was pressing tantalisingly along the moist folds of my sex. All the while the tension inside me was unfurling unbearably. Then he cupped my bottom with his strong hands and lifted me over him then lowered me, so I could feel his erection surge up inside me, filling me, making me cry out his name aloud.

I flung my arms around his neck. I rubbed my naked breasts against his chest; I was gasping for breath as he thrust his length into me, again and again. My legs were still spread wide, and suddenly I felt his palm grinding deliciously against my exposed sex; my eyes met and held his burning gaze, and my climax roared through me as he pounded into me. Only when I'd finished, when I could take no more, did he pull me down to his side and pump his seed over my thighs, the pearly liquid glistening on my skin, while his face was tense with pleasure. I was stunned. I was shaking.

He'd let me look at him. He'd let me touch him.

I didn't want a single clumsy word of mine to spoil this moment. I'd stopped moving, breathing even; I simply leaned my cheek against his hard chest with my eyes closed, my arms clasped round him, and I felt his arms around me.

'Sophie,' he said quietly.

I looked up, almost afraid.

'Thank you.' He kissed the tip of my nose, then my eyelids; he pressed my face to his, so our foreheads were touching.

'Any time.' I held him tightly.

'Don't leave me,' he breathed.

Oh, Ash. Oh, my darling. 'Never,' I said steadily.

We left Belfield Hall that day. How did I get out without being seen? It was simple, really; it turned out that Ash had ordered all the staff to be outside at ten to have their photograph taken, which was quite a ceremony. A dozen chairs were brought out for the more

277

senior members of the staff – Mr Peters, Mrs Burdett and Cook – and the older housemaids and footmen sat on either side of them while the others stood behind, all except for the boot boys and the youngest of the grooms, who sat cross-legged in front of them. James had brought the photographer from Oxford to the Hall, and everyone folded their arms and looked very solemn, apart from a cheeky boot boy who grinned away at the camera. The framed photograph is still on the wall, in the servants' hall.

So while they were all outside I slipped down the servants' stairs to the rear courtyard, where James was waiting for me with the car. I jumped in the back, and ducked low; I think James found it all a huge joke, which reassured me. Then he took me to Oxford, to the hotel where Ash and I had stayed, and I was served coffee and tiny cakes in the private sitting room, just like a lady.

Ash arrived an hour later, with James. We drove back to London, and Ash was very quiet, but he kept his arm around me. My heart was full. Mine. He was my Mr Maldon. But what now?

The answer to my question came soon enough. When we turned into Hertford Street there were photographers everywhere; they were clustered around Ash's house, perching on railings, almost clambering on one another's shoulders in their eagerness as the car rolled up.

James was swearing under his breath. 'Damned journalists. What shall I do, Your Grace? Run the bastards over?'

I was afraid it was because of me, but I was wrong – though it took me a few moments to absorb what they were actually saying. They were calling out, 'Your Grace, there are rumours that you once had an affair with Lady Beatrice. Are the rumours true?'

I looked at them wildly, then at Ash. There had been some terrible mistake, surely. Ash could just tell them they were wrong. Couldn't he? *Couldn't he?*

Why didn't he speak?

Ash looked calm but pale. He said, 'Back up, James. Get us out of here. We'll go and stay at a hotel for the night.'

Chapter Nineteen

James drove us to a hotel in Belgravia, and Ash still said nothing to me, but once he'd settled me in our private sitting room I heard him on the phone in the bedroom, and he sounded so angry. He was talking to the newspaper editors, I gathered, and then he was ringing someone else. I heard him say her name – he was ringing Beatrice.

Then he came back to me. He must have seen my expression.

'Sophie,' he said.

I was slowly backing away from him, my hands outstretched to ward him off. 'You were speaking to Lady Beatrice.'

'Sophie. Listen . . .'

I shook my head. 'It's true, isn't it?' He was coming closer but I pushed him away, trembling. 'You and her. You and her, years ago.' I felt quite sick; I was looking back through *everything* in the new knowledge that she and he had been lovers – when? Before I'd even met him?

'Listen.' He sounded desperate. 'I can't think of anything to say that will make it better for you. But the Press are my enemy, because they're hand-in-glove with Sydhurst. Even so, I can't deny that what they were saying is basically true.'

My brain was reeling; bile was rising in my throat. I whispered, 'Was it . . . was it when she was married to Lord Charlwood?' I didn't really want to know any more, but I couldn't stop the words tumbling out.

He dragged his hand through his hair. 'It was when she was married to Lord Charlwood, yes. She was never much of a one for loyalty, was Beatrice. We happened to be both in London, and it really meant very little to either of us. She was bored with Maurice, and I had no reason to feel any sense of loyalty to him. But since then, as you know, Beatrice's ambitions began to focus on me rather more, chiefly because I'd inherited the dukedom. I told her I wasn't interested. And now she's getting her revenge.'

Ash and Beatrice. Beatrice and Ash. He tried to touch my shoulder but I broke away like a cornered animal.

'There's worse to come,' he said flatly. 'Beatrice has apparently been telling the Press about you and me – including the fact that your mother was briefly Lord Charlwood's mistress when you were a girl. I'm afraid it will make life difficult for you, Sophie—'

'Not for me,' I broke in. I'd drawn myself to my full height; I think every part of me was filled now with dreadful certainty. 'Ash, I must leave you. This is . . . *impossible.*'

He looked frozen. 'You promised you would stay.'

'That was before all this. This has made me realise that I've got to leave you, for your sake as well as mine. I've realised that I can't simply erase everything that's gone before – my poverty, my mother's disgrace. It's no good. I don't fit into your world. I'll always be a liability to you.' I was already walking towards the door, but I stopped and turned. 'Ash, you must defend yourself against the wicked rumours that you were a coward. If people knew that you'd been shot down and were a prisoner of war – if they knew how you'd suffered in that camp . . .'

His reply was swift and sharp. 'I've told you, I won't lower myself to their level.' Suddenly he came closer to me and cradled me against his body, and in a terrifying moment of weakness I let him. 'Listen,' he said more softly. 'Listen. Forget about Beatrice and me – it meant nothing, to either of us. And it doesn't matter a damn about your past. I will protect you. Sophie, you must believe in me – I beg you.'

Oh, God, I couldn't bear this. His story of the war last night had both shocked and grieved me, yet had in no way harmed my love for him – rather the contrary. I had agreed to continue being his mistress, lowly as I was. But he and Beatrice. He and Beatrice . . .

The shock of it had reminded me of everything else that widened the gulf between us. Of the vicious gossip that would flare and burn and torment him repeatedly if I stayed in his life, exactly as Beatrice had warned me; of the way the Press, encouraged by men like Sydhurst, would always be probing his defences.

I was a weakness he couldn't afford. 'I'm sorry,' I whispered.

And I left.

As before, I found a room to let, this time near St Pancras where lodgings were cheap. Once I was there I scarcely glanced at my surroundings but sank down on the little bed and clasped my arms around myself.

I could hear Beatrice's bright, brittle voice ringing in my ears, that time at Belfield Hall when I'd asked her in my naivety if she'd met him. 'Oh,' she'd said, 'I met him briefly a few years ago in London . . .'

Then a pause. That long, lingering pause. Oh, God, what a fool I'd been not to have guessed. How Beatrice must have laughed at my stupidity. I had to find a job again, I had to earn my living somehow. But first . . . I had to see her.

She'd told me she was staying at Claridge's Hotel, so I hailed a taxicab to Brook Street. How I had changed, I reflected bitterly, as I paid the driver and nodded haughtily to the top-hatted doorman at the hotel's entrance when he held open the door for me. How I had changed, from the shy little scullery maid I had once been.

Inside the hotel's smart foyer the staff called me 'madam', and someone rang up to see if Lady Beatrice would receive me. The answer must have been yes, for a liveried manservant escorted me immediately to Beatrice's suite on the first floor. On the way we passed a maid, who stood back with her eyes lowered to let me pass, and I thought, *I used to be like you.* Almost I wished I still was.

Beatrice opened the door. 'Sophie.' She looked me up and down, then beckoned me in.

'You must have been expecting me,' I said steadily. 'After what you've done.'

She sat down and pointed to a seat opposite her. 'My,'

she said, 'you're quite the young lady now, aren't you? I hope you've enjoyed yourself with Ash, Sophie my dear. Because you could never have kept him – you realise that, don't you? "The Duke and the chorus girl who was once a scullery maid" – imagine if that particular story were to escape.'

I ignored her. 'Why didn't you tell me you'd had an affair with him? *Why?*'

'Perhaps because I didn't really see that it was any of your business.' Her tone had changed; suddenly she rose, walked to the window then turned on me sharply. 'As for you, don't try to preach to me about truth and honesty. At Belfield Hall you tricked me utterly, with your pretence of leaving him. Yet here you are now, his slut . . .'

I too had got to my feet. 'At Belfield Hall you pretended you hardly knew him. You let me think his burns were most likely the result of a motorcar accident. Even when we talked about him in London, and you admitted he'd flown aeroplanes in the war, you made out that he'd hardly been in any danger. But he went on to fly for the French, and was shot down and taken prisoner. You made out that he was a coward – how could you?'

'My, my.' She drew on her cigarette. 'He *has* been opening his heart to you. And yes, I have heard that he didn't have the easiest of times for a while – but as soon as he could, he travelled straight to America rather than return to England again. Don't you find that odd?'

'The war was over,' I cried. 'The war was *over* by the time he went to America. And in the prison camp, he suffered terribly. The things they did . . .'

'So you think he's a hero?' she mused. 'Then explain this to me – why on earth doesn't he tell everyone about his oh-so-daring adventures with the French air force?'

I caught my breath, remembering what he'd said to me. *I betrayed them, Sophie.* 'Because he'd rather forget the past,' I said. 'He'd rather forget *you*, that's for sure.' She repelled me so much now with her expensive scent and her cigarettes that I was finding it hard to stay in the same room as her.

'Poor Sophie.' She spoke mockingly. 'There you were, thinking you could hold on to the new Duke of Belfield, when your experience ranges from the role of scullery maid to playing the whore in Cally's Chorus Line.' She paused to stub out her cigarette then went on thoughtfully, 'For a while I gave Ash exactly what he wanted.' She smiled. 'Sensual heights, sensual depths – dear little Sophie, you've no idea – and I enjoyed his rather astonishing virility. It's quite true that once my tedious husband was out of the way, I wanted to be his wife – but not any longer, since he's somewhat diminished himself by his dalliance with you.'

'You're wrong, as usual. Because I've left him.'

Her head jerked up. Her eyes narrowed.

'It's true,' I said shortly. 'And I'm going now. I just wanted you to realise that your stories about his cowardice are utterly false.' I turned to make for the door.

'Did he give you a good pay-off?' she called. 'I hope so, because how else are you going to live? Will you be selling off your memoirs, *My Lover the Duke*? No, of course not, because you still think you love him, don't you? And if that's really so, then you'd be as well to remember, Sophie, that he's losing money hand over fist with those precious coal mines of his – hasn't he told you?'

I turned back to her slowly.

She smiled. 'Oh, my dear, I don't suppose he discussed his . . . business affairs with you – you're for entertainment, that's all. But you ought to know that his Midlands mines could bankrupt the entire Belfield estate. He should have done what the other owners did and either sell them off or shut them down, just as soon as the government passed them back to him – they're a poisoned chalice.'

'He has money,' I broke in. 'Money of his own.'

'Ah, but he's already spent most of that on setting Belfield Hall to rights. It's an expensive business, having an estate to run.' She paused. 'There is an obvious solution open to him, and he knows it. He needs, more than ever, to make a rich marriage. Admittedly that will be easier for him, now that you say you're out of his life. But you'll have to pray the Press don't find out about your friend Cora. Oh, my.' Her eyes glittered. 'I can just see the headlines: "Duke has affair with chorus girl whose former roommate is a sensation in Soho" . . .'

I felt the blood leave my face. 'What do you mean?'

'You don't know?' She looked amused. 'Your Cora is working now at a "gentlemen's club".' She gave the words a mocking emphasis.

'How do you know? Have you been following her?'

'Not personally; I employ people for such . . . distasteful tasks. She's a dancer, I suppose – of sorts – but the ingenuity of these nightclub owners knows no bounds, my dear.'

'Where is she?' I breathed.

Beatrice lifted her painted eyebrows. 'You want to join her? Sophie, darling – to think I encouraged you in your ambitions to entertain the public! I really am quite proud of myself...You'll find her,' she concluded, 'dancing at the Club Paradis.'

I slammed the door on her and hurried outside.

That evening I headed east to darker streets, where men and women loitered outside the bars and beggars lurked in doorways. Times were getting hard again in London and many were out of work and without a home.

I felt, as I'd done several times before that I was being followed, but when I swung round I was accosted by a gaunt woman with bold lipstick and brash clothing and I guessed it was she who'd been at my heels. 'Looking to earn a shilling or two, love?' she grinned. 'Nice, clean gents only, mind; none of yer riff-raff . . .'

I swept on and asked the way to the Club Paradis from a lad selling newspapers, who grinned up cheekily at me. 'Next lane on yer left, darlin'.'

And so I found the painted sign saying *Club Paradis*, above a picture of some dancing girls. There was a door that was half open, and from it a stairway led downwards. Though it was quite early in the evening, there was already a heavy smell of spirits and the air was thick with cigarette smoke. Men lounged at tables, and waitresses hurried between them serving drinks; waitresses who were either young, or pretended they were, in short black skirts and low tops in garish colours like scarlet and jade. On their feet were little high-heeled ankle boots, over black stockings.

My heart sank.

I suddenly realised that a man in a shabby brass-buttoned coat was hurrying over in my direction – some kind of doorman, I suspected, but at the same time a woman dressed like a waitress but lounging at the bar spotted me. She put down her drink and came over to say to the man, 'Leave this one to me, Fred.' She looked me up and down. 'What's your business, then?'

'I'm looking for a job. As a dancer,' I said.

'You've got experience?'

'Yes.'

She inspected me anew, curious. The man she'd been talking to at the bar had followed her, slightly unsteady on his feet. He pawed at her. 'Aw, c'mon, Susie. I've only half an hour before I'm expected back home.'

He was holding some crumpled bank notes in front of her but she waved him aside impatiently. 'In a moment, right?' Then she turned back to me. 'Come on. I'll take you to meet Mr O'Rourke.'

I followed her towards another door where I waited outside; although I could hear her voice and that of a man from within, I couldn't make out what they were saying. Moments later she was back, gesturing towards the open door. 'He'll see you now.'

She left and I went in, a little blinded by the light. Mr O'Rourke, blond and in his early thirties and presumably the owner, had got up from his chair behind a desk and was strolling towards me, his sharp eyes scouring me.

'Susie tells me you're a dancer,' he said in an East

London accent. 'As it happens, I need a few more girls for tonight – can you oblige? Chorus-line work, that's all.' He thrust his hands in his pockets. 'I'll put you on the back row for starters – you should pick up the steps quickly enough. Oh, and I pay five bob an hour.' He looked at me expectantly.

'I'll do it,' I said.

'Good girl.' He grinned. 'You'd better get changed. The show starts in half an hour.'

He took me to the dressing room. All the rooms back-stage at Cally's were cluttered but basically clean, whereas this one had heaps of stuff everywhere; pots of old make-up littered the dressing tables, and the air smelt of cigarettes and stale clothes.

Mr O'Rourke introduced me to the dressing assist-ant, whose name was Sal. Sal was a hard-looking woman, forty or so, with a red gash of lipstick and blonde-dyed hair. She eyed me suspiciously. 'New, eh? Precious little time they give me to get stuff together for you . . .' She muttered on, sweeping round the piles of clothes that lay heaped everywhere, picking things up seemingly at random. 'Here you are. This lot should fit.'

I inspected what she'd given me – a black brassiere, a pair of harem pants in black also, and a long gauzy veil. My face must have expressed my bewilderment. 'What are these?'

She was already turning to go. 'We've got a party in tonight – Turkish is the theme. Where in the name of the holy saints did they find *you?* Get the stuff on and don't look so bloomin' shocked.'

I got changed quickly, but my fingers were shaking.

There was no sign of Cora, but perhaps it was her evening off. Or perhaps Beatrice had been lying again – that was more than likely. Oh, God.

Mr O'Rourke came to lean against the door while we were still changing; no one else seemed to care that he was there, but I clutched my veil tightly over my breasts as his eyes rested speculatively on me. 'We've got a party of rich folks in tonight,' he announced to everyone. 'So you know what's expected. What's expected, girls?'

'Entertainment, Mr O'Rourke!'

'Fun, Mr O'Rourke!'

'That's the idea. Lots and lots of saucy fun. Oh, and get your tits on show, all of you – don't be shy.' He was looking at me again; he was smiling, but I thought he had a sharp face, a mean face, like a ferret.

'Well, well,' he said. 'Welcome to the Club Paradis, Sophie.' Suddenly he turned back to his dancers. 'Come on, girls, you've just had your tea break! Twenty minutes to go, then you're on stage – and kick those saucy legs of yours for the punters, or I'll break 'em for you.' He turned to Sal, then pointed at me. 'Sal, get this newcomer looking a bit less like she's just come from a convent, will you? She's taking Cora's place.'

'I'll be back in a moment,' Sal told me curtly and hurried off, but I stood there, frozen. *Taking Cora's place.* So Beatrice hadn't lied. But had Cora left? Or was she still here somewhere?

Sal came back to me to pull down my harem pants so my stomach was exposed, and tighten my black brassiere so my breasts were shamelessly thrust up, like those of the other girls. Then she shoved a sort of belt at me – it was made of silken cords, with small silver bells sewn into it that jangled at the lightest touch. An empty pouch, like a small purse, was attached to it. I silently vowed to loosen the brassiere and pull up my harem pants again the minute she was gone and I held the belt at arm's length. 'What's this for?'

'Gettin' fussy now, are we? It's for tying round your middle, of course.' Sal was clipping some cheap gilt bangles on my wrists. 'And the purse is for the coins the gents'll give you when you dance for them.'

My pulse faltered. 'When I . . . ?'

She rolled her eyes. 'Put the thing on, for Christ's sake, or Mr O'Rourke will have your guts for fucking garters. Believe me, darling, no one else objects.'

I tied the girdle and purse round my waist with a sinking, sinking heart.

Within twenty minutes I was lined up with the others, on stage in the Club Paradis in front of those tables full of eager men. *A private gentlemen's club*, Beatrice had said. Just as Mr O'Rourke had implied, the dance routines were simple to the point of absurdity. I'd learned them all in my first week at Cally's, and I had no trouble at all in following the music played by the small band at the side of the stage. After our act was over, I accosted one of the other dancers as we went off stage. 'Look, I heard there was a girl called Cora working here. Is she still around?'

She looked at me sideways. 'Cora, eh? Friend of yours, is she?'

I didn't answer; I repeated, 'Do you know where Cora is?'

Before she could reply, O'Rourke roared at her and she hurried off, following his voice. I saw that he was about to climb some stairs at the far end of the room and the girl was going after him, so I pulled the Turkish veil over my face and quickly followed. They were out of sight by the time I'd got to the top of the narrow staircase, but I saw a half-open door, from which faint light gleamed.

Making my way towards it, I edged inside and found myself in a softly lit room with a low stage that was curtained off. Twenty or so men were already seated at tables, with plenty of drinks – champagne bottles mostly, and whisky – set before them. I saw O'Rourke moving amongst them, talking and smiling, and I noted how these men kept glancing at the concealed stage expectantly. I pressed myself back against the wall in the shadows, realising at the same time that the band from below had moved up here also, and were starting to play some sultry jazz music.

In a corner, some of O'Rourke's dancing girls were collecting trays of drinks from a barman, so I picked up a tray of drinks and wandered round too, offering them to the customers with my face veiled. The curtain was still drawn across the stage, but the lamps were being dimmed, as though something was about to happen.

I jumped as a fat man sidled up to me and put his hand on my arm. I'd noticed him watching me earlier, when I'd danced downstairs.

'So,' he said. He was swarthy, with oiled black hair. 'New at Danny's, are you?'

'Danny's?' I breathed.

He put his hand on my arm. 'Danny O'Rourke. The

man himself,' he grinned. 'Good pal of mine, is Danny. And my, he's got an eye for the girls . . .'

Mr O'Rourke – *Danny*. Oh, how could I have been so stupid? Poor, poor Cora! I almost pushed the man away; his eyebrows shot up. 'Picky little bitch, are you—' He broke off. His eyes were on the stage. *Everyone*'s eyes were on the stage. The jazz trio had started playing some music with a Turkish rhythm, and the curtain was gliding back. The main part of the room was cast completely into darkness now, but a soft yellow light shone on the centre of the stage.

And . . . Cora was there. She wore a harem outfit just like the rest of us. Beneath her veil her face was ghastly pale despite the rouge and lipstick.

The music was erotic and dark. She began to dance, sliding off her veil while undulating her hips, and it was pitiful to see, because she was so clearly drugged. I wanted to run to her and stop her, but someone was behind me; I swung round, and Danny O'Rourke's hand was round my wrist like a vice.

'You. Who invited you up here?' he hissed.

I pushed him away and darted to the other side of the room; he glared at me, but could do nothing without interrupting the show.

Cora. Oh God, she had stopped dancing. There was a silk-covered settee at the back of the stage, and she went to recline there, in her brassiere and harem pants, with one hand behind her head as she smiled hazily down at her audience. Apart from the jazz trio, still playing that low, pulsing beat, there was a hushed silence throughout the room.

The next few minutes were so hateful I could hardly take it in. Some athletic-looking men had come on stage dressed as Turkish soldiers; they wore red waistcoats, loose trousers gathered at their ankles, and turbans. They danced well; their naked chests and arms were powerful and muscular. Then one by one they danced with poor Cora; they passed her from one to the other, while she smiled dazedly at them. They kissed her, each of them, with slow, deep kisses.

Then they laid her on the settee again.

And while the people at the tables sat in the dark drinking their champagne and whisky, and watching with avid interest, those men used her, one by one; unlacing her brassiere to cup her naked breasts, pulling down her harem pants to reveal the jewelled thong she wore, then opening their breeches and fondling themselves into full arousal before quite calmly using her in turn for their pleasure.

Cora didn't protest. I guessed she must have been ordered before she went on to smile and look happy. She sighed, she played in turn with her own breasts and with their erect male members; she took one of them in her mouth and let another man rub himself against her nipples until he ejaculated over her; all the time she was dreamy and hazed. The music played on.

London's a big, dark place, Sophie, once you lose your way. She'd said that to me, when I first moved into her little house. I remembered something else she'd once said: *All I wanted was love.*

Cora had lost her way. Oh, God. I couldn't watch any more. But I couldn't leave either; this was my fault, all my fault. I'd let her go from the safety of Ash's house in Hertford Street, and in my selfish joy at being at last with the man I loved, I'd dismissed her from my mind, when I should have been out there searching every street in London for her. Blindly I started to make my way to the stage, having, I think, some ridiculous notion of stopping all this, of rescuing her. But Danny O'Rourke had been edging gradually closer, with two of his men close behind.

'Hold her,' he rapped out to them.

'No. No.' I struggled. 'You've got to stop this. I'm taking Cora with me—'

'I'm the one who gives orders around here,' he cut in. 'And you're neither of you leaving yet. I've had an offer for you. Someone's paid a lot of money for you for the night.'

I thought with horror of the fat man. '*No . . . !*' I fought hard.

He nodded to his men again. 'Take her.'

I struggled all the way as they dragged me to the foyer. And there, waiting for me, was . . . Ash.

Chapter Twenty

He simply stood there as I was brought to him. He looked relaxed and spectacularly handsome with his thick brown hair and smooth-shaven, sculpted features. He was wearing a long dark overcoat that hung open, and beneath it he wore an immaculate white shirt with a tie as usual and black trousers.

But when he looked at me, I saw something that utterly chilled me in his blue eyes. I stammered a little as I began to say, 'I came for Cora. How did you know . . .'

He spoke to me so O'Rourke couldn't hear. 'James was following you.' Then he swung round to O'Rourke and said with authority, 'I've told you, I'll take both of them. This one here and the other one – the girl who was on the stage.'

O'Rourke almost laughed. 'The other one? Cora? Oh, no, no, sorry. She's in the middle of her act still.'

'I want both of them,' Ash said with deadly emphasis.

'But—'

'Believe me,' said Ash, 'I'll make it worth your while.'

O'Rourke hurried off. I turned to Ash, my blood heated with shame because of my costume and what I'd just seen. 'We're not going with you,' I said.

He took me by my shoulders and I thought he was

going to shake me. He said, in a harsh voice, 'Don't be a bloody fool. Do you really want to see your friend Cora go through all that again? She's due for the midnight show. There are more men arriving to see her this very minute. Did you intend to follow in her footsteps? Because that's what it damned well looks like, Sophie.' As he gestured at my flimsy outfit, his mouth curled with what I could only take for contempt.

'Cora,' I whispered. 'I had to help Cora.'

'Then let's get on with helping her,' he snapped. 'When she arrives, take her to the dressing room, or wherever it is you get changed, and both of you, put something warm on. I'll be waiting for you here. But be quick.'

I saw that one of O'Rourke's assistants had brought Cora to the far end of the hall, so I hurried over to my poor friend. 'Sophie!' she murmured, blinking in confusion. 'What are you – why are you . . . ?'

Swiftly I led her towards that mess of a dressing room. Cora was stumbling and exhausted. 'Danny,' she kept whispering to me brokenly. 'Sophie, Danny came back to me. He told me he loved me . . .'

I briefly held her close, then once in the dressing room I hunted for her coat and mine, and we just pulled them on over our costumes. There was no time for either of us to change fully – we needed to get out of there. That sultry music still played in the distance; no doubt some other poor girl would be on that stage dancing for them now. Sal came in to see if there was anything else we needed, feigning concern but really she was spying on us. I pushed her away and helped Cora on with her shoes – oh, God, the bruises on her legs, her breasts.

'Poor, poor Cora,' I whispered. She was weeping helplessly by then and I held her close. 'There, there, it's all right.' For a short while we were untouchable, because Ash had bought us both – whether for good or ill I didn't know, and I didn't have time to consider it, because I had to get Cora out of there. Away from Danny, the man she thought she loved.

We had our coats and shoes on, and I was clutching the dress I'd come in; I'd no idea where Cora's clothes were, but I wasn't going to waste a moment looking. I held Cora tightly as we went back to where Ash was waiting calmly still, his arms folded across his chest. And I wanted him. Oh, God, in all my fear and all my shame, my whole body was aroused and sensitised and I wanted him. Danny pretended to be bowing and scraping as he handed us over to him.

'When you bring them back tomorrow, sir,' Danny was saying, 'you might like to try some of our more sophisticated girls. You'll understand, I hope, that these two are rather inexperienced—'

'I'm not bringing them back,' Ash cut in.

'Now wait a moment. That's against the house rules—'

'Be damned to your rules,' said Ash. He turned towards the door, gesturing to us to go in front of him.

Danny tried to block our way. 'Now, look.' His voice had changed to a snarl. 'If you think you can just walk off with my girls . . .'

Ash looked down at him with contempt. 'I've paid you for them.'

'Only for one night.' Danny, starting to flush with anger, was beckoning to some of his doormen. 'There are rules in this establishment, and you're damned well breaking them.'

'Then I'll break another one while I'm at it,' said Ash, and he punched him on the jaw. Danny stumbled to the floor, his hand to his bleeding mouth. Ash's eyes were blazing with fury. 'Be glad I let you off lightly this time, O'Rourke,' he said. 'You bastard.' Then he turned and saw Cora and me shivering there. 'Come with me,' he said. 'My car's outside.'

I heard O'Rourke behind us, shouting to his men. 'Fetch the Press. I know that man, I've seen him before. We need the Press; I want them to see His fucking Grace going off with two lowlife tarts in tow . . .'

Ash was pulling me by the arm. 'Sophie. Hurry, for God's sake.'

But I couldn't move. I saw it happening in my mind's eye: the journalists gathered again round Ash's mansion in Hertford Street, the gossips agog. *The Duke of Belfield visits Soho club and hires private dancers . . .* I started backing away. I couldn't do this to him. I couldn't.

Ash grabbed my wrist. 'I can deal with this, Sophie,' he told me forcefully. 'Come with me. *Now.*'

I clutched poor Cora closer. I said to him, 'Oh, Ash, I've just forgotten something. Will you wait for us outside in your car? Two minutes. We'll be two minutes.'

I dragged Cora back down to the dressing room again, where I'd noticed earlier that there was another

299

door, a fire escape. Cora was confused. 'Oh, Sophie. That was your man, wasn't it? Your lovely, lovely man. The Duke. Aren't we going away with him?'

'No.' I bundled her through the door and up the grimy outside stairs to the street at the back of the building. 'No, we're not, Cora. We're on our own now, do you understand? We're on our own.'

So my life moved onwards, and once more it was Cora and me, in London together again.

Those first days reminded me of when I came here from Belfield Hall last autumn, and found myself all alone in this big, busy city. Cora was ill for several days, but I nursed her in my little room where the trains rattled by night and day. I had failed my mother, I had failed Ash. I would *not* fail Cora.

'Sophie,' she murmured one day. 'Sophie, have you been to see your man to explain that you were only at Danny's because you were looking for me?'

Something in my face must have warned her.

'Oh,' she whispered. 'You haven't. And it's truly over. You must be so very sad . . .'

'No,' I said quickly, trying desperately not to let my smile break. I took her hand and squeezed it. 'No, it's all right, really, Cora. I'm no good for him.'

'You're just what he needs,' Cora said quietly. 'Sophie, I'm so sorry.'

A week after I'd found her at Danny's, Cora was strong enough to go out, and I still had a little money left, so we went, not to the Lyons' Corner House as we sometimes used to, but to the Ritz, for afternoon tea. Cora's spirits visibly lifted as we took the bus down to Piccadilly. It was May by then, the sun was shining, the plane trees were coming into leaf and the pigeons were strutting and cooing in the London squares.

Cora was very nervous as we entered the Ritz; I think she half expected to be thrown out, but after the waiter had served us and she realised no one beside the staff had paid us the slightest bit of attention, she was soon chattering in her old, optimistic way.

'Perhaps we'll both get jobs as chorus girls again, Sophie. Or maybe we'll find ourselves some nice, ordinary men – the kind who go to work in an office every day and come back to their wife and children . . .'

Then I realised she was shaking. Unshed tears filled her eyes. 'Cora,' I said softly, 'we'll get over it, both of us.'

'But Sophie. Your Duke!'

I took her hand. 'I always knew it couldn't last, with Ash.'

'Oh, Sophie. He came to Danny's for you. He loves you, he must love you! He'll be back . . . won't he?'

I tried to smile. 'He did enough damage to his reputation by stooping to take me for his mistress just for a short while.'

Cora said fiercely, 'He thumped Danny for you. Yet you think he doesn't care? He'd have taken on the whole blooming lot of them that night, sweetie. For *you*.'

'Yes,' I whispered as a sudden dark, wild longing for my man surged through me. 'Yes, he would have done, I believe. But I had to leave him, Cora. It really is for the best.'

She heaved a sigh. 'So what shall we do now? What are you going to do? Will you dance again?'

I shook my head, knowing that Ash hated me dancing on stage.

'I know!' Cora's face lit up. 'We could both go into service in a grand house. They say it's so much better being a maid these days, especially in London – you get proper wages, and more time off. Or we could work in a hotel and meet lots of rich men!'

We chatted, we fantasised about impossible jobs. I did it to cheer Cora up.

And then I became aware of some marvellous music drifting through the air. Cora had heard it too, the eloquent notes of a saxophone, and quickly she was on her feet, peering through a half-open door to a wide, airy room adjoining ours, with clusters of potted palm trees set around a polished dance floor.

'Benedict,' she exclaimed delightedly. 'Sophie, it's Benedict and his band!'

Benedict – our kind neighbour in Bayswater. Eagerly we hurried through. The dance floor was crowded; the band was playing 'Any Time's Kissing Time', and Benedict was in the middle of a thrilling saxophone solo. We clapped loudly when the music ended and he caught sight of us, waving to us in delight. 'My favourite girls!' he called. 'Let's see you strut your stuff!'

Almost immediately he swung round to his band again, this time to conduct, and they briskly started on 'Tiger Rag'.

'Come on, Sophie!' cried Cora. 'Let's show them what we can do!'

As I said, the dance floor was almost full. But when Cora and I began a lively two-step, everyone else drew back to stand amongst the palm trees, and watch us with increasing delight.

Benedict kept glancing at us too as he conducted, a big grin on his face when he realised the impact we were making. My heart was thrumming with pleasure as I danced – *oh, this was the way to forget my troubles.* When it was over our audience burst into rapturous applause and Benedict insisted we come up to share it. 'Ladies and gentlemen,' he was calling. 'Two of the best dancers in London – let's hear it for Cora and Sophie!'

Cora and I made little bobs of curtseys, then Benedict took my hand and urged in my ear, 'Sing. Go on, Sophie. I mean it – I used to hear you singing when you lived next door to me in Bayswater. Just tell me what you want the band to play.'

I hesitated. Then: 'Jazz Baby, Be Mine,' I breathed.

He smiled and nodded. 'Here we go!'

I was nervous at first, but the band were so good, and Benedict kept looking round to smile his approval. The applause took me aback; they weren't just politely clapping, they were begging for more. But I shook my head and went to rejoin Cora, who hugged me tightly.

'You showed them!' she whispered. 'Attagirl!'

We returned to our table and poured ourselves more tea; we could see from there that Benedict and his band had started on another number, and the dance floor was filling up again. Cora started chattering away.

'Sophie?' I realised Cora was asking me something and I snapped back to attention. 'Sophie, you're not even listening to me, are you? I was talking about your singing . . . You must stop thinking about him, your Duke. He should never have led you on so . . .'

I put my hands to my face; my throat was suddenly aching. 'I'm sorry,' I whispered. 'I'm sorry.'

Cora jumped from her chair to hug me hard. 'Oh, sweetie. You're really suffering, aren't you? Oh, my. Let's go, shall we? Let's just go.'

We were putting on our coats when Benedict appeared in front of us. 'Girls,' he said, 'are you thinking of dancing on stage again, the two of you? A friend of mine, Max, is taking his chorus troupe on a tour of the south coast resorts in summer; I could get you fixed up with him, no problem.'

I saw Cora's face glowing. 'Yes. Oh, yes please.'

'Then I'll speak to him.' He turned to me. 'Sophie? What about you?'

I shook my head. 'No more dancing for me,' I tried to say lightly.

'No? Then how about singing with my band? You were wonderful in there – those people just adored you. And you sang as if you really meant it. As if you were really in love . . .' He broke off as he caught Cora shaking her head fiercely. 'Oh, I'm sorry . . .'

'Benedict,' I said, 'I'd absolutely love to sing with your band.'

'You would?' His kind face beamed with pleasure.

'I would. I really would.'

He hugged me and grinned at us both. 'That's just wonderful. I'll give Max a ring for you, Cora, about the summer season. And as for you, Sophie, we'll discuss the details over supper tonight, shall we? Meanwhile, how about singing with the boys again? You could look on it as a kind of sealing of the contract.'

He led me back through to the dance hall, and what else could I sing but 'All I Want Is You?' When I'd finished there was absolute silence and my heart plummeted. *They didn't like it?* Then the rapturous applause began and went on and on, Cora as enthusiastic as any. Benedict blew kisses at me, and played a jazz fanfare on his saxophone.

I was a singer.

I started taking daily singing lessons from a teacher Benedict knew. 'Your voice is superb, Sophie,' Benedict assured me, 'but you need to be trained in performance techniques, you know? It's hard work on those vocal cords, singing night after night. We want yours to be a career that lasts.'

Benedict's band was, I'd discovered, fast becoming one of the most successful in London, with regular slots at the Ritz, the Dorchester and all the other most prestigious venues. He'd come far in the short time since we'd lived next door to each other in Bayswater – and so had I, since I was, for the first time in my life, paid well.

Cora joined the chorus troupe Benedict had recommended and left for Brighton; as for me, I rented a small but smart flat not far from Piccadilly. All summer and into early September I sang with Benedict's band at afternoon tea dances and expensive evening clubs, and people flocked to see me. I was a success. But I was expecting some sort of blow all the time, and finally it came. 'Some news here, Sophie,' Benedict said to me quietly one night before the band went on stage. 'I'm so sorry.'

For a moment I didn't understand. But my ignorance didn't last long, because he was holding out a page from a society newspaper.

News is arriving from New York that a young American heiress, Miss Diana Oakley, daughter of the Chicago steel tycoon Mr Ross Oakley, is shortly to be betrothed to His Grace the Duke of Belfield. Miss Oakley's father is said to be delighted with the match.

I can't remember what I said or what I did, but I think the words must have struck me like a physical blow, because I was aware of Benedict holding me, steadying me. 'Cora told me,' he said. 'About you and him. I'm so sorry to do this to you, but oh, my poor girl, they're in town, the Oakleys and their entourage, sightseeing and shopping and all the rest of it. I thought you ought to be prepared.'

Indeed, I should have been prepared. I knew Ash needed to keep the dukedom, and that all of his workers – all those miners and the others employed by the estate – needed him. But to make the Belfield inheritance prosperous again, he'd had to make huge financial investments, and Miss Diana Oakley from Chicago would doubtless provide millions.

Benedict was still trying to soothe me. 'It doesn't mean he doesn't still love you, you know, sweetheart. Anyway, look at you – you're on your way to becoming a star! You could take your pick of lots of lovely men who adore you! Including me,' he added quietly.

'I only want him, Benedict,' I whispered. 'I only ever wanted him.'

He held me tight. 'Oh, sweetheart.'

It was time for me to go on stage and sing, though my mind was in turmoil. Would his American heiress care for him? Would she bring him devotion, always, as I would have done? Oh, it was inevitable that she would love him. And the thought of him sharing the same intimacy with her that he'd shared with me was hard – no, was *impossible* – to bear.

One night soon afterwards I was booked to perform with Benedict's band at a private party in the ballroom of the Berkeley Hotel, and just before we were due to begin I peeped out as I usually did to assess the audience. All the people there were the height of elegance: the men wore evening suits and the women were in elaborate gowns and glittered with jewels. They'd all clearly enjoyed an abundance of champagne and gossip while Benedict's band had played gently in the background, but they stopped talking when I came on.

I was wearing a new gown of pink silk with narrow shoulder straps, and below it I wore pink satin lingerie, like the set Beatrice had once dressed me in, for Ash. Every day – no, every hour – there was something new to remind me of him: a colour, a lingering scent, a haunting sequence of chords. *Miss Sophie Davis sings with a broken heart*, one of the critics had written admiringly about me, and I wasn't surprised – it was true.

And that night . . . he was there. I'd sung two songs before I saw him on the fourth row, and he was gazing at me with such intensity that I missed my entry. I glimpsed poor Benedict glancing at me anxiously, then he went through a few preliminary bars again and this time I managed to come in as if nothing at all was wrong.

I was a professional, you see. And it was as well, because by then I'd realised that next to him was *her* – it had to be her, Diana, his American heiress. I knew I ought to hate her, but I couldn't. She looked so young and timid, clinging tightly to his arm, and on her other side sat a man who was presumably her father, in an expensive suit, looking unutterably smug at the thought of having caught an English duke as his prospective son-in-law.

My next song was, as ill-luck would have it, 'All I Want Is You'. No time to signal to Benedict, *Please, not this one. Please let me sing something else.* I saw Ash freeze as the familiar notes began, and his Diana turned to him, lifting her pretty little face to his austere one. She laid her dainty fingers on his scarred hand but he pulled away sharply, and she looked, just for a moment, frightened.

You are not right for him, I wanted to cry. *He's mine. He will always be mine.*

I saw Benedict watching me anxiously again; I sang 'All I Want Is You', and it ripped me apart, my audience too; I saw some of the women dabbing at their eyes with their dainty handkerchiefs. I tried so hard not to look in Ash's direction, but near the end of the song, accidentally, my eyes met his. My voice hitched and broke slightly and I was aware of Benedict glancing tensely once more in my direction.

But I smiled as if it was all part of my act, and carried on. I was a real trouper by then, you see. I carried on.

After my final song, the audience wanted an encore, but I rushed to my private dressing room before the applause was even over, and every part of me was aching so badly with grief that I think I was shaking. I sat in front of my mirror, but I didn't see my reflection; I simply gripped the edge of my dressing table and struggled for control. Soon Benedict would come in, to see if there was anything he could do. I bowed my head. *Nothing.*

The door opened and a shadow fell across the room. I glanced in the mirror and I think my heart must have stopped beating. Not Benedict, but Ash – and just at this moment I couldn't bear it.

He stood very still behind my chair, gazing at me in the mirror, and I felt weak with shock. *I should have gone with Cora, and joined that travelling dance troupe; I should have gone anywhere, done anything to avoid this . . .*

He said, 'Why did you leave me?'

I felt my chest heave with sharp, convulsive breaths. Slowly I stood up and turned to face him.

'It was for the best, Ash. You know that. I know the dukedom means more than anything to you, much as you pretend to despise it. And I have my own life to lead, my own life to get on with . . .'

My voice trailed away as he went to close the door. He came towards me again. He was kissing me. I tried, oh I tried to push him away.

'*Go.* Leave me. Please, for God's sake, get out of my life.' I wanted him more than ever, but I couldn't let him love me, I couldn't. 'Ash,' I breathed, 'this is madness, it's *always* been madness. I'm no good for you, no good at all – you have what you want, you have your heiress. Sweet Jesus, will you leave me alone, for pity's sake?'

He kissed me hard. There was no gentleness in it, no tenderness – it was a kiss of fierce possession. 'You're mine,' he said savagely.

'No.' Somehow I kept my voice steady. 'You don't mean it. You're ashamed of me.'

'*Never.*'

I broke away from him and made for the door, but he barred my way. I said bitterly, thinking of the night at O'Rourke's back in May, 'Then you should be ashamed. You've good reason to be ashamed—'

He cut in, 'You sang that song to *me*, Sophie. You saw me here and you sang that song to me. You've stolen my damned soul – and I've got yours. Haven't I? Haven't you given me your soul?'

'Yes,' I whispered back helplessly. 'Yes.'

He gathered me into his arms. 'Tell me that you love me and no one else. You will damned well tell me.'

'I love you,' I breathed. I took his scarred hands to my lips and kissed them. I began to shudder; I lifted my own face yearningly to his. He kissed me again and I couldn't resist. Oh, God, he was kissing me as if the heat of his lips and the fierceness of his thrusting tongue could erase the hurt of all that was past, and as he slid his powerful hands beneath my gown and over my breasts, I almost ignited with need. I pulled him to me, I let my hips grind helplessly against his, I could feel the power of his erection beneath his clothes.

He put me up on the dressing table then and there. He parted my thighs and I struggled with his jacket, dragging it at last off his strong shoulders. He almost ripped my gown from my breasts and suckled them; he made love to me savagely, pushing my legs wide apart, dragging aside my panties to thrust himself into my moist flesh, as my hands roved beneath his shirt, against his smooth skin, and my cries of need mounted.

I gazed up at him while he made love to me, wanting to imprint on my eyes for ever the image of his perfect, beautiful face and burning blue eyes as I spiralled help-lessly, wildly towards my climax and he joined me, pulling himself out just before the end to spill his seed over my stockinged thighs. Then he gathered me in his arms, still standing; my legs were still clasping him, my hips resting on the dressing table, as I stroked his hair and let him kiss me over and over . . .

My beautiful, scarred man. *The last time*. I knew it was the last time.

The door opened. The door opened, and there, hand in hand, stood Lady Beatrice and Diana.

Chapter Twenty-One

I was back at Belfield, the village where I'd spent my childhood, and I stood in the churchyard in the late afternoon with my hand resting on my mother's simple but beautifully carved headstone for which, all those years ago, the man I'd known then simply as Mr Maldon had paid.

Inside the church the village choir was at its weekly practice, and the faint but familiar sound of voices and organ mingled with a blackbird's song as I laid on the grave a posy of fragrant cream roses and Michaelmas daisies. I wondered what my mother would say if I could speak to her now.

I was a success, they said. I was famous. My finger-nails were painted, my fair hair was short and glossy, my clothes were lovelier by far than those Lady Beatrice had once dressed me in, when she was preparing me to seduce Ash. I'd been offered a contract by a well-known American theatre manager to sing in New York for three months, and I was sailing there with Benedict and his band in a week's time. I should have been happy.

But my heart was as cold as the stone of my mother's grave.

I could not forget my last night in London, two weeks

before. I couldn't forget Diana's face as I realised how completely innocent she was – not only a virgin but ignorant, totally, as to the reality of physical love. She'd looked so horrified to see the two of us, half naked and still in the fresh aftermath of raw passion.

I knew – because I was once like her – that she would have had sweet and girlish fancies of being in love with her Ash, her English Duke. She would have pictured him gently kissing her lips beneath soft moonlight, perhaps, and offering her gifts. She would have imagined tender murmurings, promises of eternal devotion. But never, ever would she have pictured the near savagery of our physical union, our faces still etched with the intensity of our emotions, the air still heavy with our passion-filled coupling.

By the time we'd swiftly covered ourselves, Diana had run off with a low cry – to her father, presumably. Ash had taken one look at me, rasped out, '*Wait for me,*' then pulled on his jacket and charged off after her.

Beatrice stayed in the dressing room. Beatrice had me where she wanted me. She'd said, almost licking her lips, 'You've lost everything for him now, you fool. That girl's dowry was worth millions and was going to save the entire Belfield estate. Her father will be furious – and you can be sure that all of society will hear about this *very* quickly.'

'Because you'll tell them?' I broke in. I could still feel Ash's hands on me and his body next to – *inside* – mine.

She'd shrugged. 'Why not?' A smile had curled her mouth. 'But my dear, what an education for poor little

313

Diana, seeing the two of you in the aftermath of such passion. Quite magnificent – I wish I'd arrived a few moments earlier . . .'

I was already grabbing my coat and bag, and charging blindly for the door.

'Going so soon?' I heard her calling after me. 'Perhaps it's as well. Rest assured, Sophie – you've lost him, and ruined him. Well done, you.'

I turned to leave the churchyard. From there I could glimpse Belfield Hall in the distance, rising above the lush beech woods of the valley. Tonight I would return to London by train and start making my final preparations to sail with Benedict's band to New York. There perhaps I would forget him. Perhaps.

Because of the yew trees overhanging either side of the path, he was almost upon me by the time I realised it. My footsteps faltered; I looked up at him, my eyes wide with emotion. *Ash.*

It was a warm day, so he'd taken off his jacket and slung it over one shoulder. His dark brown hair was rumpled, and there were shadows under his beautiful eyes. Pain tightened my throat. A duke? No, he was my Ash, my Mr Maldon, the man I would always love.

'I thought you were in London,' I said.

'I left London this morning.' The heavy boughs of the nearest yew cast loving shadows across his perfect profile. 'Benedict told me you were coming here, to visit your mother's grave.'

He'd searched out Benedict? No – it was probably sheer chance. Benedict's band had perhaps been playing at some hotel or party that Ash had attended. I answered, 'I came to say goodbye to her.'

'Goodbye?'

'For a while, anyway. Because – because . . .'

'Benedict said that you're going to New York.' His voice was very steady, and as he spoke I noticed his car parked nearby. No James. He was on his own.

'I've been offered a contract there, to sing.' I tried to make it sound like the most wonderful news I'd ever heard. 'You'll realise that I can't turn the chance down.'

He'd come closer. 'Not even for me?' he asked quietly.

My heart clenched. I felt dizzy. *Anything. I'd do anything for you, I'd lay down my life for you, you know that* . . . 'It's impossible,' I breathed. 'I've done you so much harm already, Ash; I've caused you to lose so much. I've already been reminded of that, so many times . . .'

He looked around the little churchyard, then back at me, steadily. 'I'm not marrying Diana,' he said.

'No.' I lifted my eyes to meet his gaze, trying so hard to sound sensible. 'No, I don't suppose I thought for a minute that you would be. After . . . after—'

He broke in, 'Incredibly enough, her father was still willing to push her into the marriage – I can only suppose he obtained a somewhat sanitised version of the events of that night. Diana, of course, was more than happy to tell me she never wished to see me again. I was wrong to have allowed her family to pursue the match so far. It's one of the worst things I've done.' Suddenly he took my hand. 'I love you, Sophie – I'll give up the damned dukedom if you'll have me.'

Oh, those tender words – *I love you.* They almost broke my heart. And marriage? Did he mean marriage? 'You mustn't give it up, Ash. You *can't.*' My voice was vibrant with emotion. 'You've fought for the dukedom, and it's yours. And you have so many people who rely on you to run the estate with sense and with justice. You are needed.'

He looked away for a moment and I realised that, like me, he was gazing at the Hall, with its windows and pediments glittering in the sun. 'I would give it all up tomorrow,' he said. 'When I heard, in America last year, that the dukedom was mine, do you know how I felt, Sophie? I felt as if a huge, a relentless burden had been laid on me. I had no desire to take its weight on my shoulders.'

'But you were *made* for responsibility and duty,' I breathed. Almost without realising it, I'd wrapped my arms round him and laid my cheek against his chest, feeling the warmth of his body through his shirt, feeling his heart steadily beating. 'The dukedom is yours, Ash; it's your obligation, and I know you will fulfil the role with great generosity and great honour.'

He put his hands on my shoulders, and moved me away from him so I could look up into his face. 'I cannot do it,' he said, 'unless I have you beside me, Sophie. As my wife.'

The sun was shining still, the familiar harmonies of the small village choir still drifted out to us, but an almost chilly breeze was stirring the old yew trees, rustling their boughs and casting shadows, this time over both of us. I remembered when I'd first seen him on the street in Oxford, when I'd run to him instinctively. *Sir. Please will you help us, sir?*

I'd known then that he was good and strong and true. I'd always known it. But . . . 'I can't,' I whispered.

'Why?' He'd gone very still. 'Don't you love me?'

'Oh, more than anything.' My voice was passionate now. 'Don't you realise that's why this is simply impossible? You need money – I would bring you nothing. And it's worse than that. You need powerful friends around you, and on your side. My low birth and past would destroy you, Ash.'

'Not if I married you,' he said. This time he'd drawn me into his arms, and he was soothing me and stroking my hair. 'If I married you, people would simply have to accept you. The world is changing, Sophie. The old ways are passing.'

'The Duchess . . .'

He smiled, for the first time. 'Can you see her face? She'd be the Dowager once we were married, and you would take precedence over her – she would probably never set foot in Belfield Hall again. And do you think I would object to *that*?' He was cradling me tenderly now, holding me against him, pressing his lips to my forehead.

'The staff,' I said desperately. 'If I were the duchess they would never accept me.'

'Of course they would. You are gracious and beautiful and generous. You would treat them fairly, and they would love you for it. We're going to make everything better for them, Sophie – all this has to come sooner or later anyway. Will you marry me? Will you?'

I gazed up at him, at the sheer desire in his blue eyes, and for a moment I let myself dream the impossible. Then I said, and my voice as well as my heart was breaking, 'I'm going to New York, Ash. I'm going to sing with Benedict's band. It's best, for both of us.'

He dragged me to him and kissed my forehead. 'Sophie. *Sophie.*' He tilted my face up with his hand, almost savagely. 'God help me, Sophie, but I meant what I said – I'll renounce the dukedom if you don't say yes. I fell in love with you the night I arrived at Belfield Hall. When I saw you there, in that vast and empty dining room, everything fell into place – the letters you'd written, your faith in me. And you were so beautiful, so incredibly beautiful . . . Oh, Sophie.' He looked suddenly into the distance, at Belfield Hall, then turned back to me. 'I'll follow you to America,' he said, 'and make myself a fresh fortune out there and come courting you again. I'll keep asking you; you'll not know a moment's peace, until—'

I put my finger to his lips. 'They need you *here*, darling Ash. Here.'

He was silent. We held each other tightly. Then I pulled away. 'I must go now,' I said, suddenly afraid my self-control was going to shatter at last.

His arms fell to his sides. The sadness in his eyes haunted me; would always haunt me. He said, quietly, 'Very well. I'll drive you back to Oxford.'

'No. No, I have a taxicab waiting, in the village.'

'When do you sail?'

'In a week,' I whispered. 'From Southampton.'

'I'll look for news of you,' he said. 'Taking America by storm. And someday, perhaps . . .'

I put my finger to his lips again. I tried to smile so he wouldn't see how my heart was breaking in two, how the happy song of the blackbird in a nearby tree was tearing me apart. 'Some day, perhaps,' I said. I could see that the big doors of the church were swinging open now, and the members of the choir, their practice finished, were coming out into the sunshine, chattering and smiling. Soon they would see us here.

I started towards the gate. 'Goodbye, Ash.'

He didn't try to follow me. I walked away, to my new life, and he was letting me go.

All I ever wanted was you. Oh, my love. My only love.

About the Author

Elizabeth Anthony discovered historical novels early in her teens. After graduating from Nottingham University she worked as a tutor in English Studies, but always dreamed of writing. Her ambition was fulfilled with the publication of an eighteenth-century thriller, received with great acclaim in the UK and US and translated into nine languages. She has also written erotica and several Regency romances. Elizabeth lives with her husband in the Derbyshire Peak District.

Reading Guide

1. Why do you think Sophie could not forget Ash, even after he stopped writing her letters?

2. What role did Will play in the story? Do you think Sophie should have considered him more as an option for her future?

3. Do you think what Sophie and Ash had was real love?

4. Did Sophie love Ash or did she love Mr Maldon? Was there a difference?

5. Why do you think Ash's traumatic experience with the war affected him the way it did?

6. As the novel progressed, did you view Sophie as a strong or weak character? Ash?

7. Ash's want of Sophie for himself—love or a selfish stifling of her independence?

8. Do you think the couple could have had a happily-ever-after if it wasn't for Beatrice?

9. Could Ash and Sophie have overcome the difference in their social status if they'd stayed together?

10. How did you feel about Sophie letting Ash go in the end? Do you agree with her decision?